LOST. FOREVER?

"May I help you?" The man at the Red Cross desk looked and sounded like a clerk. It was oddly comforting.

James shook the misplaced feeling off. "I'm looking for my son."

The man pulled a box of file folders closer to him. "What is his last name?"

"McManis. M-C-M-A-N-I-S."

The man selected a folder and scanned the contents. "We don't have anyone by that name listed."

It had to be a mistake. "You're sure?"

"I'm sorry, sir. No one by that name has registered with us."

James took a deep breath. "What does that mean?"

"It means he did not do as the park service and the Red Cross asked everyone who was here during the quake to do."

It wasn't the man's fault Chuck was so irresponsible. James turned away and sighed. Now what? It was closing in on 10 pm, and his plan hadn't gone anywhere past finding Chuck and locking him in the car for the trip back home.

He hadn't the first clue where to look next.

BOOKS BY M.M. JUSTUS

Much Ado in Montana

Cross-Country: Adventures Alone Across America and Back

UNEARTHLY NORTHWEST

Sojourn

TIME IN YELLOWSTONE

Repeating History
True Gold
"Homesick"
Finding Home

FINDING HOME

A TIME IN YELLOWSTONE NOVEL

M.M. JUSTUS

Carbon
River
Press

Finding Home

Acknowledgements

Thanks to the staff at the Yellowstone Heritage and Research Center for helping me find the history I needed.

Thanks to Elizabeth McCoy, for copyediting even when she didn't have the time, and for the artichoke.

And thanks to Mary Downs, who didn't believe she was going to like James but read about him, anyway, then generously admitted that she did like him after all.

The two most important days in your life are the day you are born, and the day you find out why.

-Mark Twain

FINDING HOME

CHAPTER 1

August 17, 1959

The boy took off at first light, before the beam from the streetlight shut off for the day. James heard the racket as the motorcycle roared down the street. He rolled over onto his back between the sheets and wearily rubbed his eyes. He'd strictly forbidden Chuck to leave the house today. As far as James was concerned, his son was grounded until doomsday. Or until James managed to talk the board of regents into letting him back into Colorado State University again, whichever came first. After the phone calls he'd made yesterday, he suspected doomsday would win that particular race.

The boy was taking his grandfather's death hard. But then so had James, and he wasn't ruining his life over it. Granted, James wasn't taking his father's death as hard as when he'd lost his mother five years ago, but he'd always had the closest bond with her, from the day they'd met, or so she'd told him. James had been five years old, and he didn't remember a time before that, before his mother had loved him. He wished he didn't remember a time after she was gone.

He sighed and threw back the covers, sat up, and put his head in his hands and his feet on the cold floor. He supposed it didn't matter where the boy had gone. He wouldn't be gone long. Where else would he go? James ought to know, but he'd been busy, and he and Chuck had been like ships in the night since the boy'd gone off to college. Since long before he went off to college, if he was to be honest. Well, now James had to get him back there, once he came home.

If his son was to have a successful career and take over the business one day, he had to at least get his degree first.

* * *

James had showered, dressed for the office, and was halfway through breakfast when the phone rang. The housekeeper was clattering around in the kitchen, and she wouldn't answer it when he was in the house, anyway, so out he went to the hall to pick it up.

"Hello?"

"Mr. McManis?"

James sighed. He'd had more than enough of his father's lawyer yesterday, going over the will, to last him a good long time. "Pritchard. What can I do for you this morning?"

"I'm glad you changed your mind."

A niggling dread ran through him, but no, Pritchard wouldn't go against his wishes. And he'd made those clear. "About what?"

"Chuck came by to pick up the paperwork for the ashes. And the money for the trip."

The niggle churned into full-blown anger. James took a deep breath, let it out on a whoosh when it didn't do anything to calm him. "You should have called me first."

"I didn't see any need to." The idiot sounded downright smug. "The will was clear."

"He's my child. You had no right to go against my wishes on this."

"He's nearly twenty-one, James." The man treated him as if *he* were twenty. Just because that's how old James had been when they'd first met was no excuse. Besides, he'd been carrying a 3. 8 grade point average and a job at the time. Acting like the adult he was. Unlike Chuck.

"Twenty going on twelve. He's got work to do here. He doesn't need to be taking off for parts unknown on a fool's errand."

"Yellowstone is hardly parts unknown."

"That's not the point. The boy –"

"He's not a boy. And he's grieving. You saw it. Give him a few days to go to the park to say good-bye. You can shove him back into college when he gets home." Pritchard paused, as if doubting he should put his oar in, but went ahead and did it anyway. "You could use the time apart, too."

James bit his tongue, even though it went against every instinct he had. No point in letting loose at the man. He was only doing his job. Which was going over a parent's head on the orders of a dead man. Might as well call it what it was. Right then, no matter how much James had loved his adoptive father, he wanted him back so he could smack him on the head.

"Look. The park's where he grew up –"

"He grew up here," James said flatly.

"All right, the park's where he spent a good chunk of his childhood. It's where he spent time with his grandparents. Let him go say good-bye to them there. Is it really any skin off your nose if he skips town for a few days?"

No, it wasn't. Except for the principle of the thing. You're the one who left him with them until he was old enough to go to school, James thought, and sent him up there every summer afterward. If you didn't want him to care for them more than he does for you, you should have spent more time with him.

"It's none of your business whether I go after him or not."

"But you won't."

James sighed. "Why do you care?"

Pritchard didn't answer his question, just made the niceties and hung up.

James went back to his now-cold breakfast, but it had lost its appeal. He ate anyway, and refilled his coffee, and went through the rest of his normal morning routine. He paid so little attention that he was a bit surprised an hour later to find himself sitting in his high-rise office with its view of the front range of the Rockies through the floor-to-ceiling windows.

That was where mountains should be, he'd always thought. Close enough to be beautiful, far enough away to be safe. It was one of the things he'd loved about Denver from the day he'd arrived here for college, forty-seven years ago. He'd been eighteen, out to set the world on fire. And he supposed he had accomplished it in his own way, to judge by this office, the thriving accounting business, the house just off Broadway, the brand-new Lincoln every few years, the season tickets to the opera and the symphony. His client list was full of movers and shakers, his attendance in demand at charitable events. The only thing lacking was a graceful wife on his arm, but his beloved Catherine was irreplaceable.

All of which was a far cry from the cabin at Old Faithful, issued to his father as ranger family quarters, where he'd grown up, or the log cabin in West Yellowstone, not much bigger or in better repair, where his parents had retired. He'd been able to help them by then, but they wouldn't take the kind of help he'd wanted to give.

Nor did Chuck. All the boy wanted, James thought, was to go backward. Back to the boonies James had escaped from. For him. In spite of everything James had done to teach him better.

James sighed at his tidy, and full, to-do file. He didn't have time to go haring off to that godforsaken place. Time enough to try again when the boy came back. And he would come back. He had nowhere else to go.

The intercom buzzed. In the meantime, he had work to do.

* * *

He tried not to think about Chuck all day, and mostly succeeded. Tried not to let his anger loose at how things had gone badly, although that was a harder battle. Neither his employees nor the clients he saw that day deserved to be treated poorly, and they deserved his full attention as well.

But shoving his personal problems to the back of his mind all day proved wearing. Out of practice, James supposed, as he locked up his office and headed for home. It had been some time since he'd had to work at it so hard. A long time since he'd been glad for the workday to end, too. He liked his work. To spend his days creating order out of chaos, working with numbers that always responded with the same answers when you asked the same questions. Reliable, that's what they were, and James respected reliability. So did the clients he worked with. They depended on him to make those numbers work for them, and to be acceptable to the government as well as their bottom lines, and that's what he did.

Too bad the boy had to be a throwback to chaos. He should have arrived at the park by now. If he hadn't wrecked his cursed motorcycle on the way.

* * *

The house was quiet when he got home. Empty. Mrs. May was gone for the day, leaving his supper in the oven for him instead of waiting till he got home before she left. He grimaced. Her absence was clear commentary on the shouting match she'd not have been able to help overhearing yesterday. She was inordinately fond of the boy and took his side in everything, not that her vote counted. It was one reason James had kept her on for the last fifteen years.

Supper could wait a few more minutes. One thing he knew from yesterday's meeting with Pritchard was the arrangements for where Chuck would be staying for the three nights his father's will had provided for. The desk clerk at the Old Faithful Inn was pleasant and informative. James hung up the phone, relieved to know his worst nightmare hadn't come true today, so he wouldn't have to scour the roads between Denver and northwest Wyoming for a mangled motorcycle alongside the road with a dead body flung into the underbrush nearby.

His motorcycle was Chuck's pride and joy, and the only thing the boy had worked for with his own hands and brain, money earned from summer jobs and work after school as soon as he could drive. James had been so proud to see him ambitious about anything, he hadn't had the heart to fight him for something more sensible. Safer. His mistake. It had given the boy a sense of independence he wasn't mature enough for yet.

Catherine would have approved of it. But Catherine wasn't here. And hadn't been here since she'd died giving Chuck life. All the labor she'd gone through, labor that had killed her. But she still would have approved.

He was used to the peace and quiet, and it should have been soothing. It was hard to keep from thinking about what the boy was doing this evening, though. Scattering ashes. The thought was repugnant. What was wrong with a nice plot at Cherry Hills? A place he could have gone to pay his respects and leave flowers at his parents' graves, the way he'd always done for Catherine. He wasn't about to traipse off up to the park every time he felt the need.

He ate, although the meal was a bit dried out by the time he got to it. He left his dishes in the sink for Mrs. May in the morning, mixed himself a martini, and settled down in his easy chair for the evening. Tried to read, discovered he couldn't concentrate, mixed himself a second drink and turned on the television, realized after half an hour that he had no idea what he'd been watching but his glass was empty again.

Resisted making a third, and instead listened to the clock in the hall chiming hour after hour, till it was a decent time to go to bed. He was grieving, too, in his own way, he understood after a while, realizing his thoughts had gone to his parents, and to his memories. He'd taken it out on the boy, perhaps. Blaming him for something that wasn't his fault.

Let Chuck get his grief out of his system in his own way while James did the same. It wasn't as if they couldn't resolve their differences when he got back. He had to let the boy grow up sometime.

At last it was late enough to go to bed. He set his glass in the sink next to his supper dishes, and went upstairs.

* * *

He woke early again, when he heard the sound of a motorcycle on the street through the open window. It took his muzzy brain a moment to realize it couldn't be Chuck so soon, but by then he couldn't get back to sleep. He heard the milkman's bottles rattle as they landed on the back step, the newspaper thud on the front porch. When Mrs. May's car pulled into the driveway just as his alarm clock went off, he swung himself out of bed and began another day.

The newspaper sat next to his plate when he came down for breakfast.

"QUAKE JOLTS WESTERN STATES. HEBGEN DAM OPEN, VACATIONERS HURT" And further down the page, "TEMBLOR CRUMPLES MOUNTAINS IN DEATH, DESTRUCTION SWEEP" And, last and worst of all, below both of them, "PARK SCENE OF FEAR, CONFUSION Single Thought: 'Let's Get Out'" The headlines, in heavy black ink, and their articles, taking up the entire front page of the Rocky Mountain Post, stopped his breath. He didn't even realize he'd fallen into his chair until the dishes rattled from the force of his landing.

He stared at the paper, unable to touch it, unable to read any further as the words below the headlines blurred. He blinked, forcing himself to focus. The Hebgen Dam, right. His grandfather had taken him fishing at Hebgen Lake on occasion when he was a boy. It was just west of the park, less than an hour away as the raven flew from where his son was, this very moment.

He took a deep breath. "Mrs. May?" He was amazed at how calm his voice sounded, right then. He felt like he was standing in the middle of the earthquake himself, as if it were jolting him from the inside out.

She stuck her head through the door from the kitchen. "Yes, sir?"

"Did you see this?"

"Yes, sir."

God, she was cold. And he'd thought she loved the boy. "Please call the office for me. Tell Alice I've had an emergency and will be out of town for a few days. She'll need to reschedule my appointments through Thursday – no, through the rest of the week."

No, she wasn't cold. The relief on her face was palpable, even to him. So was the rare approval in her eyes.

"Yes, sir. "She strode across the dining room toward the hall, then stopped in the doorway. "You bring him home. Safe."

James nodded, grabbed the paper, and strode to the car.

* * *

He was halfway to Laramie before it dawned on him he probably should have changed his clothing, and perhaps packed a suitcase, before he left. The suit and dress shoes he was wearing were not what he'd call appropriate for a rescue mission into a disaster zone, even though his jacket and tie were now in the back seat and his shirt sleeves were rolled up to the elbows. Well, he wasn't about to stop now. He'd manage. He and the boy would be on their way home this time tomorrow, anyway. He'd pick up a toothbrush somewhere, and hang the rest of it.

The radio was full of news of the quake. It had been felt as far away as Spokane and Salt Lake City. The Hebgen dam had ruptured, then no, it hadn't. People were being rescued by helicopter from a landslide caused by the quake outside the park. The death toll was still rising. There'd been a second landslide, this one in the park, and the phone lines were down. The town of West Yellowstone had been all but destroyed. The town of Ennis was being evacuated due to potential flooding. The roads were closed into the park, nobody allowed to enter or leave. Well, they'd see about trying to keep *him* out. The Gallatin and Madison County sheriffs both asked people to stay away from the Madison Canyon area. That was all right, he wasn't going there. The park superintendent came on the air and asked people to stay away from the park as well. Sorry, Mr. Garrison, James thought, I can't. My son's in there.

The Lincoln ate up the miles. The only stops he made were for gas and, once, to grab something to eat when he realized he hadn't put anything in his stomach since the night before. He bought a perfectly wretched hamburger from a greasy spoon in Lander, wrapped it in a paper napkin, and ate it one-handed as he drove on.

The radio faded in and out, giving him too much time to worry before he could tune to another station from the next town, and the next, and the next. The last one came out of Jackson Hole late in the afternoon, and lasted until the Tetons blocked the signal at last, not far from Yellowstone's south entrance.

A steady stream of cars poured out, but not as many as he would have expected. He supposed most of the tourists were already gone and these were just the stragglers. He reached the gate only to find a line going in, too. So much for asking people to stay out. He wondered if they were all on missions like his own, or if they were just ghoulish curiosity seekers, but if there'd have been room to get by he'd have been five miles down the road by the time he finally reached the entrance kiosk.

"Good evening, sir. Welcome to Yellowstone. You should know, because of the earthquake, some of the roads are closed."

James fumbled with his wallet. "Can I get to Old Faithful?" He shoved the entrance fee at the ranger, who took it.

"Yes, but the West Entrance —"

"Thanks. I'm not here on vacation. My son is here."

"I'm sure he's fine, sir. As soon as the phone lines are back up they'll be letting people call through —"

He wouldn't have stopped in the first place if he'd had a choice. James put his foot on the gas and roared off into the deepening shadows. No, he won't be fine, he thought, but only because I'm going to ground him forever after I find him myself.

* * *

He'd never have known anything happened to look at the place so far, even if he was still a couple of hours from Old Faithful. But the park looked just as it had the last time he'd seen it, the last time he'd brought Chuck to stay with his grandparents here for the summer, five years ago. Miles and miles of monotonous endless forest, every lodgepole pine straight as a toothpick and indistinguishable from all the others. The road was the same, too, no buckles, no cracks. He was going faster than was safe, but one of the reasons he'd always bought Lincolns as soon as he could afford them was for their handling. He didn't see a single animal, which was just as well. Probably all scared back into the woods where they belonged.

Lake Yellowstone, enormous and ringed with jagged mountains, gleamed in the fading light behind him as he made the last turn toward Old Faithful and began the climb over the Continental Divide. He had to slow down now, to navigate the twists and turns. The Lincoln growled as he wrenched the wheel back and forth.

He'd made the two crossings of the divide and was on the downward slope when he saw the first crack in the pavement in the beam from his headlights. Not much to look at, a long, narrow split that caused the outer edge of the asphalt to tilt slightly. If this was the kind of damage all the panic was about –

The next crack was a bit wider, and ran diagonally off the road into the forest, its path marked with trees tilted at crazy angles. He shrugged the sight off as the car bounced over it and several more like it and kept going.

Even when he came around the last corner and saw the buildings at Old Faithful, it didn't seem that awful. A number of emergency vehicles were scattered about, but no one seemed to be doing anything. People were wandering around. Some were even seated at the benches at Old Faithful, for all the world as if it was a perfectly normal evening.

James let out a deep breath and swung the car into a surprisingly empty parking space in front of the Inn. But he'd no more than opened the door when a man in uniform – not a ranger – walked up.

"I'm sorry, sir, but you can't park here. We need to keep this area clear for emergency vehicles."

"I'm just here to pick someone up. I'll be back and gone before you know it."

"I'm sorry, sir –"

But James was out and past him before the man could finish whatever he had to say.

The tremor hit when he was halfway up the stone steps to the porte cochere at the front of the Inn. He grabbed the metal pipe railing, but the shaking was over almost before it started. Well, and that wasn't so bad, either. What a fuss. He headed on up, but when he reached the door, it was blocked by another man in uniform.

"I'm sorry, sir, but no one may enter the building. It's too dangerous."

Dangerous? Nothing even seemed to be damaged. "I'm looking for my son."

"The building has been evacuated. No one is in there."

James waited. When the man did not continue, he could not keep the exasperation out of his voice. "Where were they evacuated *to?*"

"Excuse us." The door swung open, and several more men strode out, their clothing covered with dust, hard hats on their heads. Their boots muddy. *Muddy?* "Get out of the way. Another rock just fell from the fireplace."

James caught a glimpse of the interior of the massive lobby, stones scattered helter skelter across the now deeply gouged wooden floor, dust still settling in great clouds, water running across the floor. *Water?* The man James had been trying to pry information out of grabbed James by the arm and pulled him back. James shook the hand off and turned on the man.

"Where were the people staying here evacuated *to*, young man!"

The fellow blinked. "Most of them went to the lodge, sir."

"Thank you," James flung over his shoulder.

"Sir, you still need to move your car —"

* * *

The people milling about were not acting like tourists after all, James realized as he strode the few hundred yards down the road to the lodge, his eyes scanning them fruitlessly for the boy. They weren't admiring the scenery or wasting their time waiting for Old Faithful to go off. He guessed they were the ones stupid enough to hang around instead of leaving like sensible people after the place blew up on them last night. Even at this hour after dark they didn't seem to have the sense to go indoors.

Although he supposed indoors probably didn't seem very safe to them right now. The glimpse of the damage he'd seen inside the Inn would have made him dubious about going indoors in this place if he had the time to think about it or care.

The lodge looked the same as ever, and there weren't any emergency vehicles in front of *it*. People, none of them Chuck – good grief, where *was* he? – coming and going as if everything were perfectly normal. Until he went inside.

Controlled pandemonium was what it looked like. Crowds milling, no blond bespectacled kids sticking up above the rest. The place looked like a disaster shelter, and, indeed, a table with a Red Cross sign was set up in a corner of the big room, next to the closed photographic shop. It looked completely incongruous, but perhaps they knew where people were.

James strode over and caught the attention of one of the three men behind the table.

"May I help you?" He looked and sounded like a clerk. It was oddly comforting.

James shook the misplaced feeling off. "I'm looking for my son."

The man pulled a box of file folders closer to him. "What is his last name?"

"McManis. M-C-M-A-N-I-S."

The man selected a folder labeled with a big black M, pulled a sheet with a list of names out of it, and scanned them. "We don't have anyone by that name listed."

It had to be a mistake. "He was staying at the Inn. Arrived last night."

"I'm sorry, sir. No one by that name has registered with us."

His irritation was beginning to feel just a bit like panic. "His first name is Chuck."

"It's all by last name, sir. He's not on the list."

James took a deep breath. "What does that mean?"

"It means he did not do as the park service and the Red Cross asked everyone who was here during the quake to do."

Of course he hadn't. "Which was?"

"To come here and give us his name and tell us what he was going to do, whether he was leaving or staying, and where he could be contacted." The man paused, obviously taking in whatever James looked like by that point. James didn't want to think about what he

21

looked like. Or care. It was just like the boy. Heaven only knew where he'd gone by now. "For just this purpose."

"What?"

"The purpose of the registration process."

"Yes, I know." It wasn't the man's fault Chuck was so irresponsible. James managed to calm his voice. "Thank you. I'm sorry."

"What is your name, sir?"

"What? Oh. James McManis. M-C-M —" The man waved him to stop, and James did, feeling a bit foolish.

"Where will you be, sir? In case your son does show up?"

"Looking for him."

"Where should we tell him to go?"

James snorted. "Chain him to the table."

The man looked sympathetic." I'll do my best."

"Thanks. I'll keep checking back."

"That sounds like an excellent idea."

James turned away and sighed. Now what could he do? It was closing in on 10 pm, and his plan hadn't gone anywhere past finding Chuck and locking him in the car for the trip back home.

He hadn't the first clue where to look next.

CHAPTER 2

Weary both mentally and physically, James headed back outside. The sun, and most of the people, were long gone as he trudged toward the Inn. But the moon was shining enough to show the way, bright enough that the stars behind it were faded almost to invisibility. Not that he cared about the beauty of the moon, the stars, or anything else.

Where on earth *was* Chuck? Come to think of it, he hadn't seen the boy's motorcycle, either. If he'd taken off without leaving word with anyone – James shook his head. Punishment was beside the point now. All he wanted to do was take him home.

He supposed he ought to go get his car. But when he got back to the Inn, it was gone, and when he went to find out what imbecile had had it towed, all he got was polite stonewalling from the only person he could find to ask, a young man in a ranger's uniform.

"I told your colleague I'd be right back."

"And I'm sure he told you not to leave your car parked in an emergency zone."

"Fine." No point in arguing, especially since he had let it sit there for the better part of an hour. "Where is it and who do I have to pay to get it back?"

The man handed him a small square of pasteboard. James glanced down at it as he took it. It appeared to be the business card for the service station manager here at Old Faithful. "The gas station?"

"It's impounded. You'll have to wait till morning." Was the kid smirking at him?

"I will not."

"If you go in to retrieve it without permission, sir, you'll be charged for it."

"Fine."

"With breaking and entering."

James took a deep breath. He hated to plead, but there wasn't any help for it. "My son is missing. So far no one seems to know where he is. For all I know he could be dead."

"No one at the Inn was injured except for one lady who fell out of bed and broke her ankle. Have you checked with the Red Cross at the lodge?"

"Yes. He's not listed."

At least the kid, young man, he couldn't be much older than Chuck, James thought, had lost the smirk. James wasn't sure if the sympathy on his face was much of an improvement.

"You haven't seen him, have you? About this tall –" James raised his hand to about four inches over his own head, trying not to remember the first time he'd noticed Chuck had grown taller than he was. "Blond, wears glasses? About your age?"

At least the young man appeared to give some thought to the question. But he shook his head. "No, I haven't, I'm sorry. Do you have a place to sleep?"

It was the last thing James was worried about. "I'll try at the lodge."

"Good luck." The radio on ranger's belt beeped. "I have to go now. Maybe your son is there, and just didn't check in."

"Maybe." It was possible. Even likely.

"I'm sorry about your car." And he sounded sincere, now. "Contact Mike at the service station in the morning. He'll get it out of hock."

"Yeah." Belatedly James thought, there's no point in shooting the messenger. "Thanks."

"You're welcome." The young man strode off.

"Wait."

The young man turned back. "What?"

"Have you seen a motorcycle?"

"No."

"Where would someone park one, if he was staying here?"

"Depends on which wing he was in. "He turned again and was gone before James could quiz him further.

James trudged back to the lodge. Again. He'd look for the motorcycle in the morning. It wasn't as if he could go anywhere tonight, and with the luck he was having at the moment, if he went searching for the thing in the dark he'd probably fall over a rock and break his neck.

* * *

The woman at the lodge registration desk, who was the first person over forty James had spoken with since he'd arrived, was sympathetic but firm. No, she hadn't seen any tall young men with spectacles, not that he'd expected her to, but she also didn't have a cabin for the night. "We're full up, what with the Inn being shut down. I'm sorry."

He should have expected it, too, given the lack of line at the desk, but now he didn't have anywhere to go. Not even the car.

"Check at the Red Cross desk. They'll find you a place."

So he did. What else could he do? His first question was answered quickly. Chuck hadn't shown up, but then James hadn't expected him to. When he asked if there was somewhere he could sleep, the young woman who'd taken over for the other fellow didn't bat an eyelash.

"Most of the people who were staying at the Inn have left altogether, so there's more than enough cots," she told him.

He tried to feel grateful. "Thanks. I'm sorry to be imposing on you like this, but I can't leave till I find my son."

She gave him the same look of sympathy that sprang from politeness but not understanding that the young man at the Inn had given him. "Of course not."

She took out a chart and asked him his name, then wrote it down on one of the many empty rectangles. "You'll be in the recreation hall, row six, cot three. It should have blankets already on it. If it doesn't, come back and I'll find you some."

"All right." Row six, cot three. How many cots did they have crammed in there? He supposed it didn't matter.

In spite of the exhaustion dragging at him, he walked through the entire building, in case Chuck had holed up somewhere without telling anyone. No luck, of course. By the time he made his way to his bed he was weaving on his feet, and even his worry couldn't keep him awake. Two blankets lay folded on the narrow aluminum-and-canvas cot, with a small pillow atop them. It all looked like army surplus from Korea, and probably was. James took his shoes off, carefully tucking them out of the way underneath the cot, spread blankets, stretched out fully clothed on top of them, tried to get comfortable and failed, and fell asleep anyway.

* * *

He woke with a start. He was lying on his back with a lump under his head and a dusty-smelling cover wrapped around his legs. He shivered and pulled the blanket up to his neck, feeling the cold air seep in around the edges. Where was he? Where was his electric blanket? His double bed with its thick mattress? This thing was so narrow he'd almost fallen out trying to roll over, and it sagged in the middle.

The room wasn't pitch black, not quite, not with his eyes adjusted to the dark. He could make out the high timbered ceiling above him, and when he looked around he saw row upon row of more nasty little cots, some with people sleeping on them, most empty. The various sounds of snoring and heavy breathing bounced around the room.

His memories of yesterday came rushing back to him. The news of the earthquake, his mad dash up here to rescue his wayward son who refused to be found. He let out a long breath and pulled his left hand out from under the blanket. He peered at his watch. Five in the morning. He tucked his hand back down and attempted to roll over without tipping the cot. When he was as comfortable as he was going to get, he tried to drop back off, but all he managed was an uneasy doze.

Finally, light began streaming in through the clerestory windows and people around him started stirring and sitting up. James threw back the blanket and wished he'd hung onto his suit jacket instead of leaving it in the car. The air was – crisp, he decided, rolling down the sleeves of his wrinkled shirt and fastening his cuffs. Not as cold as it could have been, even in August, although why no one had turned the heat on in this benighted place was beyond him. Maybe the electricity had broken in the earthquake. But the lights had been working last night.

He pulled his shoes on and laced them up, wincing as he bent over, then rose from the cot, stretching and creaking. Sixty-five was too old to be sleeping on a sheet of canvas, and surely too old to be chasing after his late-in-life son. He scanned the room, and all the other people waking up. Half a dozen blonds in his range of view, but none of them was the right one.

A bathroom first. Then coffee. He needed coffee more than he needed air right now. Then he had to go get the Lincoln out of impound and try to find Chuck's motorcycle. Maybe it would give a clue as to where he'd gone. Or, if he couldn't find it, that would be a clue, too. One leading to a conclusion that would make him want to strangle the boy, but a clue. If he called home this morning and discovered he and the boy had crossed paths – Oh, he'd be angry, he thought. But even the very idea had relief rushing through him. Yes. A pay phone. A pay phone was exactly what he needed now.

His stomach growled. The hamburger he'd eaten yesterday afternoon was long gone. A bathroom, a pay phone, then coffee and breakfast, then the car. In any sane world he'd get the coffee first, so he could be civilized enough to keep from climbing through the telephone lines and strangling the boy when he heard Chuck's voice. But first things first. James folded the blankets neatly, to leave the cot the way he'd found it. He wouldn't be back here tonight. And went in search of a restroom.

* * *

Three pay phones in the hallway of the lodge, and twenty people waiting to use them. He should have known. At least the phones were working again, which was more than he should have expected.

He was wishing he'd gone and gotten coffee first by the time he reached the head of the line, but he wasn't about to lose his place for it. He stuffed a nickel into the slot and dialed home, then added more coins to pay for the long distance call.

"McManis residence."

"Mrs. May? This is Mr. McManis. Has Chuck come home?"

"Oh! No, sir, he hasn't." Even thinned out by distance he could hear the worry in her voice. "You haven't found him?"

James swallowed the knots in his stomach again and tried to stay calm. No point in upsetting her, too. "Not yet. Please stay at the house in case he does show up, and if he does, tell him I said to stay put till I get home or else."

"Yes, sir." A pause. "Is there anything more I can do?"

"No. Thank you. I'll stay in touch."

"Thank you, sir. I appreciate it."

And that, thought James in frustration, was that.

The lodge cafeteria was open for business, and the line – no Chuck there, either – was much shorter than it had been for the phone. James loaded up on coffee and some rather dubious-looking scrambled eggs and cold toast, and took it to an empty table. As he shoveled the food in as quickly as he could and drank the vile coffee for its caffeine content, his eyes constantly scanned the room. Surely, if Chuck was still at Old Faithful he'd have to come here for food sooner or later. Unless –

James flagged down the young man clearing the table next to him." Is this the only place here open for food right now?"

"So far as I know, sir." The kid paused. "They did say something this morning about reopening the soda fountain at the lower Hamilton store later today."

"Thanks. Have you seen a tall blond kid with glasses? He'd be about your age."

"No, sir."

Of course he hadn't. James was beginning to think the boy had vanished into thin air. He finished his meal. After he rescued his car, the Hamilton store was as good a place as any to try next. The boy had mentioned the place once or twice, if James remembered correctly. And maybe he could buy a toothbrush.

* * *

He supposed the process of getting his car unimpounded could have been worse, but as it was it took precious time away from his search, and cost more than enough to have paid for a decent bed the night before, if one had been available at any price. James shrugged his suit jacket on as protection against the morning chill and politely asked where he could park and leave the car where it would be left alone.

The Lincoln safely stowed in the lodge parking lot, James trudged back down the road he'd already walked five times in the last twenty-four hours, past Old Faithful, which was erupting, not that he cared, past the Inn buzzing with workmen, and on to the log building housing the Hamilton store. Another tremor struck on his way there, this one just enough to make him widen his stance to keep from falling down. It only lasted a few seconds, and James regained his balance and strode on.

The store's door was unlocked. No one tried to stop him as he entered, either. This place certainly did look as if it had been in an earthquake, unlike the lodge. The shelves which hadn't had their goods dumped all over the floor still looked as if someone had been rooting through them to get to the very back, shoving everything out of his way. Nothing was in a straight line. The clothing racks and souvenir shelves looked like someone had been playing bumper cars with them, and the part of the store holding groceries and other goods for campers was all out of kilter with its contents strewn about. The refrigerator cases were the only furnishings that hadn't moved, probably because they were bolted to the walls, but they'd been emptied and their doors hung open.

James picked his way through the minefield toward the soda fountain at the back of the store, past clerks cleaning the mess up and putting things back in order, who ignored him as he passed by. At least none of them told him he had to leave.

He slid onto one of the round red stools and leaned his elbows on the counter. "Anyone here?"

"We're not serving till this afternoon," said a voice from behind the pass-through.

She sounded like the second person over forty he'd spoken to since he got here. James almost brightened. "I just wanted to ask you a question."

Her head became visible through the pass-through as she rose from whatever she'd been doing. Cleaning up the mess on the floor, he supposed.

She was over forty. Probably over fifty, actually. Her hair was graying from a black as dense as his own had once been. She wore it in a braid down her back. The buttons of a blue and white striped shirt strained over her full figure, and she looked as if she'd been working all night. Come to think of it, she might well have been. James searched for patience and, amazingly enough, found some.

"I'm looking for someone."

Her mouth quirked. "Aren't we all?"

He supposed so. "His name is Chuck McManis."

She shook her head. "Doesn't work here."

"No, he doesn't. But you might have seen him. He's twenty. About six-two, kind of skinny. Blond. Wears glasses."

She started to shake her head again, then stopped. For a second so did James's heart. "Kid like that was in here recently." But before he could open his mouth, she added, "But it was before the earthquake. About eight, night before last. I was already closing up for the night, but Alice took his order, anyway."

His heart sank. But – "Was he here? Did he say where he was going?"

"Yeah. He asked me where he could get a beer. I remember because he looked under age." She smiled reminiscently. "Also because he barely got started flirting with Alice before the lummox showed up and scared him off."

James waved this away as irrelevant. "Where could he get beer?"

"Only bar in the village is at the Inn, which is what I told him." She gave him a curious glance. "What's he to you?"

"My son."

She looked taken aback, then sympathy, real sympathy, not just the polite kind, shone in her eyes. They were dark brown, he noticed, not that it mattered. "I take it you've checked –"

Impatiently James cut her off. "With the Red Cross, yes. They haven't seen him." He slid off the stool and stood up. "Thank you."

She shrugged. "No skin off my nose."

James started back toward the door, but he only went a couple of steps before he turned around and asked, rather belatedly, "Do you know where I can find the bartender? The Inn's shut down."

"Yeah, the chimney took a header into the dining room, and a water main broke. It's all flooded." She sighed. "It's too bad. That place is special. I hope they can fix everything."

James waited. She sighed again. "I might be able to help you find him."

"Now?" Or did she have to stay here?

Her upper body disappeared from the pass-through. He heard some thumping and a couple of muttered curse words, and he had just come to the conclusion she'd gone back to work when the door at the end of the counter swung open and she strode through. She stopped halfway across the floor and James realized she was waiting for him. He hurried to catch up.

Her lower half was clad in blue jeans stained at the knees, and her feet were shod in worn hiking boots. Practical, he supposed, considering, but not very ladylike. She shouted to tell someone she called Fred she'd be back in a few, and they stepped out into the bright sunshine. Without pausing, she headed back toward the Inn. "Most likely he'll be cleaning up, same as I am. I hate to think what the quake did to all those bottles."

"You think he's in there?"

"They've let the maids back into the east wing, or so the scuttlebutt says. The water didn't get that far, and they say it's safe. Most of the pillow punchers don't agree with 'em, though. They're going to have a hard time getting enough people to stay to keep the place open the rest of the season."

He was starting to gasp. Ridiculous, to be bothered by the altitude. It wasn't much higher here than in Denver, but she was striding fast enough that he was having a hard time keeping up with her. "Most of the what?"

"Pillow punchers." She grinned at him. She was almost his height in her boots. "Local term."

He'd forgotten all about that nonsense, as if he'd ever wanted to know in the first place. Pearl divers and dude heavers and gear jammers. The first time he'd ever kissed a girl was after he'd asked her to go rotten-logging with him. What a repulsive thing to call a date. If you could call a walk in the woods a date, not that he'd had many other options here. He only nodded, letting his shortening breath speak for him.

When they reached the entrance to the Inn, the fellow who'd had his car impounded was back. He glared at James, and James glared right back.

"You again?"

But before James could say anything, the woman said, "Hey, Pete, let us in."

The kid smiled at her, but said, "You know I'm not supposed to, Jo."

"But you will, anyway. You seen Stan?"

"Yeah, he's in there. The quake made some cocktail out of the bar."

She laughed. "I bet." She stepped forward. James followed.

The kid frowned, then said, "Oh, what the hell. Don't let him –" he jerked a finger at James "– go wandering off by himself in there."

"I won't. We'll just be a few minutes."

The young man rolled his eyes.

"Thanks." James aimed it at the kid, but it was Jo he meant it for.

The water was gone, or at least it wasn't running across the floor anymore, but the wood was stained and still damp. The water was the least of the visible damage by far. James would have gaped at the hole the fallen chimney stones had put through the wall between the lobby and the dining room if he hadn't been so intent on following Jo to the bar, tucked away in one corner of the cavernous place. He wouldn't have had trouble finding it on his own, however. The fumes alone were enough to get drunk on.

"Stan?" Jo called. "Hey, Stan?"

James's breath caught. The fellow was tall, thin, blond, glasses and all. But older. He wasn't Chuck, wasn't Chuck. "Come to give me a hand, Jo?" He gave James a passing glance, then ignored him.

"Sorry. I've got enough of a mess at the grill." She shrugged, then gestured at James. "Fellow here wants to ask you a question."

"Well? Shoot."

"I'm looking for someone," James said, then as the man opened his mouth, he held up his hand. "Yes, I've checked with the Red Cross people. They haven't seen him."

"Then why the hell would I?"

"Because I sent him here night before last, before the quake," Jo added. "Give the guy a break, Stan. He's looking for his kid."

The fellow shrugged, but said, "Go on."

James said, "He looks a lot like you, only younger. He's twenty. Tall, thin, blond, glasses. Would have been wearing jeans and a leather jacket."

Stan nodded. "Oh, yeah, I have seen him. He looked underage, but wasn't. Said he'd come all the way from Denver in one day. Looked like it, too."

James swallowed against hope. "That'd be him."

"What about him?"

"Did he say where he was going when he left here?"

"Back to his room, I guess. He wasn't in shape to do much more." Stan smirked. "When you're as tired as he was at this altitude, it doesn't take much to get you drunk. Especially if you're not used to it."

"Did he say anything else?"

Stan thought for a moment. "Something about his grandfather and ashes. Sounded weird, but he was pretty out of it by then."

Calm. He needed to stay calm. "He was here to scatter his grandparents' ashes. His grandfather was a park ranger here."

"Oh," Jo said, sounding enlightened. "I thought the name sounded familiar. Your dad was Will McManis?"

"Yes," James said shortly.

"I've heard about you." Great, he thought. She grinned. "You ran away from home."

"No, I didn't." The denial was automatic, even after all these years. The difference between escaped and ran away mattered to him, if it hadn't to anyone else.

"And Chuck came back. I hadn't seen him in years before the other night. I didn't recognize him. He probably didn't recognize me, either."

"Probably not. But he's still missing."

She sobered." True. "She turned back to Stan, who was looking curious. "So he said he was going back to his room."

"Yeah."

"Thanks, Stan."

"Sure." He went back to work.

"Well, come on." She started to stride away again, but not toward the door. Instead she headed toward the front desk, or what was left of it.

Helplessly, James followed.

CHAPTER 3

When they reached the desk, Jo went around behind it and swept the dust off of a ledger.

"What was your name again?" James asked.

"Jo Bennett." But she was concentrating on the page in front of her, running a finger down the list of names.

He certainly didn't recognize her, but he doubted he'd recognize anyone here after all these years. "How did you know my parents?"

"This place is like a small town – ha!"

"What?" James leaned over the counter.

"Is that him?" She pointed.

He peered down at what was unmistakably Chuck's almost illegible scrawl. Even more unmistakable was his name next to it, printed in someone else's clear block letters. "Obviously."

"Then he was in room 267." She dodged back out from behind the desk and strode away again, stepping over debris as if she did it every day.

He felt like he'd created a monster as he trailed after her. "Don't you have to get back to work?"

"You didn't tell me you were looking for Will and Karin's grandson."

A man in a hard hat approached her and said something, but James's head was buzzing. She brushed the fellow off, at any rate. A moment later he returned with two more hard hats. Miss? Mrs. ? Bennett – Jo, James thought irritably; if she was going to be informal with him she could do without the proper respect – took the hats and handed him one as she headed up the peeled log staircase. James fumbled with the chin strap as he puffed up after her.

He hoped the floor wouldn't collapse beneath their feet, especially when everything rumbled and rattled again just as they reached the mezzanine with nothing but a log railing between them and the lobby below.

The shock didn't last more than a few seconds, however, and she was already shoving one of the water-swollen doors open. It led into an unlit hallway, and he counted the dusty wrought iron numbers on the rows of doors as the carpet runner squelched under their feet. 245, 253, 261 – 267.

He didn't even have time to wonder if they were going to have to break in when she produced a key and shoved it in the lock. The door creaked open, the damp wood catching on the jamb, then giving way.

He took a deep breath and stepped through. Jo was already inside. "This look like his stuff?" she asked.

"Yes." Even in the poor light he recognized the boy's duffel bag, slung across one of the two beds. It looked like someone had been ransacking it, but that was as likely to be from Chuck's own disorganized attempts at packing as anything else.

Without thinking James reached up for the pull chain on the lamp mounted to the wall above the bed. Jo's sharp, "Don't touch that," stopped him, and he went to the window instead. Pulling the curtains back gave some light, but not much.

"Does anything look like it's missing?" she asked.

"With him it's hard to tell," he admitted.

"Well, come take a look," she demanded, and he went back to the bed.

Two pairs of jeans, several shirts, underwear, socks, shaving kit. He opened the kit. Nothing missing there, not even his toothbrush, except if the boy had gone off voluntarily surely he'd have taken the whole duffel with him. He nudged a familiar pair of sneakers out of the way. "I don't think so – Wait." The corner of an envelope stuck out from under the shaving kit.

James tugged it out and opened it. "That's strange."

Jo had been wandering around the room as if it could tell her where the boy had gone, but she stopped. "What's strange?"

"The ashes are gone."

"He brought them with him?"

"Yes," James said impatiently. "That's why he's here, to scatter them. His grandfather arranged it all before he died."

"When did he die?"

"Six days ago." It seemed longer.

"I'm sorry." She sounded like it, too. But then she'd known his parents, apparently.

"Me, too. But right now I'm sorrier he decided to send Chuck off up here." He finished his fruitless perusal of Pritchard's letter. It was a simple document requesting the release to Chuck of his grandfather's and grandmother's ashes from the crematorium, and accompanied the crematorium's brief form stating the release. He shook his head ruefully. "Don't get me wrong. My dad and I had our differences, but I am sorry he's gone. Right now, however, I'm more angry with him than anything else. If he was still here, Chuck would still be in Denver, and none of this would have happened."

He put the letter back in the envelope and straightened.

She raised an unplucked eyebrow at him. "So now what do we know?"

He shrugged. "Not much more than we did. I knew he'd gotten here all right, because I called the front desk the evening of the 17th, and he'd already checked in."

"What about the ashes?"

"What about them?"

"Where are they?"

He drew a deep breath and almost choked on the damp dust. "Somehow I just don't care right now."

"If he went out night before last to scatter them somewhere and got caught in the quake –"

"He was drunk, according to your friend."

"So? He could be out there somewhere."

James gazed at her in mounting horror. "No."

"I'm really sorry, Mr. McManis, but he could be."

* * *

They were downstairs and outside by the time James started thinking again. Not because he was so wrought up he couldn't think, of course, but because another man in a hard hat stuck his head through the open door and told them firmly they had to get out. Now.

Jo was still moving. James slung the duffel over his shoulder and followed her, not to the lodge this time, but toward the ranger station on the other side of the road.

"Now what?" he puffed.

"Now we get a search and rescue started." She sounded too matter-of-fact for his taste.

"Oh."

She glanced back at him. "Out of shape, aren't you?" He glared at her. She wiggled her fingers. "Give me that."

He hung onto it. "I can manage."

"You collapsing in a heap is not going to help us find him." She solved what she seemed to see as the problem by stopping for the second or two it took him to catch up, then snagging the thing off of his shoulder.

And nearly taking his fingers with it. "Ow."

"Sorry. Come on."

He was beginning to lose track of how far he'd walked, back and forth, going absolutely nowhere, in the last twelve hours. "Wait. I'll put it in my car."

"There might be something in it that'll tell where he went."

She seemed incapable of simply opening a door, but shoved this one open and gestured him inside.

This was by far the calmest-seeming place he'd been since he'd arrived here. It took James a few moments to realize it was an illusion. It wasn't crowded. He supposed most of the rangers were out clearing roads and dealing with recalcitrant tourists and whatnot. But the place hummed like a hive, anyway.

Jo strode up to the main desk. "We have a missing person," she informed the middle-aged man in a ranger suit who was sitting there.

He glanced up, startled. "You're sure?"

She slung Chuck's duffel onto the desk, where it almost took out a lamp, and gestured at James, presumably so he could explain.

The man, who turned out to be the district ranger, was disinclined to believe him at first. Jo's indignation and the McManis name were all well and good, but it was the call to the Red Cross at the lodge that finally convinced him, James thought. It certainly wasn't anything *he'd* managed to say.

"Will McManis's grandson. I knew Chuck back when he was about so tall." The ranger raised a hand to a bit more than the height of the desk. "I haven't seen the kid in years, not since his grandfather retired." Then eyed James. "Who are you?"

James straightened his spine." Chuck's father."

The ranger's eyes widened. "The one who ran —"

It wasn't worth the argument. "James McManis." He stuck out his hand, and the ranger shook it.

"I am sorry, sir. We don't have many men to spare for a search right now, but he can't have gone far."

"If he hasn't gone far," Jo put in, "then he's hurt. Or he'd have come back on his own by now."

The ranger nodded. "All right." He didn't need to get the attention of the other men in the room. As James had told the story, they'd drifted up and begun listening, until he had an audience of half a dozen. "One more question." He nodded again, this time at James. "Did your son tell you where he had in mind to scatter the ashes?"

James shook his head. "No. We'd had something of a disagreement before he left." No need to go into detail about that. "He took off without telling me he was leaving, let alone anything else."

That raised an eyebrow under the ranger's flat-brimmed hat, but he didn't ask anything else. "Okay. Patterson, you drive down to Riverside. Ford, you go back around by Giant and Grand, and Mirovski, go up to Observation Point. Ranger McManis was fond of the view, and the boy might have remembered that."

As the men scattered, the ranger picked up the telephone. James put a hand out. "Thank you, sir."

The man set the receiver down. "Ranger McManis was well-loved here, and so was his wife. And your son. But even if the boy was a perfect stranger, we'd be out there looking for him."

James acknowledged that with a soft, "I know."

The ranger hesitated, then asked, "When did your father pass away?"

James sighed. "Last week."

"My condolences on your loss."

"Thank you."

"Now I need to report this to the superintendent's office." He reached for the phone again.

"Is there anything I can do?"

"Stay where we can find you. Don't go haring off yourself." He looked stern inquiry at James.

James nodded. "I'll keep checking back."

The ranger frowned, but let this pass.

As they left, however, Jo didn't. "You ought to go back to the lodge. Check with the Red Cross."

She'd done more than enough. "I can take it from here. Not that I don't appreciate all the help," he added quickly when she scowled at him, "but your boss is probably wondering what happened to you."

"Fine. Let me know when you find him, will you?" She turned on her heel and headed back toward the store.

James watched as she strode briskly away. Then he stared around blankly. Now what could he do? He couldn't simply wait helplessly for others to find the boy. But what could he do that the others couldn't?

He nudged Chuck's duffel bag with his foot, then bent over to pick it up. James didn't think there'd be any clues to the boy's whereabouts he'd missed before, but he supposed it wouldn't hurt to take it back to the car and look.

* * *

Half an hour later he'd emptied the duffel bag down to the canvas shell, gone through everything, not that there'd been anything much to go through, and repacked it rather more neatly than its owner had. The boy wouldn't dare complain, though, not this time.

He stared at the letter, willing it to tell him more, then shrugged, folded it neatly, and put it in his pocket. He closed the Lincoln's trunk. More than ever, James wished he'd stopped long enough to pack a bag of his own before he left Denver. Even to change his clothes. Or his shoes, which were not designed for hiking. Not much to be done about it now, however. He supposed he could buy something at the gift shop, but he just didn't have the energy.

Slowly he headed back toward the lodge, then kept going on past it. Between the low-slung log building and Old Faithful, steaming quietly in the late morning sun, following the trail to the wooden bridge across the Firehole River. He stopped for a moment and stared down at the clear water. He wasn't sure why. It wasn't as if he expected to see Chuck's drowned body there. Or a clue.

He continued on his way, his steps on the bridge as hollow-sounding as his heart. Up the hill. He remembered hiking the geyser basin with his father as a teenager, complaining all the way about being dragged from his books. He still didn't understand the mentality that preferred scrambling around out in the woods to the chance to learn something new. Resolutely he shoved the memory away and kept doggedly on, even as he reached the turnoff for the trail to Observation Point.

Someone's been sent up there, he told himself. You don't have to do this. But he began the climb up the switchback trail anyway, stopping occasionally to catch his breath and call the boy's name. His once-shiny black shoes slipped and slid on the loose soil and pebbles, and he knew he was going to end up with blisters, if not flat on his face.

At least the park service had put up a railing since the last time he'd been up here. He grabbed onto the wooden handhold gratefully, pulling himself step by step until at last he reached the top.

The view was spectacular, so far as such things went. James ignored it, scanning the ground, hoping for something, anything, that would tell him the boy had been here. Footprints were everywhere, but he had no way of knowing which of them were Chuck's. So far as he could tell, the raggedy-looking brush at the edge of the overlook didn't look like anyone had fallen through it. He peered over the edge of the cliff but saw nothing, no bodies, no waving arms. He heard no cries for help. He shouted Chuck's name, anyway.

"You shouldn't be up here," said a deep voice behind him.

Startled, James almost fell down the cliff himself. A strong hand grabbed his upper arm and steadied him as he turned around. "I can't just sit and wait."

The ranger – what was his name? – something Polish, James thought, about Chuck's height but much broader across the shoulder and at least ten years older, said, "I've checked the area. He's not here. We don't want to have to add another missing person to the list. Go on back down. We'll let you know the moment we find him."

"I know you will. Thank you." What else could he say? He didn't turn back, but kept on going. The trail was a loop, so at least he could keep up the pretense of going back, even if he wasn't.

He kept his eyes on the trail the entire way back down, only stopping periodically to call the boy's name and peer through the trees as if he thought he was going to find Chuck's body lying in the woods. The dust was thick in places, and some of the footprints were large enough to be from Chuck's motorcycle boots, but that didn't mean they were. When he reached the main trail again, the boot prints turned right across a small open space. James didn't hesitate, but turned right, too, and kept going, kept calling. Away from the lodge. A few yards later, he entered the woods at the base of the hillside.

Lodgepole pines were too tall and skinny to make much of a gloom no matter how closely together they grew, and bars of sunlight sprayed across the path from between the trees. The trail was dry and dusty, as if it hadn't rained in some time. The large boot prints were headed this way. James wasn't sure why he was so positive they were Chuck's, but he kept following them, anyway. When the trail passed out from under the trees and onto open ground dotted with hot springs and holes in the ground with signs labeling them geysers, the trail turned into boardwalk, and the footprints disappeared.

It was as if something had been jerked out from under him. He stopped and stared out across the river.

He hadn't come that far, but he had another choice in front of him. Several, actually. He could turn and go back along the river toward the lodge, or down the hill to another bridge and the road, or he could keep going ahead, to God knew where.

The last time he'd walked these paths had been over forty years ago. Once upon a time he might have known where he was going. Once upon a time he might have even cared. James shrugged and took the God knew where choice. He was quite sure if Chuck had made it this far he wouldn't have turned back. Wherever he was going.

The boards clunked hollowly under his feet, but at least they were solid, unlike the ground beneath them. A few yards past the intersection, he passed a small geyser, chugging and churning, the thudding noise hard enough he could feel the vibration through his feet. It, like everything else here, smelled like rotten eggs.

Everything about it made him feel sick. Everything in this place made him feel sick. It always had. The stench, the steam, the powdery white dust. The way a person couldn't trust the very ground to stay stable under his feet. Why anyone wanted to visit here had always been beyond him. Why his parents wanted to work here, why his son of all people had fallen in love with the place, was beyond his ability to comprehend.

The first explorers had called it hell with the fires burned out. And yet people came in droves to visit this hell. It made no sense.

A pine tree, looking like it was barely surviving, grew next to the boardwalk. James stopped in its shade and took his jacket off. It was getting hot out here. Shading his eyes with his free hand, he scanned the area.

A small sign read "Grand Geyser." The memory assaulted him. It was one of his earliest. It had been before his parents came back from the Klondike, because he was with his grandmother and grandfather. They'd ridden horseback down from the Fountain Hotel, James perched in front of his grandfather on the saddle.

They'd left the horses in the meadow and strolled about. It had been early spring, and cold, snowbanks in the woods, the wind sharp, the sky a deep, deep blue. His grandfather had carried James – Jem – he'd been called Jem, back then – on his shoulders until he'd squirmed down and run off before either of his grandparents could catch him.

Past the trees, across the gray ground ringing hollow beneath his feet.

His grandmother had been the one to catch him, he remembered, and just before he'd run through a big pool that had been rippling, ground that had been thudding, and yanked him back and ran just before the pool that wasn't just a pool erupted, throwing boiling water everywhere.

He'd jerked loose again, but he'd run away this time, till his grandfather's arms caught him up and held him until the tears of sheer terror had stopped.

He was breathing hard even now, just thinking about it. But this wasn't helping to find Chuck. He shouted the boy's name again. And again. His voice was getting hoarse, and his throat dry as dust.

Then suddenly he realized he was staring at something lying on the ground, half under the boardwalk. His eyes couldn't make sense of it at first. It was dirty white, not all that different from the color of the ground. But the angles and corners of it were too square to be something natural. James squatted down on the edge of the boardwalk and picked the object up.

It had been sitting in the water, and it dripped on the boardwalk, making darker patches on the warping wood. An odd catch held the lid closed on one side, and a printed label, half-smeared by the wet, was stuck to the other.

James peered at the writing, then dropped the box. It landed with a splash back into the thin layer of water flowing beneath the boardwalk. His legs buckled under him, and he went to his knees, heedless of splinters or wet spots or anything else.

The words on the box were his parents' names.

CHAPTER 4

James wasn't sure how long he sat there, staring at the box in the water, before he picked it up again as carefully as if it held dynamite. It was light. Empty. So the boy had scattered its contents before he'd disappeared into what was beginning to feel like thin air. James read the rest of the printing on the label – not that there was much more to read. His parents' names were handwritten in thick black ink. The name and address of the crematorium was printed, like the letterhead on the document he'd found in Chuck's duffel bag. No more clues than that.

At least he knew Chuck had gotten this far. Was this where he'd scattered his grandparents' remains? Not up at the viewpoint? Not that it mattered.

He levered himself to his feet, getting a grip on the scrawny tree with his free hand and stumbling when it rocked, its roots apparently loosened by the quake. Whatever the boy had done, it wouldn't have been like him to just drop the box here. Something must have happened.

He stared around, getting a good look at his surroundings for the first time since he'd stumbled to this point. The boardwalk was in terrible shape. Oh, he'd half-noticed when he'd first stepped on it that it wasn't level and was even broken in places, but he hadn't thought about the reason. But here in front of the geyser the boards were splintered and split, sticking out at odd angles. Some of them had even washed away.

The ground, well, he didn't know what the ground was supposed to look like, but right this moment it looked as if someone had dropped a bomb. The crater was empty and dry, but deep ragged channels ran from it under what was left of the boardwalk, and down the hillside to the river many yards away.

Had the boy been caught here during the earthquake? If so, what had happened to him? And where was he *now*?

James shouted Chuck's name over and over, for the first time hearing a note of panic in his own voice. He couldn't suppress it. If the boy had been injured, or, or killed, his body would still be here. But it wasn't, and –

He had to be close by. He had to be.

* * *

He jumped at the sound of a voice.

"I thought I told you to go back." It was the ranger, the one with the Polish name, from up at Observation Point.

James looked up at him. He was taller than Chuck. "Would you, if you were in my place?"

The ranger shook his head. Only then did he seem to notice the dripping box James held in his hands. " What's that?"

"The crematory box."

"What?" The man gave him a confused look.

James supposed it did sound rather odd. "The box my parents' ashes were in. Chuck must have dropped it here."

The ranger held his hand out. James shook his head. "It's empty. He must have scattered them here, before the earthquake."

"After the earthquake."

"What?"

The ranger gestured. "Look. It's obvious the Grand went off when the earthquake hit." He glanced around in obvious appreciation for the damage. "Must have been quite an eruption."

James let his breath out in a huff. "Can we get back to the point?"

The ranger didn't roll his eyes, but to James's irritation he looked like he wanted to. "If he'd dropped the box before the earthquake, it would be in the Firehole River by now."

"Oh."

"Yeah." The ranger's face reflected the hope he must have seen in James's expression. "If he was still calm and cool enough to hang onto the box after the eruption that did this, chances are he's fine."

"But if he's fine," James asked plaintively, "where *is* he?"

"We'll keep looking, sir." Now the ranger's face took on a determined look. "But you need to go back to the lodge. For all you know, he might be there by now."

It had been several hours since the last time he'd checked in with the Red Cross. And he never had gone looking for the boy's motorcycle. If it was missing, too, then chances were he was on a wild goose chase out here. And the rangers, too. Somehow he couldn't quite bring himself to care about them.

"All right, all right. You *are* going to check the whole area thoroughly, right?"

"Yes." The ranger pulled a walkie-talkie out of a loop on his belt.

James waited to hear what he was going to say, but the ranger gestured him on. "Be careful, sir."

Now James wanted to roll his eyes. Reluctantly, however, he picked his way over the broken boardwalk and limped – cursing his now-battered dress shoes – back toward the lodge.

* * *

James was not surprised to find out that Chuck hadn't checked in with the Red Cross. The young woman staffing the table gave him one of those sympathetic looks he despised, and then a longer once-over of more genuine concern.

"You should sit down and rest, sir."

"I need –"

"Let me get you something to drink. You don't want to get dehydrated. You'll make yourself sick." Turning to her fellow worker, she added, "I'll be back in a minute," then took James by the arm. "You need to rest."

Bemused, James let her lead him over to one of the Mission-style cushioned wooden chairs littering the lobby, and didn't object when she nudged him down into it. She took the crematorium box from his clutched hand and plopped it on the table at his elbow. "Stay there," she told him, as if he was some sort of trained dog, and went off.

He wasn't sure he was going to be able to get back up again. He watched people come and go, knowing somehow that none of them would be Chuck but unable to keep from hoping, anyway. Except for the Red Cross table, the place looked as if it were getting back to normal. He wanted to shout and yell, and tell them nothing was normal, tell them, my son is missing, you idiots!

The young woman came back with a steaming cup of coffee, some packets of sugar and thimbles of creamer, and a large paper cup of ice water. James reached for the coffee, but she said, "Drink the water first."

Obediently he picked it up, even though his system was crying out for caffeine, and took a sip. Suddenly he realized how very thirsty he was, and drained the entire thing.

She smiled. "Have you had lunch?"

James thought about Chuck, wandering around God knew where for two days without food, and shook his head. "I need to get back out there."

"You won't do anyone any good if you don't eat something."

"I'm fine." He leaned his head back and let the pulse of his throbbing feet create a sort of rhythm in his head. "I'm just going to rest for a few minutes, then I need to get back out there."

She smiled. He closed his eyes. Just for a few minutes.

* * *

When he opened his eyes again, the angle of the shadows had changed. Not only because it was later in the afternoon, James discovered, but because clouds had rolled in, obscuring the sun.

A plastic-wrapped sandwich and an apple sat on the table next to his now-cold but untouched coffee. He should have drunk it first. James levered himself to his aching feet. Might as well take the food with him.

Taking a bite of his sandwich, he checked back in at the Red Cross desk. They appeared to be packing up. "Are you leaving?"

"Yes, sir. We're going to go help at West Yellowstone now that the road is open again and things are getting back to normal here."

"Oh," James said, feeling stupid. He'd forgotten that things were much worse elsewhere. "Is it bad there?"

"A lot of damage and a number of injuries, but so far as we know," she gave him that now-familiar sympathetic glance, "no fatalities except for the people up at Rock Creek. Where the landslide was," she added.

"Well, thank you for the help." What else could he say?

"I hope you find your son soon," she told him, and stood as her partner folded the now-empty table.

He nodded, but he couldn't help but feel that they were giving up. On Chuck. On him. James fully expected, as he headed to the ranger station, to find out that the search had been called off there, too.

When he arrived there, he was grateful to find out it hadn't been, not yet, although the district ranger seemed to feel the need to vent his frustration on James. James understood. He wished he had someone to vent his frustration on, too.

"That boy of yours pulled a real vanishing act. Was he running away?"

James sighed, and tried to get comfortable in the straight-backed chair he'd been offered. And there it was. The boy was technically an adult, even if he didn't act like one most of the time. "He's twenty years old. I'd hardly call it running away."

"You said you'd had an argument before he left Denver."

"Not anything serious." Not any more serious than any of the other arguments they'd had recently about the choices Chuck had been making. "I just didn't see the necessity for the trip up here, and he had his heart set on it."

"Why?"

It wasn't any of the man's business. James opened his mouth to tell him so, then shut it again.

The ranger waited. "Maybe he was just following your example?"

"What do you mean?"

"You –"

"I did not run away. I went to college."

"That wasn't how your father told the story. He said –"

James rose, trying not to let the steam escape from his ears. Of all the – "I appreciate your efforts. I'll check in again later."

"Wait."

"What?"

"Do you really think he's still out there?"

"You found his motorcycle." The machine was now parked next to the Lincoln outside the lodge. He had no idea how he was going to get it home if Chuck wasn't able to ride it. If he even found Chuck. No, he told himself. He would find the boy if it was the last thing he did.

But if he was injured – Firmly, James squashed his churning thoughts. "How else would he have left?"

The ranger shrugged. "He could have hitchhiked. If he was trying to cover his tracks –"

"That motorcycle was his pride and joy. He would never have left it behind."

"He obviously did."

"No, he's obviously still here, somewhere." James pointed at the crematorium box, which was now sitting on the ranger's desk. "We have proof he was out there. Who do you think would have given him a ride in the middle of the night?"

"Do you have any idea how many people tried to leave the park after the earthquake? As soon as the road opened back up, it was like a parade. What would you have done if someone had asked you for a ride out?"

James shoulders slumped.

"We're going to keep looking for him. We're not giving up yet."

"I know." The words stuck in his throat, but he forced them out. "I'm sorry."

The ranger's voice became more sympathetic. "What you are is worn out."

"Not yet."

"Please don't go back out there and get lost yourself."

"I'll stay on the trails."

The ranger sighed. "I can't stop you, can I?"

James almost smiled. "No."

And so James found himself limping across the bridge and up to the boardwalk once more, with no idea where to go or what to do, the only certainty in his mind that the boy hadn't taken the opportunity to run away.

Certainty. No. That was an illusion. James trudged along in the fading light, calling Chuck's name, oblivious to the curious stares from the people he passed. The longer this went on, the less certain he was about anything.

Helplessly he began replaying that meeting at Pritchard's office, and the aftermath. Perhaps he'd overreacted when he'd put his foot down so hard. Chuck had spent much of his childhood here, and James had never objected before. But the boy's grandparents had always been here before, to watch over him. He'd trusted his mother to take care of Chuck when he was small, the way she'd taken care of James after they'd taken him in. He'd trusted her to have Chuck safely waiting for him to go back to Denver every fall after he grew old enough to go to school. He'd trusted her.

No, he was sure this was something concocted by his father after she'd died five years ago. She would never have approved of such a cockamamie scheme.

If it weren't for the occasional new sign warning hikers away from damage done to the trails by the earthquake, he'd never have known it wasn't an ordinary evening in Yellowstone. People wandering the trails, staring at muddy springs and steam clouds, gathering around the occasional spurt of water to exclaim over it. He wanted to shout at them, to tell them it *wasn't* an ordinary day, it was a dangerous place where people could get killed or go missing, where someone *had* gone missing and might be dead or injured, all because no one could find him.

Because *James* couldn't find him. Couldn't save him from whatever horrible thing had happened to him. Couldn't help the son he loved so much. Tears stung his eyes for the first time, and he stumbled.

A hand grasped his arm. "Hey."

He tried to jerk away.

"You shouldn't be out here."

So everyone kept telling him. He stared at his shoes. Everything he hated about being here was in those shoes.

"Are you all right?"

Something about the voice sounded vaguely familiar. Slowly he raised his head. "What are you doing out here?" Wherever here was. He'd walked farther than he thought he had, clear down almost to the other end of the trail.

The woman from the soda fountain – Jo? – answered matter-of-factly, "I'm off shift now."

"How nice for you."

"I'm helping with the search." She didn't sound angry with him for his sarcasm. He didn't want to think how she sounded.

"Oh. Thank you." He knew he sounded inane, but he was more grateful than he could express. That she would use her precious time off to search for a stranger –

"You're welcome. But first I think we'd better get you back to civilization."

He stared at her. "I can't go home without my boy."

"The lodge is civilized enough for now, I think." She was tugging him along the trail. He thought about resisting her, but he was very much afraid she'd be able to overpower him, and wouldn't that simply top his day off.

"Is that how you think of him? As a boy? How old is he?"

"He turned twenty a few months ago," James admitted.

"Hardly a boy, then."

"That depends on your point of view."

She laughed. Instead of irritating him, it sounded almost comforting. "You're almost old enough to be his grandfather, if I don't miss my guess."

James shrugged. That was what came of not meeting the love of your life until you were almost too old for it, or at least so it had seemed when he was forty years old, and Catherine strode into his office looking for work. He'd ended up marrying her instead. It had been almost embarrassing, like some sort of Tracy/Hepburn movie, the sharp, beautiful young secretary and the hidebound old boss. He'd been so lucky. For a while, at least.

Jo cleared her throat.

"I married late. We weren't going to have children."

"But you did."

"Yes."

"Where is your wife?"

James sighed. "She died in childbirth. But if you knew my parents you probably already knew that."

She didn't make any of the usual trite responses he'd heard the few times he'd made that admission over the years. He appreciated it. "I didn't know them that well. Your father retired only a couple of years after I started working here. But I liked them." She smiled.

"Everybody did."

"He used to come in to the store with your son whenever your mother was out of town, to get hamburgers and fries."

"I know. That's why the fountain was one of the first places I started looking for him."

They'd reached Old Faithful. James shook Jo's hand off of his arm and sat down on one of the benches. "Go on. I'll be fine here. Thank you so much for all your help."

"You sure?"

I'm just going to rest for a bit." He gestured at the lodge entrance a few yards off. "If I can't make it the rest of the way on my own, I'll get help, I promise you."

She smiled. She had a nice smile. It made him realize the lines around her mouth were there because she did it so often, because they crinkled right up and added to the effect. It was strangely familiar somehow, too, and that wasn't a bad thing, either, even if he couldn't explain why. "All right. Get something to eat."

"I will. "Why was everyone so determined to keep him fed? No one was doing that for Chuck, at least so far as he knew.

"Hey." Jo sat down beside him. "We'll find him."

"Go on."

"As soon as I know you've got yourself back together."

All right, now he *was* embarrassed. "I'm fine. Really."

She stood up, but the expression on her face was still dubious.

"Go on."

"All right."

After James watched her walk back the way they'd come, he levered himself to his feet again, but instead of going to the lodge he crossed the road back to the ranger station.

The door opened as he approached it, and the young ranger gestured at him, then turned to shout inside. "Here he is, sir."

James's heart leaped up into his throat, and he had to swallow it back down before he could get his feet to move. He barged past the young man and stared about the room. No Chuck. He let his breath out. Maybe someone was bringing him back and they just hadn't arrived yet.

The district ranger stood up from his desk and walked up to him. He didn't look like someone with good news.

James swallowed again. "Yes?"

"I have a message for you."

"What?"

The district ranger held out a piece of paper. "Apparently he couldn't think how else to get hold of you."

"What did he say?"

"Just asked for you, and when I told him you weren't here, he asked to leave a message."

"Oh." James took the small pink rectangle. It was just like the ones used in his office, a standard while-you-were-out form. The name printed on it in square black letters read "Michael Pritchard." And a phone number. Pritchard. Surely the boy hadn't contacted *him*, even if he was running away. Which he *wasn't*, dammit. Although given the events surrounding William McManis's last will and testament, it was as likely as anything else that had happened in the last three days.

James glanced over at the district ranger's desk. The plain black telephone stood out as if it was lit up in neon. He looked back at the ranger.

The ranger shook his head. James gave serious thought to strangling him. But the man was pointing to another desk in the back of the room, with another phone." You can use that one."

"Thank you." He moved in a stumbling rush.

CHAPTER 5

He had to go through the park operator for the long-distance call, then he had to wait as the ringer threshed endlessly. Finally a female voice. "Pritchard Law."

"Let me speak to Pritchard."

"May I ask who is calling?"

"James McManis, and I'm calling long distance."

"Yes, sir."

Silence over the line, another interminable few seconds. "Yes?"

"Pritchard, if you know where my son is –"

"Hello to you, too, Jem."

Jem? Why on earth would Pritchard be calling him that? The childhood nickname barely registered through his anger, but his response was automatic. "Don't call me that. Where *is* he?"

A few more seconds silence, then, "It's not something I can explain over the phone –"

"Oh, yes, you can. And you will." He was about to climb through the telephone lines. "If this is some asinine instruction my father left you, then forget about it. Where *is* he?"

"I don't know."

"Then why are you wasting my time?"

"Don't hang up."

"Give me one good reason not to."

"I have something for you."

"I'll get it after I bring the boy home. Is that it?"

"He's not there."

It was like a punch straight to his solar plexus. It took James a second before he was able to wheeze out, "How the – how do you know?"

"I'm not going to explain this over the phone."

"Then you're going to have to come here. I'm not leaving until I find him."

"Je – Mr. McManis." That was more like it. "He's not there. At least not –" he broke off.

"At least not *what?*"

"Fine." He paused. "Fine. I'll be there tomorrow night. Where can I meet you?"

So far as James cared, the man could meet him in hell. He was already there, anyway. "At the lodge, on the porch. At six."

"I'll do my best. If I'm not there by then, wait for me."

"If I'm not there, you can just wait yourself."

"Yes, sir."

Definitely more like it. James didn't bother with the niceties himself, but put the receiver back down with a gesture just short of a slam. If Pritchard wanted to waste his time, he was more than welcome. He probably didn't know anything useful, anyway.

* * *

It was almost full dark by the time he stepped back outside, a lavender line on the horizon all that was left of sunset. The moon wasn't up yet, but light gleamed from the windows of the various buildings, so at least he could see well enough to make his way back to the lodge. He glanced at his watch. It was almost nine.

The woman at the front desk hailed him. "Mr. McManis?"

Sighing, James stopped. "Yes."

"I have a message for you."

He couldn't help it, he – It was another idiotic pink piece of paper. He picked it up and saw the name Pritchard on it. He crumpled it in his fist. "Thank you."

"Sir?"

He glanced back at her pleasant face. "Yes?"

"We've had some cancellations due to the earthquake, and I have a cabin available if you'd be interested."

Oh, he'd be interested, all right. A bed. A real bed, not a canvas cot. "Yes, please. Thank you." It came out a bit more heartfelt than he'd intended, and the woman smiled at him. "Do you have one with a bathroom?"

She did, thank God, and a few moments later he stumbled back out into the dark, the key clutched in his hand.

The cabin wasn't much, certainly not up to his usual standards, but it was clean and private. He stripped off his wrinkled, smelly suit and shoes, ran the water in the tiny shower until steam rose, soaped off two days of dirt and grime, and fell face first onto the springy mattress.

* * *

He was woken by a discreet knock on the door. "Housekeeping," said a young voice on the other side.

James rolled over and rubbed his eyes. "Can you come back later?"

"Sure." The sound of wheels on rough ground trundled away.

He didn't want to know what time it was, but he checked his watch, anyway. Nine in the morning. His stomach growled in spite of him. The last thing he wanted to do was put that suit back on, but it wasn't as if he had much choice. The sun almost blinded him when he stepped outside.

First things first.

The district ranger wasn't in, but the ranger on duty was full of that now-familiar sympathy without understanding, and had no news whatsoever. If James hadn't known he meant well, he'd have given the young man an earful. He almost did it anyway when the fellow asked, probably in all innocence, "Is there anywhere he would have gone? If he didn't want to go home?"

"No." James bit down on 'you young idiot.' The last thing he needed to do was offend these people.

"Ranger Willis said you and your son had a fight before he left home."

"That is none of your business."

The ranger glanced up. "Maybe he didn't want to go home."

James took a deep breath. "I've got a cabin at the lodge. Number 411. If you find anything, anything at all, please contact me there."

The ranger made a note. At least that was something. "Thank you." The telephone rang. "Excuse me." He picked it up.

James went back to the lodge and the pay phones. The call to the house, where he spent more time trying to reassure a worried Mrs. May than anything else, and what should have been a brief phone call to the office to let them know he was going to be gone longer than expected, but turned into another, if more discreet, worry fest on the other end. He hung up the phone and rolled his shoulders to try to relieve the tension. He supposed he should eat something. Jo Bennett was right. He wasn't going to do anyone any good if he didn't put at least something in his stomach occasionally. He would kill two birds with one stone and check in at the soda fountain. Not that he expected news, but perhaps she would be there and he could ask her for more information than that obnoxious young ranger had had time to give him.

It wasn't until he tramped down the road yet again that the oddness of Pritchard's willingness to drive clear off up here at a moment's notice dawned on him. What was so incredibly important that the man felt the need to drive twelve hours from Denver just to give him something he could have handed him at the meeting on the sixteenth? Unless he hadn't had whatever it was he had now at the meeting. Could Chuck have given Pritchard something the next morning when they'd conspired behind his back? But that didn't tell James why Pritchard couldn't have simply told him what it was. If Pritchard had known Chuck was going to run away and hadn't told him, James would not be responsible for his actions when the man showed up.

James took a deep breath and shoved the door to the Hamilton store open in a manner Jo would have approved of. Indeed, he could see her glance up and nod in his direction as he strode forward.

What a difference twenty-four hours made. He'd never have known there'd been an earthquake the day before. Except – he glanced over at the grocery section of the store, at the empty refrigerator cases and the only partially-filled shelves. He supposed getting them restocked wasn't all that high on anyone's list of priorities right now. But everything else looked absolutely normal, even the couple of tourists browsing through the souvenirs.

He aimed straight for the soda fountain.

Jo smiled at him. "Good morning."

James clenched his teeth for a second, then deliberately relaxed his jaw. "Not precisely. Have you heard anything?"

Her expression changed to puzzlement. "Haven't you checked in at the ranger station this morning?"

"Yes."

She shrugged. "Then you know more than I do."

"I doubt it. I think they're about to call off the search. It hasn't even been forty-eight hours." He took one look at the disbelief on her face. "They've got it into their heads that Chuck took off. That he ran away."

"Sit down, Mr. McManis."

"I don't want —"

"Sit down, anyway."

He sat. What was it about her that she could order him around like this? She wasn't anybody, just a short order cook at a soda fountain. *He* was someone people obeyed. Who owned his own business, who told other people what to do.

"Have you had breakfast?"

"No."

"All right." She disappeared behind the pass through.

James leaned his elbows on the counter and put his head in his hands.

"How do you like your eggs?"

She had eggs? What did it matter? "Scrambled."

"Bacon or sausage?"

"I don't —" She turned and eyed him through the pass-through. "Sausage."

"One more question."

"*What?*"

She smiled. "White or whole wheat?"

"Why are you *doing* this to me?"

"Whole wheat it is." In a moment she came around through the swinging door carrying a coffee pot. He would have clawed through glass for coffee just then, and gladly burned his tongue on the thick black brew as soon as she set his cup in front of him.

He watched her swing back through the door, and a few moments later come back through with a loaded plate. She plunked it down in front of him. "Eat."

He wasn't sure he could now, for all that his stomach was growling, but after the first bite it went down all right. "Thank you," he told her a short time later as she took his now-empty plate away.

"You're welcome. Feeling a bit more human?"

"I – Yes." He was, he realized. "But now what?"

"For one thing, I can tell you they're not giving up the search." She picked up a cloth and started swiping the counter down. "Pat – the district ranger – is a friend, and he told me last night they're pretty convinced he ran away, but they're not giving up on the off chance that he didn't.

"Could he have?" She set down her cloth and gave him her full attention. He found it disconcerting. "Run away?"

She wasn't asking because she thought she knew already. She was asking because she genuinely wanted to know.

He tried to sidle up and glance at the possibility without admitting it. It was impossible. He took a deep breath and closed his eyes and stared at it full on, hating what he saw but unable to deny it any longer.

When he opened them again, she had other customers. The feeling of relief was almost palpable. He started to get up.

She glanced over. "Wait."

He sat back down. What *was* it about her?

When she had taken their orders, she came back down to him. "I'm only working the breakfast shift, and I'll be off in an hour." She refilled his coffee cup. "You stay right there until I'm done."

"I have to go –"

"Go where? Back out where we've all looked already?"

He slumped, and had to grasp the counter to keep from sliding off the stool.

"You're not doing him any good this way."

He almost groaned. "I know."

"One hour. It's not going to make a difference one way or the other."

His breakfast churned in his stomach. But she was right. So he sat, and waited, and after she'd completed her work, she pushed through the swinging door in her jeans and flannel shirt and boots, untying her apron and tossing it at the young woman who was taking her place.

"Come on, let's get out of here."

As if he had no mind of his own whatsoever, he got up and followed her.

* * *

They went back to the ranger station and checked in one more time, although it seemed a waste of time to him. The ranger on duty appeared to be relieved to see her, for some reason, and as she chatted with him James found himself realizing that her method of interrogation, for that's what it was, was much more effective than his. The old saw about catching flies with honey slid through his mind and out the other side without stopping. He simply wasn't capable of the kind of thing she was doing right now.

But he could listen, and he did, between the lines as well as what was being said out loud. The district ranger, when he joined them, seemed to have come to the same conclusion that his underlings all shared, that Chuck wasn't lost out in the wilderness somewhere, but that he'd planned to run away all along and took advantage of the unexpected confusion to cover his trail. It wasn't that the man didn't care, and it wasn't, James realized, even that he begrudged using the time and energy of his staff to search for the boy. It was that he was running out of logical places to look and was hoping for a happier ending to the story. Happy from his perspective being that they hadn't failed because Chuck wasn't there to be found in the first place.

James swallowed, and then almost choked on it when Jo turned to him and asked, "Why didn't you tell me you'd talked to your lawyer?"

Because it wasn't any of her business? "It slipped my mind. Besides, he's not my lawyer, he's my father's lawyer. Or was."

The district ranger said, "I meant to ask you if he'd had any information."

James sighed. "He says he does, but he refused to give it over the phone."

That startled both of them. Well, it had frustrated the daylights out of him, too, James thought. Not that his frustration had done any good.

"Are you going back to Denver, then?" asked the ranger. It was probably only in James's imagination that the man's voice sounded hopeful.

"No," James said slowly. "He's coming here."

"Must be important," Jo put in. "For him to drive all this way."

"If it was that important he could have told me over the phone," James snapped.

"When will he get here?"

"He said tonight."

"Well," the ranger broke in. "We'll keep looking. You stay where we can find you, and if the lawyer has any useful information at all, you come tell me. I'll be here." He sighed. "I suspect I'm going to be here every waking hour for a while yet." He looked over at Jo. "You working today?"

She shook her head. "I just finished my shift."

"Good." His glance at James was so quick James almost missed it, but it was telling. So was Jo's nod in return.

James followed her out, but as soon as they cleared the door, he came to a stop. "I don't need a babysitter."

"No, you don't," she agreed, but nudged him forward, anyway.

"I'm sure you've got other things to do, after spending all day yesterday searching." She raised an eyebrow at him. "Not that I don't appreciate it. You have no idea how much I appreciate it."

"*De nada.* I just wish I'd found him for you." She nudged at him again, and, almost against his will, James started forward. "And, as it happens, I have the rest of the day ahead of me and nothing else to do." She led him to a shaded bench at the side of the museum. He could see Old Faithful from here, deserted now between eruptions. "Why don't you sit down and tell me what you and Chuck were arguing about?"

* * *

Jo Bennett was utterly wasted as a short-order cook, James thought sometime later. She should have been a psychologist or maybe a private investigator, in spite of being a woman. She didn't badger him, or push him. She just asked in that persuasive way of hers, and he found himself telling her pretty much everything, as the crowds ebbed and flowed past along with the geyser.

But at last she smiled at him, and said, "I agree with you. I don't think he was running away. He just wanted some time to say good-bye to his grandparents, and I don't think anyone can blame him for that."

No one but him. "I did."

"It's hard to blame you for that, either."

"I should have been more understanding –"

"But you were angry because he was ruining what you wanted for him."

Well, that was one way of looking at it. "His future, yes."

"We all have goals for our kids. I certainly did for my daughter."

He didn't know why he was surprised. She had to be in her fifties. "You have children?"

"Just the one. She's grown now."

"Where is she?"

"I don't know." She smiled again, but it didn't go to her eyes this time. "She ran away when she was eighteen. So I do have a little experience with this kind of thing."

"Oh. I'm sorry. Couldn't you find her?"

"She was of legal age. I didn't feel it was my place to try." He wasn't sure if the criticism was intentional or not. "It wasn't the end of the world. And I'm sure she's doing fine."

He didn't believe he was going to ask the question, but – "Where's your husband?"

She laughed. That took James aback. "I ran away, too."

"You're divorced?"

"Yes. Years ago."

No wonder her daughter had run away. "What happened?"

She moved her shoulder as if she was pushing the question away, but she answered readily enough. "He wanted one thing, I wanted something else entirely." She paused. "You remind me of him." Then added hastily, as his dismay must have shown on his face, "Not in a bad way."

He wasn't going to ask, wasn't – "How?"

She laughed again. "I think it's the suit."

He suspected his favorite Brooks Brothers suit was going to end up in the ragbag by the time he made it back to Denver, if only because he'd never want to see it again. "I was about to go to work when I heard about the earthquake, and I didn't stop to pack a suitcase."

Her face softened. "You care about him."

What did she think? "He's my son."

"Of course he is." She took a deep breath. "I'm sorry."

Why did he have the feeling she didn't say that very often?

Her next question made a sharp right turn. "What do you do for a living?"

"I'm a CPA."

Now the smile went all the way to her eyes. "So that's why you remind me of him. He was a lawyer. Rules for law and rules for numbers aren't that different."

He hadn't quite thought of it that way before. "It's a good living."

"More respectable than short-order cook out in, didn't you call it the middle of nowhere?"

Wait, he hadn't meant – She sounded downright defensive. He just looked at her.

She shook herself. "I hate apologizing."

"You don't need to." He knew he sounded stiff, but he couldn't help it.

"I'm putting his words in your mouth." She shook her head. "After all these years. I had no idea anyone could still do that to me."

"I didn't mean to."

"Of course not. How would you know?"

James stood. "I have to do something. I'm sure this has all been fascinating for you, but I can't just sit here anymore." He glanced at his watch and sighed. "Still hours before that idiot Pritchard can possibly be here." He gave her a defiant glance. "I'm going back out there."

She stood, too. "I'll come with you."

"Look, I know your friend the ranger wants you to keep an eye on me, but if I promise to stay on the trails and not fall in a hot spring, can you just leave me alone?"

"I sort of promised –"

"Well, I didn't." He started off.

She kept pace.

"Please, just go *away*."

"I think we should go back to Grand Geyser and see if he left any other traces behind."

James glared at her.

"He might have dropped something the rangers missed. Or left some footprints."

"On the boardwalk?" He didn't even bother to keep the sarcasm out of his voice.

She put a hand on his shoulder. He shook it off, but stopped and faced her.

She faced him right back. "No. If he was flung off the boardwalk by the quake, which isn't unlikely at all given what it looks like now, he might have tried to climb the hill instead of going back to it." She looked him up and down. "Now I wouldn't recommend trying to climb that hill in your shiny shoes —" he glanced down at his scuffed, battered dress shoes "— but I could probably find a pair of hiking boots in your size. Maybe even a pair of jeans. But not unless I come with you."

How – "Where?"

She smirked. "I have my sources."

* * *

She did. They walked back into the woods across the road, past the campground and through the trees to the cabins and bunkhouses where the employees lived. She led the way to one of the bunkhouses and up the stairs, then down a hall full of doors, to one at the end.

She swung it open. "Welcome to Aladdin's cave."

He peered inside and sneezed. "Hardly." But at her gesture he stepped inside and reached for the pull chain to a bare bulb hanging from the ceiling, then blinked in the glare.

The place was lined with floor to ceiling shelves, each one so loaded with piled boxes it amazed him they didn't bow in the middle. The boxes were labeled with numbers.

"What is this?"

"Clothes. Don't worry, they've all been washed. What's your size?" She waited. He told her. And the next thing he knew, she was waiting outside in the hall while he changed from his suit to a pair of jeans and a shirt that looked like they belonged to his son, and a rather disreputable-looking pair of hiking boots that were, amazingly enough, more comfortable than his own shoes had become.

When he stepped out, his suit over his arm, she said, "That's better."

And he had to admit she was right.

* * *

He could only wish the hike out to Grand Geyser and up the hill behind it had been as fruitful. They'd spent the entire afternoon out there, searching for something, anything else besides the box now sitting on the table in his cabin, to show that Chuck had even been there. The sun had angled back over the hills to the west when Jo finally said, "we've got to give up, for now, anyway."

James only shook his head and peered more closely at a spot on the ground. "I think I found something. A footprint."

She came over." That's yours. Just like the others you found."

"You're sure?"

"I'm sure. Come on." She took him by the arm. "You're going to keep your lawyer waiting if you don't."

He didn't want to. There had to be something out here. The boy couldn't just vanish into thin air. Unless he wanted to. It was getting harder and harder to believe otherwise. He had to give Chuck credit, though. If he had run away, he'd not only been an opportunistic young pup, taking advantage of the earthquake that way, but he'd obviously had a plan. James wouldn't have given him credit if he hadn't seen the results himself — it had to be one more argument against the whole scenario, James thought. He knew the boy, knew him better than anyone else, and he would have put good money against Chuck having the ability to disappear so completely. So utterly.

He was thinking as if the boy really had done it, he realized. As if he didn't know his own son at all. He swallowed, and put one foot after the other. The boy wouldn't have done this to him. He wouldn't have just straddled his godforsaken motorcycle and ridden away for good. Not without telling his father what he was going to do.

And if he'd told you, what would you have done? You know how angry he was the night before he left, James reminded himself. How angry they'd both been. How he, James, had tried to assert authority over Chuck as if he had no will of his own.

"Come on," Jo said.

"What?"

"We're almost there. Don't stop now."

James glanced up. So they were.

"Is that your lawyer?"

"He's not –" The man striding toward them certainly didn't look like the buttoned-down lawyer he'd seen, was it only three days ago? He was about as underdressed for a meeting as James was at the moment.

James matched his pace until they were standing nose to nose, right there in front of the lodge. "All right, you're here. Now tell me what on earth's going on."

CHAPTER 6

"Hello, Mr. McManis." Pritchard looked him up and down, and smiled. "Is there somewhere we can sit and talk?"

James bit down swearwords. He wasn't going to lower himself to that point. "What was *so* important that you couldn't tell me over the phone?"

"Mr. – Pritchard?" Jo broke in. "Come this way."

"Excuse me?"

"Come on," James growled.

They followed her to the bench where he'd spent his morning telling a perfect stranger what felt like his life story, and sat down. Jo remained standing.

Pritchard gave her a puzzled look.

"I'll just –" Jo said.

"Sit down," James said wearily. "I know you're not going anywhere."

She did, on the very end of the bench, looking uncomfortable for the first time since James had met her. He dropped her from his radar and turned to Pritchard.

"*Tell* me."

"Not tell, Mr. McManis. Give." He lifted his briefcase to his lap and opened it. Took out a paper-wrapped parcel, shaped and sized like a single shirt box from the cleaners, tied with string. He held it out. "Your grandfather wanted you to have this."

James took it. "My grandfather – What?"

"Open it." Pritchard rose.

James sprang to his feet and grabbed Pritchard by the arm. The parcel fell to the ground. "If you think you're going anywhere before you explain yourself, you've got another thing coming."

"Mr. McManis, I've been driving nonstop since six this morning. I'm just going to get something to eat. You need the time to go through it, anyway. I'll answer any questions I can when I get back." He pulled away, turned on his heel, and walked away. James stared at his retreating back in utter disbelief.

"Open it," Jo said.

"Why? If it's from my grandfather it's not going to help me find Chuck." James sank back down on the bench. He felt as if all his strings had been cut. He'd been counting on Pritchard knowing – something, anything. On Chuck having confided in him, the way he hadn't confided in his own father. If I could take back everything I said to you on Monday, James thought, I would. I'd have come with you. No. I'd have trusted you.

But wouldn't he be in the same situation now? Yes, he thought miserably. But the last words I said to you wouldn't have been in anger. I wouldn't have pushed. I'd have –

"Come on," Jo said. "Open it. You never know." She picked the parcel up and pulled the string off, then handed it back to him as the paper loosened. No tape, no writing, just the paper wrapped around something soft, two small lumps, and a large flat rectangle. It all but unfolded in his hands.

James stared down at the contents. A pair of small, battered, red Converse All-Star high-top sneakers lay atop an equally small, equally battered t-shirt. A faded sepia-toned photograph behind glass in an old-fashioned frame, bigger than an 8x10, and proportionately taller than it was wide for a standard size.

"Hey, that's Grand Geyser," Jo said. "May I see it?"

Silently he handed it to her, only then seeing another flat, paper-wrapped parcel hidden underneath, with his name written on it in an achingly familiar handwriting. He couldn't bring himself to pick it up.

He picked up one of the shoes instead. God, they were tiny. He thought about the size 14s Chuck wore now. Jo glanced over from her perusal of the photograph. "Were those Chuck's?"

"They could be."

She gave him a questioning look.

"After my wife died, my parents took Chuck until he was old enough to go to school. They aren't like anything I'd have bought for him."

"Oh." She handed him the photo, and picked up the other shoe. "They're adorable. Is that a t-shirt?"

He didn't bother to answer her. He was trying to get up the courage to open the inner parcel when she saw it.

"What's that?"

"That's my grandfather's handwriting."

"Well?"

"Do you mind?"

"Sorry." But she didn't look repentant. "I'm just naturally curious."

Nosy was more like it. But he picked the parcel up. It bent like a stack of paper. He just looked at her.

Jo grinned." I'll be back in a bit," she told him.

James watched her as she walked away, but the heat of his anger had blown out of him with his first sight of his name. Jem McManis. Jem McManis didn't exist anymore, hadn't for decades. Not since Granddad died, James thought. Not since long before his grandfather had died.

He took a deep breath and slid his finger under the tape holding it closed.

It was a stack of paper. Actually, it was half a dozen yellow legal pads, stacked one atop the other and all dense with his grandfather's handwriting. Atop the stack was a single sheet of white unlined paper. A letter. James picked it up.

June 1, 1939

Dear Jem,

Since you're reading this, August 17, 1959 has come and gone, and you're in Yellowstone searching for me. I hope you weren't here for the earthquake. It was a humdinger and no mistake.

James's mind came to a screeching halt. His breath caught in his

throat and stayed there. His fingers loosened and the letter dropped
to his lap. Legal pads went every which way. He stared blankly at the
words, which suddenly were no more readable to him than hieroglyphs.
Searching for me? he thought wildly. Searching for his grandfather? He
shook his head. Why would he be searching for his grandfather, who
had been dead for twenty years? How had his grandfather known he
would be here now?

It was a hoax. A horrible practical joke. It had to be. James had
no idea why anyone, his son, that lawyer, anyone, would pull a stunt
like this on him, but it was the most cruel, the most insane, the nastiest
thing he'd seen in a lifetime of cruel losses. He picked the letter up, and
headed toward the lodge, leaving the legal pads, the photograph, and
the shoes in a forlorn pile on the bench.

He had but one single thought in his mind, and that was to find
that son of a gun Pritchard and strangle him. But not until he found
out why his son – his *son* – was so angry with him that not only did he
have to run away, but set up this elaborate scheme to what? Distract
him? Drive him crazy?

"Mr. McManis?" He ignored the voice behind him. It was just that
busybody babysitter, and he no longer had the time of day for her or
anyone else.

"Mr. McManis?" She came up beside him, holding the rest of the
package. "Don't you want these?"

"No."

"But don't –"

"No." James knew he was shouting, and couldn't help it. "Go
away, and take that practical joke with you. It's not funny." He shoved
the door to the lodge open, heedless of the tourists who jumped back
out of his way. On across the lobby, into the dining room, shaking off
the young woman at the door, leaving her plaintive "may I show you a
table, sir?" in his dust.

There he was. Eating calmly like he hadn't just been part of
something so heinous – James strode up to him and jerked his plate
away. Flung it. Heard the crash and an indignant "hey, mister!" and
ignored both. Grabbed Pritchard by the collar and yanked him to his
feet as his chair went over with a bang. Jerked him forward until they
were nose to nose.

"Who the hell do you think you *are*?!"

"Sir! Sir!"

"Well?"

Pritchard stared at him. Not in surprise, James realized. No, not in surprise at all. "You were waiting for me to do this."

"If you'll let go, I'll explain." Pritchard's voice sounded choked. As well it ought to.

"There *is* no explanation for this."

"Sir." The new voice was male, and deep. A hand came down on James's shoulder. He tried to shake it off, but couldn't. "I must ask you to take this outside."

"Fine."

"And for you to unhand this man."

James pulled his gaze from Pritchard long enough to glare at the interruption, then let go only long enough to grab the lawyer by the arm. "That better?" He headed toward the door.

"It's not a joke," Pritchard panted at him as soon as they were outside. Dark had fallen, and so had the temperature.

James jerked Pritchard around to face him. "You can't expect me to believe that."

"Mr. McManis?" Jo's voice came from behind him.

"*What?*"

"Don't you want –"

"*No.*"

"Yes, you do," Pritchard said, his voice unsteady. "Let go of me."

James flung the man's arm away from him. "Fine. Explain."

Pritchard shot the sleeves of his corduroy jacket as if it was a suit coat. The gesture seemed to give him some spine. When he spoke, he sounded far calmer than he had any business being. "Have you read the whole letter?"

"No."

"Or the document? No," he answered himself, "you haven't had time. Read the letter, at least."

Pritchard gestured at Jo, who held it out. James did not take it. "Why should I?"

"Your grandfather –"

"My grandfather had nothing to do with this hoax."

Pritchard just stood there, waiting. For what? For him to break down and give in? To go along with this cruel joke? I can wait you out, too, you, you – James clenched his fists to keep from strangling the man again.

At last, Pritchard shook his head. "I can't make you do anything. But at least don't throw it out." He turned away.

"Oh, no, you don't." James got a firm grip on the lawyer's arm. "Not until you tell me where my son is."

"He said you'd react like this," Pritchard said. "I can't say as I blame you. If it weren't for the proof, I wouldn't have believed him myself."

"Proof? What proof?"

"That what he described actually happened. Inside the back of the picture." Pritchard took the photograph from Jo, who was still standing there gaping as if this was the best show she'd ever seen. "You're going to need light for this. Besides, you're normally not one for making a spectacle of yourself."

James glanced around for the first time since they'd left the lodge building. Jo wasn't the only one enjoying the show. "Fine. Come on." He led the way to his cabin. Pritchard followed with the picture. Jo, still holding everything else, brought up the rear.

When they reached his cabin, she held the pile out. James just looked at her, unlocked the door, and gestured them both in.

* * *

The place had been tiny with just him in it. With three people it felt as if he had no room to breathe. James turned on the lights and pulled out the only chair, a small ladderbacked wooden affair, from where it was tucked under the tiny desk in the corner. "Jo?"

She gave him a bemused look and a "thank you," and sat down. She watched him as she toyed with one of the little red sneakers.

"Sorry, Pritchard, my current lodgings don't run to room to entertain."

Pritchard perched on one corner of the freshly-made bed, looking extremely uncomfortable, but he said only, "That's all right."

James couldn't have sat still if his life had depended on it. He paced two steps. "Explain." And two steps back.

"It would be much easier if you'd just read the letter."

James just watched him.

"Fine." Pritchard took a deep breath, glanced around the cabin as if looking for an escape route, and said, "Your son is no longer here. Somehow, during the earthquake, he was in the wrong place at the wrong time, and by some sort of temporal anomaly, he traveled to –" another deep breath "– 1877." He spoke so fast now that James could barely understand him. "Where he rescued your grandmother from the Nez Perce Indians, and eventually married her."

When he stopped speaking, the silence rang. James tried to speak, couldn't, then tried again. "Temporal anomaly?" His voice sounded like a croak, even to him. "What in God's name is a temporal anomaly?" It wasn't what he'd meant to ask, but the rest of the line the lawyer was trying to feed him was so obviously a lie –

Pritchard looked relieved. Idiot. James wasn't quite sure what was keeping him from putting his hands around the man's neck and squeezing, but, no, his fists were clenched instead. He'd never been a proponent of violence, but then he'd never been so tempted before. "Nobody's quite sure. Your son, your grandfather, tried to research it later on. Your dad, too, but neither of them could find anything that made any sense." He went on, talking fast again. Probably because he figured he wasn't going to get enough time to get it out otherwise. He figured right, James thought. "Chuck – Charley thought it might have had something to do with the volcano we're standing on. Something geological might affect time –" He stopped again. Dared to look up from where he'd been staring anywhere but at James as he spoke. "Look, I know it sounds ridiculous. Your grandfather knew it sounded ridiculous. But there's proof. I've seen it. And it's not the only time it happened."

Behind him, Jo squeaked. It was the first sound she'd made since she'd thanked him for the seat. James ignored her. "What. Proof."

Pritchard leaned over, took the framed photograph from Jo's hands. Turned it over and peeled a corner of the paper backing off. It came away easily, as if it had been stripped away before, more than once. He extracted something from under it, a piece of paper. An oddly familiar-looking piece of paper. He handed it to James. James took it.

He'd seen that document only days ago. On August 16th, to be precise. That piece of paper had caused the argument that made his son run off up here without so much as a see-you-later. But it looked different now. Old. More than old. Battered and worn and creased. Puffy along one edge as if it had gotten wet and then dried. Yellowed, with the foxing of age. Fragile. Crumbling. But it was unmistakably Chuck's report card, from Colorado State University. With its two Fs, and its two As. The As were in forestry and surveying - electives he had insisted on taking, with his grandfather egging him on. . . Automatically James cradled the fragile piece in his hands. It might be the last thing he ever had of his son – no. It was a lie. All of it. "What is this, some kind of joke?"

"Your son's report card was in his pocket when he – well, when whatever it was that happened to him happened. He hung onto it through everything he went through, through all the decades, as proof he wasn't crazy, that he really had traveled through time. He showed it to your grandmother when he told her who he really was, and where or when he really came from. To your father, too. He wanted you to have it, so you'd know it really happened, too."

"And you're just now giving it to me? He's been dead for twenty years."

Pritchard looked him in the eye. "Your grandfather asked me to wait. Until after the 17th. He was afraid you'd try to stop him. And he was afraid of what would happen if you succeeded."

James tried to take that in. "And you believe all this."

"He was very convincing, but no, I didn't. Not until he showed me that paper. And the other things." With the photograph, Pritchard gestured at the items Jo had set on the little desk. The small red high-tops and the t-shirt. The legal pads covered in handwriting. "If I could figure out another way to explain it all, I still wouldn't. But I can't." He stood. So did Jo. "I'm going to go check in at my own cabin. I'll see you tomorrow. In the meantime, just read it. The letter, and the account your grandfather – your son – wrote. And if you can come up with another explanation for the whole thing, you have no idea how glad I'll be to hear it."

He opened the door and gestured at Jo. She held up a hand. "Mr. McManis? James?"

He stared up at her. He'd all but forgotten she was there. "Yes?"

"I'll be back. You need to eat."

He shook his head.

"I'll bring something here. But you need to eat."

She stepped out, Pritchard on her heels. James stared at the tattered grade report in his hands as the door closed behind them.

* * *

He didn't know how long he sat there, staring at it in disbelief, but he was only roused by a knock at the door, and Jo entering the room with a tray of food. She set it on the desk, then carefully took the paper from his hands and set it aside.

"Come on. Eat." She took his hand and pulled him over to the desk, then nudged him down into the chair. She'd brought enough for two people, he noticed, and two sets of dishes and utensils. He glanced up at her.

"Hey, I'm hungry, too." She sat down on the bed, within reach.

James shrugged. They ate in silence, and when they were done, he said, "Thank you."

"Are you going to read it?"

"What's the point?"

"You don't want to know what happened?"

James rounded on her. "You know this can't possibly be the truth. Time travel is impossible."

She tilted her head at him. "How do you know? Are you a physicist?" That left him speechless. She grinned at him.

He wanted to pick her up and dump her out the door. "Would you just go now, please?"

"I don't think that's a good idea."

"No, you think this is the funniest thing you've ever seen."

She sobered. "No, I don't. I admit it's fascinating, and I admit it's right out of a science fiction novel, but I don't think it's funny. Not at all." She hesitated. "I remember how I felt when Stacey ran away. I would have given my eyeteeth back then for an explanation that meant she hadn't done it on purpose."

He couldn't help asking. "Even one this unbelievable?"

"Yes."

"Well, I'm not you." He went to the door and opened it. "I appreciate everything, but I need you to go now. Please."

"All right." She picked up the tray. "Don't do anything foolish. I'll see you in the morning."

It wasn't until after he closed the door behind her that he thought, no, you won't. But it was for the best. The last thing he needed right now was to get into another argument with her he knew he couldn't win.

Wearily, he sat down on the bed, and stared at the little pile of, he supposed he could call them artifacts, of his family's past. Or present. What he wanted them to be was just one big hoax, a practical joke at his expense. Except he knew that handwriting. And he was deathly afraid it wasn't.

Dear God, he wished this was all a nightmare and he could just wake up. Back in his house in Denver with the sun coming up, Chuck asleep in his room down the hall, and Mrs. May letting herself in the back door to start her day's work.

He'd never been so afraid to face anything in his life.

His hand avoided the letter as if it was coated in poison. He picked up the framed photograph and peered behind the backing where it was still peeled away. Nothing else there. No scrap of paper with Chuck's handwriting on it, telling him it was all a joke. For lack of something better to do with it, he tucked the grade report back inside and pressed the backing onto the frame. It didn't stick, curling up again when he took his hand away. He turned the picture over.

He remembered this photograph. It had always hung in his grandparents' homes, wherever they'd lived. Seeing it over the parlor table in their quarters at Mammoth Hot Springs was one of his clearest early memories. The image had been captured on a glass plate by his father's partner, the photographer Thomas "Bird" Calfee, in the early days before film photography, and he had caught the geyser in full eruption backlit against a bright sun. It almost looked as if someone was stepping out of the clouds of steam, half-obscured by them, although James knew it was only an illusion.

That photo had been one of his grandmother's most prized possessions, and, James supposed, rightly so. Calfee's original prints from his early plates had become valuable in the decades since his death, and it was probably worth a considerable sum. That the photo's beauty and value might not be the only reason which caused her to treasure it so made him feel a bit ill.

Setting it down, he picked up one of the little high-top sneakers. These utterly baffled him. They hadn't been Chuck's. He didn't know why he was so deadly certain about that, but he was.

Not that his mother wouldn't have thought them cute. She had enjoyed her grandson, and James had been grateful to her, and to his father, for taking the boy in while James attempted to work through his grief after Catherine died. He'd probably let the boy stay with them for too long, though. He could have brought Chuck home sooner. But it had been so easy to let him stay. He'd been so happy here with them. And, he knew, he hadn't had the faintest idea what to do with the boy until he'd reached an age when he was old enough to reason with. Which, apparently, he still hadn't gotten to. No, there had been no reasoning in their last argument. On either side. He sighed in regret.

They were just shoes. He set the one down, and took a deep breath. Ignoring the letter and the little t-shirt, he picked up the first of the legal pads, with its square black writing covering the page from edge to edge.

He closed his eyes, then opened them and grabbed a pillow in his other hand, propping it against the headboard. Leaning back, he set the pad in his lap and began to read.

CHAPTER 7

"August 15, 1959: My summer school grades
arrived the day after Granddad's funeral."

This was no better than the letter. James thumbed through the
legal pad, densely packed with writing, and then glanced over at the
others, their pages equally creased from the press of the pen. How
could the boy have had the time to write so much? Why would he have
done so? And the handwriting. It could have been Chuck's, or it could
have been Granddad's. James honestly couldn't tell.

And why would these pages, while not as obviously old-looking
as the report card, look old enough that his grandfather could have
written them? James shook his head. Real or hoax, they were the only
clues he had right now.

He read on, through one legal pad, then the next, and the next,
deep into the night, drawn into the story despite himself. It was like
reading a novel, except he recognized too many parts. He found
himself anticipating what would happen next, from the stories he'd
been told as a child. He found himself grinning in some places, and
gasping in others. A few times he winced. He hadn't realized how
deeply the boy resented what he stood for.

And when he finished the last page, he set the pad on top of
the stack next to him, and looked up to see the early morning sun
beginning to glint around the edge of the curtains.

He felt as if his world had been turned upside down. Nothing was as it seemed. Everything he trusted, took for granted, was – not a lie, he supposed – trying to feel hurt and failing, but incomplete. Hidden.

James tried to remember his grandfather. The old man had died twenty years ago, after all, the week before Chuck was born and Catherine died, but the image of his face popped into his mind as if it had been waiting there for him. James couldn't tell if he was imprinting his son's features on top of the face he remembered, but the blue eyes, the hair which had never quite changed all the way from sandy blond to the gray so pale it was almost white, the nose dominating the face which had taken most of Chuck's childhood to catch up with it, all seemed the same to him now.

He thought about the old man's mannerisms, and his smile, and his frown. His attitudes and beliefs, what was important to him. The way they'd enjoyed each other's company, and the odd twinkle in his eye when Jem said something that amused him. James's eyes stung.

He could have been Chuck. If it was possible for him to *be* Chuck. He was losing his mind. But was he? Or was the world simply not the sane sensible place he'd tried so hard to make it be?

James rubbed his eyes, gritty from lack of sleep. But he wasn't sleepy, not now. He took a deep breath, and, at last, picked up the letter. It couldn't be that bad now, if he went on the assumption that this whole fairy tale was true, could it? He wasn't quite ready to do that. But he began to read, anyway.

June 1, 1939

Dear Jem,

Since you're reading this, August 17, 1959, has come and gone, and you must be in Yellowstone searching for me. I hope you weren't there for the earthquake. It was a humdinger and no mistake.

I know you don't believe this, but I'm not there. So you're going to need to figure out a way to stop whatever search the rangers are running. I guess you can tell them I did run away, after all. Chances are good they'll believe you by now.

But I want you to know, for the record. I wasn't running away.

James leaned back and briefly closed his eyes. He supposed it was something, at least.

> I was mad at you for trying to run my life, but I wasn't running away. I just wanted to get away for a bit. Say good-bye to Grandmother and Granddad. And try to figure out how to get you to let me be who I wanted to be, not who you wanted me to be. You are a bulldozer, Jem, and no mistake. You've been one since the first day I met you.
>
> That's the other thing I need to tell you. I don't know how much you remember about how we found you. About how you came to live with us and how Will and Karin came to adopt you. We never talked about it when you first came to us because it upset you so much, and, well, it was easier not to. And later on, it seemed to make more sense to let sleeping dogs lie.
>
> I'm sorry about that now, in some ways. But I wonder how it would have changed things if we'd told you. If you'd have taken steps to break the loop or if you'd have understood and let me go, anyway.
>
> But there's something you need to know. What happened to me, happened to you, too. I don't know where you came from, but if you look at the t-shirt, it's dated on the back.

James picked the small, holey t-shirt up gingerly and shook it out. *1983 World Tour*, it said in silver gothic lettering faded almost to invisibility. *1983. 1983*??? Below it, the columns of smaller type blurred in his vision. He dropped the t-shirt as if it would burn him, and took a deep breath before he picked the letter back up.

> I can tell you I first saw you on October 23, 1897.

My fourth birthday, James thought inanely. My birthday is the day they found me, not the day I was born. Didn't they know the day I was born?

> I took a job winterkeeping at the Fountain Hotel that year after your dad headed for the Klondike, and your grandmother and I just happened to decide to go exploring that day before the snow set in. We were the only people for miles in any direction. I don't want to think about what would have happened, to you or to me, if we hadn't made that jaunt, but I guess it was fate, or destiny, or part of what was meant to be. Thank God.
>
> We found you sitting on the ledge above Iron Creek, next to the geyser they call Cliff nowadays. You were all by yourself, shivering and crying. You were wearing that t-shirt, shorts, and those little red sneakers. Mind you, it was just beginning to snow at the time. After we took you back to the hotel and got you calmed down and warmed up and fed, Eliza asked you your name and how old you were. You told us it was Jem Whitehorse, and held up four fingers. And that's everything I know about where you came from.

And that, thought James stupidly, explained the middle name he'd never understood.

> Asking you to explain how you'd got there, especially when you were only four years old and scared to death at the time, was pretty much impossible. But from that moment on you were ours, our family's, and you still are. No matter what.
>
> Don't miss me. If you've read my story, you know things turned out all right for me. I hope they turn out all right for you, too, Dad.
>
> Love,
> Chuck

James leaned back and tried to remember how to breathe. It wasn't easy. His head was spinning and his heart was pounding. He closed his eyes, only to have them pop open again when someone pounded on the door. Housekeeping, already?

"Go away," he called, his voice cracking.

"Mr. McManis, it's me," said a now-familiar voice. Pritchard. Great.

"Go *away*."

Instead, the idiot knocked again. "We need to talk."

James let his breath out. Swung his feet to the floor and sat up, then put his head in his hands as the room spun around him.

"Mr. McManis – James –"

"I'm coming, hold your horses."

Slowly he stood, walked to the door, undid the lock. Walked back to the bed to sit down before he fell down, as Pritchard opened the door and strode in.

"Good grief, you look awful."

Pritchard looked like he'd slept the sleep of the conscienceless, fresh as a daisy and not a hair out of place. "Good morning to you, too."

He came in like he owned the place, and plunked himself down on the chair. "Been up reading all night, I see."

James eyed him. "How much did you know?"

"About your grandfather's wild tale? No more than he told me."

"So you haven't read these." James gestured at the legal pads strewn across the bed.

"No. Not that I didn't want to, but he made me promise I wouldn't."

"What made you go along with it?"

Pritchard shrugged. "He paid me generously, warned me what he thought would happen."

"So you just agreed. Sure, Mr. McManis, I'll put your grandson through hell over some cockamamie story about time travel."

"It wasn't that easy." Pritchard shifted on the chair. "I told you, I didn't believe him at first, either. Who would have? But he, and your dad, were pretty persuasive."

"My dad?" Not my dad, James thought. He'd always known he'd been adopted. They'd never hidden that part from him. It had always been something of a relief to him, once he'd gotten old enough to realize he didn't fit in with the rest of them. It had explained why he'd always felt like a changeling. Gave him something to blame. "So he was in on this, too?"

"He had to be." Pritchard shrugged. "But I understand he had something of an experience of his own, sixteen years ago. He saw something he couldn't explain. It wasn't long after your grandmother died. Will told his wife, who'd been on the receiving end of Eliza's confidences, and she –"

"Dragged him into the whole fantasy," James interrupted.

"If you want to look at it that way," Pritchard said blandly.

"What made you believe him?"

Pritchard propped one ankle on the other knee and leaned forward. "I took over my father's practice after he retired. He handled your grandfather's business, then your dad's, for a very long time. He always wondered why your grandfather contacted him, clear off in Denver, when it would have been much more practical to hire a lawyer in Helena, or even Bozeman, but he didn't ask." He grinned. "At least not until it was time to put their wills together. I'm not sure how your grandfather persuaded him to set all this up, but he did. And when it became time for my father to explain his oddest client to me, he was well into the conspiracy, and wouldn't let me back down, either." The grin went crooked. "My father and your grandfather were well met, James. I think Father envied him for the adventure he must have had."

Obviously Pritchard did, too, because he was glancing wistfully at the stack of legal pads. James shoved them at him. "Somebody might as well get the use out of them."

But Pritchard was shaking his head. "I'd like to borrow them when you get back to Denver. But you hang onto them now. You might need them."

James took a deep breath. "You ought to know my grandfather was convinced I did the same thing."

Pritchard's eyebrows went up. "Do you remember?"

"No." James handed the letter over. This, he noticed, Pritchard was willing to read.

The eyebrows had climbed nearly to Pritchard's receding hairline by the time he handed it back. "So you were too young to remember."

"So my grandfather tells me."

"What do you remember about your early childhood?"

James shook his head. "About the same as any kid, I guess. Not much."

"Do you want to?"

"No." James was quite sure of it.

"Why?"

It wasn't any of the man's business. "Look, I'm sure you need to be getting back to Denver. My father wasn't your only client." *James* wasn't Pritchard's client at all.

"Are you sure you don't want me to stick around?" James just looked at him. "No, I suppose you don't." He rose." Is there anything else I can do for you before I leave?"

"I think you've done plenty."

"Or when I get back to Denver?"

"No." Then James remembered the motorcycle. "Wait. What did you drive up here in?"

Pritchard grinned again. "My pickup."

Of course he drove a pickup. "Would it be possible for you to take Chuck's motorcycle back with you?"

"Sure."

"And don't tell me my grandfather told you I'd ask you to do that."

"All right. I won't." Pritchard paused. "Your grandfather loved motorcycles. Bought one of the very first ones on the market, back around 1895 or so, and kept one around till he got to the point where he couldn't ride anymore. Your grandmother was terrified he'd kill himself on it, but he told her he wouldn't. That he knew he wouldn't."

James shook his head. "It would have served him right if he had. I remember those bikes."

"I'll take the motorcycle, and leave it at your house."

"Thank you."

After Pritchard left, James picked the letter back up off the desk and stared at it, then wrapped everything back up in the parcel and left the cabin, taking it with him. All he wanted now was to go home.

But if he did, it was as good as admitting he believed the story. And he couldn't believe the story. Could he?

* * *

He was in no condition to drive home today, at any rate. What he should do, he thought, was go pay for another night, and try to get some sleep. But, as exhausted as he was, he'd never felt less like sleeping in his life.

He did pay for another night, and he did call home and the office. But then he steeled himself and headed for the ranger station. He shouldn't have been surprised to see Jo Bennett there, he realized, but he was.

"You look like you've been up all night," was all she said, but her inspection of him was eloquent enough.

"I was. Is the district ranger available?" he asked the now-familiar young fellow at the desk, mostly for form. He could see the man sitting back there, and the frustrated expression on his face when he noticed James.

James nodded to acknowledge the ranger's "go on back," and headed toward him. He saw Jo step forward and follow him out of the corner of his eye, but ignored her.

"Ranger Willis?"

"Yes?"

James took a deep breath and said what he knew he had to say. "You can call off your search. I appreciate –"

The ranger stood abruptly. "You found him?"

James exhaled." No."

"Then why?"

Hating himself for it, he used the line the letter had suggested. I'm sorry, son, James thought. "You were right. He did run away."

Willis didn't look as pleased as James had expected him to. "You're sure?" He supposed it wasn't the ending the man wanted, even if it was what he'd suspected all along. You're wrong, Willis, James thought. It's because you know what I'm telling you is wrong.

"Yes, I'm sure." James didn't have to turn around to feel Jo's gaze on the back of his neck like it was drilling into him. "He's not here. I don't know where he is, but he's not here."

"I'm going to need you to sign a statement making it official that you requested the search be suspended," Willis said in a warning tone.

James closed his eyes. And this was the finality of it. If he signed the statement, his last chance of ever seeing Chuck again vanished. All on the 'evidence' of a story so unbelievable it wasn't possible to take it seriously.

But he was taking it seriously. He didn't have a choice. His head pounded and his gorge rose and he almost sank to the floor. Would have if someone hadn't shoved a chair up behind him and pushed him down into it.

"Are you sure you're ready to do that?" The voice was Jo's, and it was gentle. "To give up?"

James gazed up at her, and the sympathy in her face just about did him in." Yes," he managed finally. And when, some indeterminate length of time later, someone handed him a pen and a form and showed him where to sign, he signed, his hand shaking his name into illegibility. He leaned back in the hard chair, closing his eyes, feeling every one of his sixty-five years, and more alone than he ever had in his life.

* * *

The conversation drifted past him as if it made no difference.

"Can you see he gets back to his cabin for me?"

"Sure."

"Thanks, Jo. You're one in a million."

"Well, since the powers that be, in all their wisdom, have decided keeping most of the concessions, including my soda fountain, open without adequate staff and supplies isn't a good idea, my time's my own until I move back to Mammoth next week. So I might as well be of some use to somebody." James felt a hand under his elbow. "Come on, Mr. McManis. Let's get out of here."

He opened his eyes. "I can manage."

"Sure you can. Give me a hand."

Another hand, bigger and stronger, under his other elbow. Against his will, James rose to his feet.

"Got him?" the ranger asked.

"With one hand tied behind my back." She sounded positively cheerful.

James shook her off. "I can walk by myself, thanks."

"If you say so."

They were halfway back to the lodge when his keeper said, "I bet you haven't eaten yet, either."

James turned on her. "What is this obsession of yours for keeping me fed?"

"Somebody has to. Come on."

The cafeteria was practically deserted in the middle of the morning, but it was more than that. "Looks like they're cutting back here, too," she commented.

"Why?"

"Mostly for the same reason everything else is. This place runs on college kids and teachers off for the summer, and most of the kids, at least, went home. Worried parents and all that." She glanced at him over her stack of pancakes. "I'm surprised Chuck didn't apply for a summer job here, seeing how attached he is to the place."

"He was in summer school." James supposed it didn't matter now. "He flunked out of two of his required classes last spring and was supposed to be making them up."

"Was supposed to be?"

James snorted. "He failed both classes again."

"That takes effort."

"He didn't like his major."

"Then why —" Jo smirked. "Let me guess. His major was your idea."

"Accounting is practical. And I hoped —" James reached for his coffee, in a, he suspected, vain attempt to hide his feelings on the subject "— he'd come work with me after he graduated."

"That would have been nice for you."

"Yes. And inherit the business eventually."

"I'm sorry." And he could tell she meant it genuinely, no matter what she thought of his relationship with his son.

"So am I. But that's the least of it now."

"It is." Jo reached over and set his coffee aside. "Don't drink too much of that."

His system was crying for it. "Why not?"

"Because after we finish here, I am taking you back to your cabin, where you are going to sleep. For at least a few hours. Then you can decide what to do next when you're rested."

He leaned his chin on one hand, elbow on the table against all good manners. "Why are you doing this? Really?"

"Really?" She smiled at him. "I like you. And I know what you're going through. It's tough, no matter how it happens. And no matter how much we deserve it."

James tried to drum up some anger at her statement, but he couldn't. He wasn't about to accept the blame for Chuck's disappearance. The boy would have wanted to come up here even if he'd gotten straight As. And now James knew he wouldn't have been able to stop him. Apparently some force larger than all of them, not that he'd ever believed in one, was in charge here. A force of nature. And here he'd always thought the phrase a mere figure of speech. If he really believed his son had gone back in time, then no, he didn't deserve it. But no one was to blame. Not even his son.

"Penny for your thoughts."

"I don't deserve this."

"I'm sorry. I shouldn't have said that."

"It's all right." James pushed his plate away and stood up. He felt a bit steadier now, but never so tired in his life, not on April 14th, not even in a foxhole in France during the Great War. "You are right, though. I need to get some sleep."

Jo began to rise, too, but James waved her back down. "I can find my own way. I promise you won't find me collapsed on the ground halfway back to my cabin."

She smiled at him. She had a nice smile, James thought. One of the kind that went all the way to her eyes, almost hiding the concern there. "I'll check on you later."

"You don't have to –"

She waved his feeble objection away. "*De nada*. The way things are going, I won't have anything else to do this afternoon."

"If that's the case," James found himself saying, "Come on back with me." Her eyes widened, and he added hastily, "That's not what I meant. I know you were curious about what my," he hesitated, "son wrote. If you want, you can read it."

"Are you sure?"

"Yes." He didn't know why, but he was. And he knew he wanted her opinion of it. If she'd think he was crazy for believing it. Because even though in his own opinion he'd utterly lost his mind, he did believe, James thought. God help him, he did.

CHAPTER 8

He slept hard, and only woke to Jo's hand shaking him on the shoulder. "Come on," she told him. "You want to be able to sleep tonight, too."

James gazed blearily up at her. She was smiling down at him. "Timezit?"

"About three." She sat back in the chair and gestured at the pile of legal pads. "That's quite a story your grandfather spun."

That brought him awake faster than he'd thought possible. "So you don't believe it, either?" he asked hopefully.

"I don't know." But she sounded like she wanted to.

He deflated, and closed his eyes.

"Hey, don't go back to sleep on me."

He wanted to. "I'm not."

"Aren't you curious?"

He couldn't imagine anything he felt less right then than curious. "What about?"

She picked up the letter."D"on't you want to know what happened to you?"

He opened one eye. "No."

She shook her head. "No wonder your son ran away."

James sighed, opened both eyes, sat up, and swung his feet to the floor. Odd, he didn't remember taking his borrowed boots off. "He didn't run away."

She grinned. "Ah. So you do believe this. The time travel and everything." The grin became unholy. James began to wonder why he'd ever found her smile attractive. But even now, he did.

"I don't know what I believe." It wasn't a lie. Not completely.

Her smile softened. "And that bothers you. A great deal."

"Wouldn't it bother you?" Obviously she was willing to believe anything if it was entertaining enough. And it wasn't *her* child who had vanished into thin air, with no explanation except this cockamamie story.

At least she took his question seriously. "I don't know. Maybe. It's better than no story at all, which is what I got when Stacey left."

He didn't think she'd intended to make him feel small, but she had. "I'm sorry."

"Oh, I pieced a few things together. She used dope and hung out with a bad crowd even before she took off. I'm pretty sure she was pregnant when she left." Her expression grew inward, and he could only imagine what she was thinking. And there lay another hurt, one big enough that he couldn't face it now. *Grandchildren*. He hadn't realized how much he'd been looking forward to seeing Chuck happy with his own family someday.

"And yet you didn't go looking for her?"

Her expression went wry. "It wouldn't have been a good idea at the time, and now? I wouldn't know where to start."

They were a pair, James thought, but he did not voice that thought aloud. If someone had told him even a few days ago that he'd have this much in common with a half-breed minimum-wage fry cook he'd have thought them crazy.

But here he was, and here she was, and, yes, their stories felt very much the same. With one important difference. She could have gone looking for her daughter and didn't, and he had gone looking for his son, only to reach this awful dead end.

She shook herself, as if shaking off the problem. "So, what are your plans now?"

"Plans?" He stared at her blankly.

"I have to assume you're not going to hole up in this cabin forever. For one thing, it'll get expensive after a while."

James started. How many meals had she bought him while he was distracted? "How much do I owe you –"

"*De nada* –"

He was beginning to hate that phrase. "Look, I appreciate your help, but I don't need your charity."

94

"And I don't want your money." When he began to protest again, she quirked an eyebrow and added, "Let me keep the credit balance – there's a term you ought to understand. I'll collect on it when I'm ready. In the meantime," she stood and put out a hand, "it's too late in the day for you to start for home."

James let his shoulders slump. "I suppose it is." There wasn't much difference between the cabin here and a motel on the way. Neither held much attraction for him. And, besides, the cabin was paid for already.

"I have an idea."

He didn't really want to know, but she seemed to be expecting him to. Leave me alone, he thought. Just leave me alone. "And what's that?"

"Let's go out to Black Sand Basin and take a stroll."

"I really don't feel like it – where?"

"That's where Cliff Geyser is." She took a step back, as if waiting for him to explode.

He felt as if he ought to, but somehow he simply didn't have the energy to manage it just then. She watched him, obviously expectant. He dragged himself to his feet.

* * *

Jo insisted on driving over his feeble protests. "It's only a mile or so. I won't wreck your car in that short a distance."

If he was stuck going, he might as well go all the way. "I can walk it."

"You've done enough walking for somebody who isn't used to it."

So she'd noticed. James wished she hadn't. But she was observant, he had to give her that. And he had to admit, it was easier just to sit back and let someone else do it. Not just the work, but the thinking.

All too soon, she parked the car. "Come on." She was out while James was still opening his door.

"I'm coming, I'm coming."

The late afternoon sun was still high over the cliff wall to the west as they made their way to the boardwalk. James was conscious of her watching him as they started down it, the boards rattling under their feet.

"Anything look familiar?" Jo's tone was light, but the glance she shot at him was anything but.

He glanced around, only half seeing his surroundings. "Vaguely. But you've got to realize, after my dad got out of college we moved here for his work, and I lived here until I went away to college, too."

"Ran away." But her lips quirked as she said it.

James shrugged. He was in no mood to fight over semantics or anything else. "The reason it looks familiar is because I spent time here as a kid." Not because this was where Granddad and Grandmother found him. Where his son had found him. *No.* His own emphasis startled him.

Because he *was* remembering. Oh, not the day he'd supposedly been found here, but walks here with his grandparents. With his parents. They'd always come back to this spot every summer, first of anywhere. "To see what's erupting this year," his dad always said. Never mind that if a person wanted to see water gushing out of the ground around here, there were much more likely places to go.

Like the Grand, which had been one of his mother's favorites, and hence his. He'd loved anything she loved, because she'd loved him so.

"Your parents must have adopted you when they were still pretty young. Didn't they want children of their own?"

He shrugged again, this time against the hurt of the suggestion he wasn't theirs. But he hadn't been, had he?

When he didn't answer right away, she turned to look down at the stream and he followed suit. Iron Creek, its name was. It was swift, but not as cold as it looked. Not nearly, with the water from all those hot springs flowing into it. He'd put his bare feet into it on hot summer days, always surprised at the water being almost the same temperature as the air. Remembered being perched on the edge of the ledge separating the empty basin of Cliff Geyser – *no.* He wasn't remembering; it was the power of suggestion. That letter suggested pretty strongly.

"You do remember something," Jo said, startling him.

"No." At her crestfallen expression, he almost smiled before he stopped himself. "At least not what you're hoping I'll remember."

"Come on, then." She gestured him forward. "Let's walk around a bit before we go back."

* * *

She insisted on making sure he ate again before she left him. Sounding more diffident than any time since he'd met her, she said, "I know you probably don't want this, but I'd feel better if you stayed in touch, at least for a while." She handed him a piece of paper. "I share the telephone with the others on my floor, but if you're persistent enough, they'll take a message. I have my own quarters at Mammoth, where I'll be moving next week." She pointed at the second number. "If you decide to come back and poke around some more, let me know and I'll come with you."

He didn't want to take it. "I doubt I will. There doesn't seem to be much point."

"Then throw it away when you get home if you like." She set it down next to his plate. "But take it now, please."

Almost against his will, James found himself pulling a business card out of his wallet and handing it to her in return.

"McManis and McManis, accountants," she read, sounding amused. "I didn't know you had a brother."

"I don't."

"Jumping the gun?"

James didn't want to admit it. "He would have graduated next June." He'd had the new cards printed up a couple of weeks ago, way too soon to be using them, but he'd been excited. One of the few things he'd been excited about lately. He'd bought them for Chuck, and shown them to him for the first time only a week ago.

"No wonder he felt trapped," Jo commented, as if she could read James's mind.

"It was meant as encouragement," James said through his teeth.

"I'm sure it was."

James started to pick the card back up, but Jo beat him to it.

"I wanted to add something to it. Do you have a pen?"

Jo waved down one of the few waitresses, who fetched one, and handed the card back to him with some reluctance, James thought.

He turned the card over, writing his home address and phone number on the back. "If you ever get to Denver —" his voice trailed off.

She smiled and nodded. When she wasn't mocking him, he enjoyed that smile. "Thanks."

"And if anything, anything at all, comes to light about Chuck, call me, please. Collect if you have to. Right away."

"Pat has your telephone number, doesn't he?"

James had to think a moment to remember 'Pat' was District Ranger Willis. "Yes, he does." But I trust you more than I do him, he thought. At least about this. "Will you?"

"Of course." She didn't add the 'not that it will.' That was understood. By both of them, unhappily. She inspected the back of the card. "Your handwriting doesn't look at all like your grandfather's. Or your son's."

"No, I don't suppose it does." He stood. "Well, I guess this is good-bye."

She stood, and took his hand to shake it. It was warm and firm, and more calloused than he was used to on a woman's hand. "I guess it is. For now, anyway. Good luck, James. And don't forget where you come from."

How could he? "I don't think there's much chance of that."

And before he could think of anything else stupid to say, he left.

* * *

The ride back to Denver the next day was a long, slow blur. He left just after dawn, but it was after dark by the time he pulled into his driveway. He'd only stopped for gas and a meal. He could have sworn the shade of Jo watched him in approval as he sat at the diner table, eating properly instead of inhaling a sandwich as he drove.

He climbed out, feeling more than a bit stiff. It should have been good to be home, but right then it felt like just another place.

Chuck's motorcycle leaned forlornly on its stand in front of the garage, barely visible by the glow of the street lights. The part of James who didn't know better wanted to be glad to see it, because for the last three years its presence meant Chuck was home from college for the weekend, and James wouldn't be rattling around in the house alone. His eyes stung and he stopped, put a hand on the worn seat, wondering vaguely what he should do with it. Put it in the garage for now, he supposed. And figure out the rest later.

He had just pulled the door up when the door from the garage to the kitchen thumped open and Mrs. May stood there, silhouetted against the bright light. "Sir? Did you find him? Where is he? Is he hurt?" Her words ran over him like the bike's tires on the concrete driveway as he wheeled it inside out of the way and went back to get the car. "Sir?"

James pulled the car into the garage and climbed out. She had come down the steps and was standing by the motorcycle, still talking. "When Mr. Pritchard brought the motorcycle back, I thought, oh, dear, the child must be hurt. Is he? Where is he?"

Mrs. May had had as much to do with raising the boy as James had, had been working for James since just after Catherine died. She deserved to know as much as he did. But even if he could think of a way to explain the inexplicable, he wasn't up to it right now. He wearily held up a hand to stop the flow. "I don't know."

Her voice went up an octave. "You don't know? Then why did you come back?"

James took a deep breath. "Can we take this conversation inside, please?"

He could feel more than see her draw herself up before she headed back in the house. He took the rewrapped parcel out of the trunk, and followed her.

As soon as they were in the kitchen, she turned on him again, obviously ready to give him the haranguing she had every right to, but after she got her first good look at him she snapped her mouth shut. Before he could say anything else, she shook her head, and said, "I'm sorry, sir. You must be worn out."

"I couldn't find him." The words simply fell out of his mouth. "The rangers searched, too. Everywhere." He dropped the parcel on the kitchen table and sank into a chair next to it. "I'm sorry." He folded his arms on the table, put his forehead against them, and closed his eyes.

* * *

He ate the food Mrs. May set in front of him, and thanked her, and at his insistence she left for her own home, casting backward glances at him, sparing one or two for the parcel. James took it upstairs with him, and tucked it carefully away in the bottom of a drawer, still in its original wrapping. He didn't want to look at the contents again. Not now. Not for a long time, he suspected.

In the morning, he fell numbly back into his routine as if nothing had ever happened, as if Chuck were at college and a mere telephone call away, instead of being so far out of his reach James would never see him again.

He found work piled high on his desk when he entered his office. His secretary took one look at him and closed the mouth she'd just opened. He hadn't hired her because she was dense, and he knew his frown was the sort which told anyone who looked at him to leave him alone or face the consequences. Anyone but Catherine. She'd always been able to cajole him out of his bad moods. But she wasn't here, hadn't been for twenty years. And, for the first time in all those years, he was relieved she wasn't. Having to explain to her that he'd given up searching for her son would have been more than either of them could have borne.

Because he *had* given up. Either Chuck, who did not possess a calculating bone in his body, had devised a plan to cover his tracks so baroque as to be unbelievable, or that unbelievable yarn he'd spun was true. Either way, what more could he do? In either case, it was vanishingly unlikely that the boy was lying out there dead or dying. If it hadn't been, the rangers wouldn't have been so willing to give up the search. But it had become more than obvious they'd felt they'd searched everywhere he could possibly be, and Willis had begun to suggest the runaway theory before Pritchard even showed up.

A throat cleared in the doorway, and James started.

"Mr. McManis?" Sally, his secretary, whose normal voice was brisk and whose normal manner was as efficient as the watch on her wrist, stepped in, looking and sounding more tentative than he'd heard her even when he'd interviewed her for the job.

James smiled at her. He expected it looked more like a grimace, but she smiled back at him. "Yes?"

"We're glad you're back. Is Chuck all right?"

James took a deep breath, then let it trickle back out. He hadn't thought about what he would tell everyone else about Chuck's disappearance. Mrs. May had caught him off-guard last night, and even then he hadn't said much. What *could* he say that wouldn't make people think he was crazy, or slander his son?

Apparently he'd waited too long to say anything. He could almost watch Sally's face fall as she came to what? conclusion? "I'm so sorry, sir." That conclusion. "Should you be here? We can manage until –" She let the sentence hang.

I will *not* have a funeral for him, James thought stubbornly. "He's missing, Sally. Not dead, at least not so far as I know."

Now she simply looked mystified. Well, so was he. And so, evidently, were his other employees, standing with their faces framed in the doorway. So Sally had volunteered to approach him first again, had she? James hesitated, but before he could figure out what to say next, the phone on her desk rang. With one last worried glance at him, she ducked back out through the door, parting the people standing there. After a moment, one or two of them made as if to step in, but then his phone rang, and he gestured them away as he picked it up. Saved by the bell, James thought, shaking his head. "Who is it, Sally?"

* * *

He had no trouble staying busy enough throughout the day to avoid being buttonholed by any of his employees. Not even Stan Miller, whose nosiness about things that were none of his business had been almost enough to get him terminated at least once. God only knew James had enough work from the last few days it would take the better part of a week before he'd be completely caught up.

He was grateful to Sally, and told her so, for being deliberately vague about the 'family business' that had taken him away from his clients, relieving him of having to field questions from the curious and well-meaning. Not to mention the clients he'd been working with for so long they seemed to consider themselves friends. None of them knew him well enough to understand he had no family now except for his son. No family now at all.

He wanted to hold onto his anger, but it was draining away as if something inside him had become unplugged and he couldn't find the stopper. As long as he could stay angry at the boy, he could somehow hold onto hope.

He hung on through the day, aware of Sally running interference for him. Not that doing so wasn't part of her regular duties, but when he overheard her telling Stan for the third time that now wasn't a good time to disturb the boss, he realized he was letting her do more than he should, and called the man into his office.

And, as it turned out, it was a fire only he could put out, which both distracted him and kept him occupied past his normal quitting time. He caught himself thinking he should thank Stan for it, and barely stopped himself before opening his mouth and all but inviting the barrage of questions that would have been the inevitable result. Not to mention the precedent it would have set.

It wasn't as if he *wanted* more problems, after all. James had always prided himself on a professionally-run business.

At last he pushed back his chair and headed out. The office had long since closed, his employees gone, even – no, there Sally sat, still at her desk.

"What are you doing here this late?"

Her smile as she looked up at him was genuine, but behind it lurked a certain wariness. "I just wanted to finish up a couple of last-minute things."

"What things?" He hadn't been aware of any emergencies other than the one Stan had so conveniently provided.

She stood. "They're taken care of now, sir. Nothing to concern yourself about."

"You were waiting for me." James didn't know whether to be touched or annoyed.

"Why, no –" But her gaze fell, and she reached into a desk drawer for her purse.

"Afraid I'd spend the night trying to catch up?" he asked lightly. It wouldn't have been the first time. But he didn't think that was it. More she didn't want him left alone and he suspected he knew why. "Let's go," he told her. "It's the wrong season for overtime."

She smiled again, looking relieved. "Yes, sir."

It wasn't quite dark yet, but he escorted her to her car, anyway. And as he drove himself home, he wished he had somewhere else to go. Anywhere.

* * *

James's days fell back into his normal routine, almost as if he'd never been gone. Part of him kept expecting to hear from Ranger Willis, that some hapless tourist had seen something, had found something, that meant this was all a bad dream. When the first Friday after his return rolled around, he found himself half-expecting Chuck's motorcycle to come roaring down the street instead of sitting in the garage acquiring dust.

He caught up with the work stacked up from his absence, and his employees, even Sally, finally quit hovering as if he were going to fall apart at an awkward moment. Perhaps in front of Mrs. Chodak, one of the wealthiest widows in Denver. She normally flirted with him during their otherwise strictly business appointments in spite of the fact that he was nearly twenty years her senior. She also normally asked after Chuck, but did not this time. James wondered, after she'd left, if Sally had warned her not to. He didn't dare ask either one of them, but it left him unsettled.

He pulled all of the new business cards but one out of his wallet, and put them with the rest of the boxful in the back of his bottom desk drawer. He couldn't quite bring himself to throw them away, but he was glad he'd not given them to Sally yet. Keeping a supply of business cards on hand was her responsibility, not his. If Chuck had been – well. She'd have been sweetly amused at James's expense, and he'd have probably enjoyed it.

Yes, his life was back to normal. Almost as if nothing had happened. As if he hadn't lost the most important thing in his life forever. And the anger he'd lost gradually turned to despair.

CHAPTER 9

Not that he'd been expecting to hear from anyone by then, but the phone rang nearly a month later, one evening after supper. It wasn't Ranger Willis, though, with good news or, far more likely, bad. It was Jo Bennett.

"Hello, James." Her cheery voice was only slightly dimmed by the long distance transmission.

James leaned back in his armchair and let his breath out. "Is this a social call?"

"Right to the point." She laughed. "No, although – well. How are you holding up?"

She probably did want to know. "All right, I guess."

"You sound tired."

"I had a long day at work." Not any more so than usual, although he'd gotten into the habit of driving himself harder than the edging-toward-retirement pace he'd been aiming at in the last couple of years. Back to his old pace, actually. And more. He frowned.

"On purpose, I assume."

"Of course." He wondered if she'd ask him if he'd been eating properly next.

"I meant – Never mind."

She was being uncharacteristically hesitant. Not like the Jo he'd gotten to know so quickly in those few intense days. "Spit it out, Jo. Whatever it is, it can't be worse than keeping me in suspense."

Her breath huffed out. "I'm sorry. That's not what I meant to do –" she stopped, then said, "and here I am doing it again." He could hear her inhalation, even on the phone. "I know it's none of my business, but I did some poking around in the park archives after I moved back to Mammoth a few weeks ago – they're in the basement of the visitor center there – and when I went up to Bozeman to the dentist last week, I stopped at the university library and went through some of the old copies of the local newspapers for 1897 and 98. There wasn't much, but more than you'd think –"

"Jo."

"Right. Sorry. Anyway, did you know your dad's return from the Klondike made the front page of the Gardiner paper?"

"No." But James wasn't surprised. That was how small towns worked.

"I'm sure you know he met his wife up there."

"Yes. She was from –"

"Seattle."

"Ballard, actually, but she was born in Norway."

"Oh. The newspaper –"

"I'm sure it didn't go into the gory details."

"Or the reporter didn't have them." She paused. "You didn't tell me your parents were still teenagers when they took you in."

"I didn't think it mattered."

"I know it's silly, but I couldn't make the dates work out. They were both nineteen when he brought her home with him, according to the newspaper article."

"Yes."

"How old were you?"

"Almost five. At least according to the birthday they gave me." That still bothered him more than he wanted to think about.

"Do you remember meeting them?"

"Vaguely." Actually it was far more than vaguely. The first really vivid memory he had of the people who'd become his parents, his first memory at all, actually, was of blonde, beautiful Karin Myre McManis stepping off the train platform and the shock of recognition he'd felt when he'd set eyes on her for the first time. He'd never been able to understand why he'd clung onto her. All he'd known was that she was the one, the one person he recognized in the strange world he'd arrived in, and in spite of having never set eyes on her before, she was his, and he was hers. It had been all they could do to pry him off of her, that moment and for ever after. It was why he'd gone to live with her and Will instead of staying with Will's parents, who'd become his grandparents instead.

Karin hadn't recognized him, not in the same way, or at all, she'd told him years later. But she'd wrapped her arms around him and held him, and made him feel like he belonged somewhere, for the first time in his life. That he belonged to someone for the first time in his life. And she'd continued to try to make him feel that way, even after they'd almost lost her. He was the one who'd stopped. He still didn't understand why she'd gone back, why she'd *wanted* to go back, to Yellowstone, the place that had almost killed her. Why she'd still loved it, in spite of everything.

Jo cleared her throat, and James found he needed to follow suit before he could speak. It amazed him, every time he was reminded, how much he still missed his mother, even after five years. "Sorry. Yes, I do remember, a bit. What's this all about?"

"I couldn't find anything about how you were found. Just a mention on the back page of the Gardiner Enterprise in the spring of 1898 about how Charley and Eliza McManis had stopped in town on their way back from winterkeeping the Fountain Hotel, and how they were going to Helena to see relatives before coming back to open their photo shop at Mammoth for the summer. The only mention made of you – at least I assume it's you – is that they had a 'young relative' traveling with them."

"Oh."

"I wonder how they explained where you came from."

"I have no idea." But he did. Some of his earliest memories had been of the stares, although he'd never understood them. Now he did, and he wished he didn't. First Eliza, although her bafflement had been tempered by kindness and had changed quickly and abruptly to a fierce protectiveness. Then the occasional soldier or other visitor over the course of the winter, then the people of Gardiner and Helena in the spring. He remembered how Charley and Eliza had stared every single one of them back down until at last they'd quit asking. Until they'd had to accept him at face value, without explanation. His grandparents hadn't given people any other choice.

"Too bad you didn't know to ask in time."

"Yes." Suddenly he was very tired. "Thank you for the information. I appreciate it." Such as it was. Although it did cast a bit of light on his past. A candle, at any rate.

He could almost hear her smile. "Oh, I enjoyed poking around. I'd forgotten how much. So thank *you* for reminding me, and giving me something to poke at." He was sure she had enjoyed it, for some strange reason. But she wasn't through, with either the conversation or the poking, apparently. "I'm thinking about taking a little trip up to Helena in the next few weeks. Now's a slow time at the park, what with the snow starting to fall and all. I don't suppose —" and now she sounded hesitant and all un-Jo-like again. "I don't suppose you'd like to come with me. We could see what else we can find out."

Now that startled him, although he wasn't sure why. It was just like her, come to think of it.

"I know it's a long way for you to come, but you might find it interesting."

Helena? He rather doubted it. His memories of the place weren't as bad as the ones he had of the park. He supposed it wasn't the town's fault they weren't wonderful, either. Still. No, it probably wasn't a good idea. "I don't think I could get away, but I appreciate the offer."

Was that a trace of disappointment he heard? "Well, if you change your mind, let me know. I'll probably head up sometime after the first of October. That's when things start shutting down."

"What do you do after that?"

She laughed. "Oh, I've made myself indispensable. It was nice talking with you again, James. Take care of yourself."

"You, too."

"Oh, I do. I'll let you know if I find anything interesting."

He didn't think he wanted her to, but he thanked her anyway.

She hung up. James set the receiver down carefully into its cradle, and wondered idly if Sally could jimmy his schedule to get him another week away. No. He'd barely caught up from the last time. He had clients. Business. Work to do.

James leaned back in his chair and closed his eyes. What was the point now? He was set financially for retirement and had been for a while. He'd basically been waiting till Chuck graduated and came to work to let go altogether and retire. He'd planned on staying on for a couple more years, just until the boy got his feet wet. The rest of the staff was more than competent, and Stan, the most senior of them, could and had taken over most of the day-to-day administration as James had lightened his own load over the last few years. The clients liked Stan, and he'd brought in plenty of his own. James had even thought of allowing him to buy into the business at some point. Become his partner. God knew Stan had hinted at it once or twice. Or three times. But James had thought it should be the boy's eventual decision since he'd be the one living with the results.

James hadn't planned for any future for the business which didn't include his son. The events of last month had put an enormous Chuck-sized hole in his own future. And he truly didn't want to deal with the consequences himself. Wearily he heaved himself from his chair and headed upstairs. He wished Jo had never called.

* * *

It annoyed and worried James, as October approached, how he was losing his concentration. Fall was a slow time in the accounting business. Time to catch up and prepare for tax season, to meet with clients when he had time to think about long-range plans instead of the madhouse of getting everything done after the first of the year. He'd always enjoyed this part before. It was the time of year he'd always been able to spend the most time with Chuck. The last three years he'd looked forward to the boy's weekends home from college, which had gradually become fewer and farther between. Until now they, like everything else taken from him on August 17th, had vanished forever.

He had too much time on his hands. He hadn't realized how much he'd structured his life around the boy's visits home. And instead, he was thinking about being utterly irresponsible and running away up to Helena, a place he hadn't visited since the last time his parents talked him into bringing Chuck up there, to visit his McManis relations and renew his acquaintance with them himself.

It had been at least a dozen years. Chuck had still been in grade school. And how would he explain the boy's disappearance to them? Or did any of them know the story?

If they did, and if he found out they'd been part of a conspiracy to keep him in the dark, he wasn't sure he would be able to control his anger.

James gazed at the photo of his wife that had sat on his desk for the last twenty-four years. It had been taken on the trip she'd insisted they make to Helena not long after they'd married, at the top of Mt. Helena, with the wind blowing through her blonde hair and her smile beaming out at him. Catherine hadn't had much in the way of relatives herself, and saw them as something of a novelty. They'd loved her and she'd loved them. So, Catherine, he thought wistfully, looking at the face forever young before him, *I can't take you, and now I can't take him. What's there for me?*

Comfort, James, he could almost hear her say. *And family. You don't have to be lonely unless you want to be.*

* * *

It took an embarrassingly short amount of time to make the preparations. To have Sally hand his appointments over to Stan and Mike, to give Mrs. May some time off. Unlike the last time, he had no need for her to stay at the house while he was gone. He wasn't expecting anyone to show up, not now. And perhaps if he didn't expect – no. He didn't believe in sympathetic magic. *You didn't believe in time travel, either,* he reminded himself. *And still wouldn't, if he'd been given the choice.*

He spent some time closeted in his office with Stan, and they both emerged, James thought, with what they wanted, even if his colleague's perpetual curiosity had been whetted more than appeased. He winced, thinking of the questions he had sidestepped and outright lied in answer to.

"You really don't think he's coming back, do you?" Stan's voice had been more astonished than anything else, not a trace of the satisfaction he must have felt knowing he was going to be allowed to buy in to the business at last. To own it all someday, most likely.

"Even if he does," James told him, "I think this proves he doesn't want the business." *He never had. James simply hadn't wanted to believe it.*

"You've got a point." Stan shrugged. "His loss."

No, mine, James thought, then hesitated. "I don't think that's how he sees it." Then wished he'd bit his tongue as Stan gave him a sharp glance. "Never mind. So the terms are satisfactory to you?"

"Oh, yes. More than I thought I'd ever get." Stan paused. "I'll be honest with you. I wasn't looking forward to working with your son.

The idea of calling him boss never appealed to me. I'd been putting feelers out around and about."

"To jump ship?" James supposed he couldn't blame the man, looking at it from his point of view.

"Just seeing what my options were." Stan grimaced slightly. "You've been good to me, McManis, but only up to a point. I've liked it here, which is why I've stayed. That and a certain amount of inertia."

"Will you be putting out more feelers?" James asked. He didn't think the man would be, but then he hadn't realized the animosity he'd been creating with his desire to pass the business to Chuck. He'd been overlooking the obvious: passing it on to someone who was as passionate about it as he was.

"Not now. And I'll be saying 'no, thank you' after all to any responses to the ones I've already put out, too. This is always where I wanted to stay. I just didn't think I'd be able to.

"So," Stan continued, quite as if his words weren't about to drop a bombshell, "you're going to take some time off, are you? Will you be back in time for tax season? Or are you going to stay gone till you find him?" He took one look at James and looked like he wanted to laugh.

James wanted to take back every bit of the generous offer he'd just made and kick Stan through the door to boot.

Stan went on, apparently oblivious. "I'm not dense, McManis. If one of my kids" – and he had three, two girls and a boy, all grade-school-aged –"had run off like that, I'd raise heaven and earth to get him back. I was beginning to think less of you for just giving up like that." Another sharp glance. "You're not giving up, are you?"

James shook his head. Not the way you mean, Miller, he thought. "No. I'm not."

Stan nodded, one sharp satisfied jerk. Why did it matter to him? James didn't dare ask. "Good. You take all the time you need, then. I'll keep things running sharp and smooth here while you're gone."

If nothing else, James thought wryly, this would be a good trial run for his retirement.

But Stan wasn't done. "And when you make the pup see sense and bring him back, there'll always be a place for him here if he wants it."

Stan sounded as if he already owned the whole place instead of just a share. James couldn't bring himself to mind. The pup, as Stan called him, wouldn't be coming back. It will be all yours, Miller, he thought. You may as well begin as you mean to go on.

They set an appointment with his lawyer for the next day to start the paperwork, and James left the office early. He wished he could leave town right that moment, but he still had too much to do.

He did call Jo that night. If she wasn't delighted with his change of mind she hid it well, he thought, cheered almost in spite of himself at her enthusiasm. He was surprised she'd gone along with his suggestion that he drive, and pick her up along the way. Actually, he was surprised he'd made the suggestion in the first place, but he suspected by the time he reached the Livingston depot, where they agreed to meet, he'd be just stir crazy enough from the long hours behind the wheel to want the company.

They set a date, and a time, and the trip began to feel more concrete. The depot, she assured him, was still the same big stone edifice he remembered, right in the middle of town, and as close as he was willing to get to the park.

James said a reluctant good-bye, sat back in his chair, and gazed around at the comfort of his living room. He wasn't much of a traveler, hadn't gone anywhere on vacation in a very long time, preferring to spend his free time at home. Well, it wasn't as if he was going to outer Mongolia, he thought ruefully. Helena possessed comfortable hotels, and if they weren't home, they'd do for the duration. However long that duration turned out to be. He still wasn't sure why he was going, except he needed to, somehow.

And he was looking forward to seeing Jo again. Which was ridiculous. He'd known her what? Four days? It had been quite an intense four days, granted, but he'd been distracted beyond redemption, or should have been. Had been. And she'd been a rock. He wondered if he'd still be glad she'd been there for him when he got back from this junket.

* * *

At last his departure day wound around, and James had made every preparation he could think of, from having the Lincoln's oil changed to calling Sally at the last minute to make sure he hadn't left any threads untied at the office. Which he hadn't, she told him, her voice sweetly amused.

The weather was cool, but dry, with no storms predicted, when he pulled out of his driveway and headed north. The sky was clear and blue as it could only be at a mile high, without a cloud in the sky. The traffic was light, and James soon left the city behind.

He wondered, briefly, if Chuck had felt the same sense of freedom six weeks before, and hoped he had, almost in spite of himself. If there was one thing James was rock solid sure of, it was that Charley McManis had loved motorcycles.

James settled himself into the luxury of the Lincoln as it cruised smoothly along. The boy had never had much sense in that department. Or in many others, for that matter. From what James knew of his grandfather – his son, he thought wonderingly – he'd never gained it, either.

CHAPTER 10

The small railroad town of Livingston, Montana was quite as James remembered it, if a bit shabbier and slower paced since the branch passenger line to the park's northern entrance had been discontinued a few years ago.

The depot looked a bit more rundown, too, and he received his first check when he discovered it was closed up tight, windows boarded and door locked.

He'd assumed he'd be meeting Jo inside the big old-fashioned waiting room. He stared around blankly. Now what? Maybe he was early? He checked his wristwatch. No. She could be running late, though. He thought about going back to the Lincoln and waiting for her there, then discarded the idea. He'd been sitting in it for too many hours already. The long bench in front of the depot was bathed in sunshine. He sat down and leaned back, face tilted up to the warmth, elbows propped on the slatted back.

It wasn't the first time he'd sat here, waiting. He could almost sense the pile of luggage at his feet, feel the excitement of going off to college for the first time, then a few years later the mingled dread and anticipation of leaving for officers' training camp, and at last the unknown of Europe and the Great War. The war which had been supposed to end war for all mankind, and made them proud of what they'd done, until it turned out their accomplishment was a lie when war broke out again a scarce twenty years later. But at the time the mingled joy and relief of arriving back was what mattered, of getting back to the people who were home, even though the place wasn't. The parents who'd surprised him by coming all the way here instead of waiting in Gardiner, here for *him*, and so happy he was all in one piece they'd about hugged him until he wasn't anymore. That his body was all in one piece, at any rate. It had taken much longer for his mind to feel all in one piece again, too.

James wasn't sure how long he'd been sitting there, lost in his memories, when he realized something, or someone, was blocking the sun. A throat cleared. Reluctantly he opened his eyes, to find a form silhouetted in the sunshine. "Yes?" His voice felt scratchy, as if he'd been there for days, not a few minutes.

"Mr. McManis? Mr. James McManis?" The voice was young, but it came from high up. James squinted against the light and made out a figure and features. Too much messy brown hair, tall, thin, in pedal pushers and a striped shirt. She grinned down at him.

"Yes?"

"I have a message for you." She thrust a piece of paper at him.

Reflexively, James took it. "Thank you."

Before he could pull coins for payment out of his pocket or even say anything else, the waif had disappeared.

He unfolded the paper. The message was short but not sweet. "I'm sorry, James, but my ride reneged on me. I hate to ask it of you, but could you please pick me up at the visitor center at Mammoth instead? Jo."

He wanted to curse. He'd had no intentions whatsoever of going back to the park on this trip. When he'd left the place in August, it was with the intention of never setting foot there again. He'd rather wait here for hours if he had to, or go on by himself. But it would be rude not to go get her now, especially since he had no way to reach her and let her know he wasn't coming. And Jo had no inkling of the resolve he'd made. Or perhaps she did. Now he wanted to curse her in spite of the notion he should probably give her the benefit of the doubt.

It being almost noon, he stopped at a greasy spoon in town before he headed south. The place wasn't what he'd had in mind – what he'd had in mind was Jo knowing of some nice little bistro in Bozeman, but he supposed that could wait until supper. His meal sat like a lump in his stomach as the Lincoln purred down the road to Gardiner.

Paradise Valley, long and narrow, lay trapped between two sharp, jagged mountain ranges scraping at the sky. It was knee deep in thick golden brown grass this time of year. Dry and windblown, it undulated constantly, almost as if an unseen hand was stroking down the back of some enormous, furry animal. The narrow gray ribbon of highway crossing and recrossing the river seemed almost an insult, a raw interruption to the sleekness of the landscape. But James remembered when the route had been nothing more than a dirt road running alongside the railroad tracks, and it had taken a full day to travel between Livingston and Gardiner by wagon. He remembered as well when the road had first been paved. Now paved roads were commonplace, something taken for granted. Still, he felt smug when he passed a road repair crew just north of Gardiner, taking advantage of the unusual weather to get some last minute work done before winter set in.

It had taken him a day and a half to get here from Denver, and now this extra jaunt was adding another half day. Still, this late in the season it could be snowing. Instead it was almost balmy. Not a cloud in the glowing blue sky, just enough breeze to keep the air moving. He didn't even need a jacket when he stopped in Gardiner to fill the gas tank.

He passed under the big stone arch, remembering Mr. Roosevelt's visit and how Granddad – Chuck – Granddad had insisted they be there when the cornerstone was laid, and the speeches made. The crowds and the dust and the words had gone on interminably. And he remembered Mr. Roosevelt's teeth. Good god, the man had had teeth. Between them, the spectacles, and his mustache it was all anyone could see of his face.

No line at the entrance station a few yards further on. James suspected the ranger manning it was about as bored as it was possible to be. If the fellow was anything like his father – and, given his choice of work, James thought he probably was – he was daydreaming about the hikes he wanted to take and the exploring he wanted to do, and only put up with this part of the job because someone had to do it.

Nobody's fault but his own, James thought, paid his fee and drove on.

* * *

The narrow, winding, five-mile drive up the Gardiner River canyon hadn't been improved much since they'd first paved it years ago, all sharp curves and blind spots. He came around one hairpin and almost rear-ended a car stopped in the middle of the road with its window down, its occupants feeding something to a bear with its front paws propped on the car door, its nose halfway inside. Two other bears were trying to crowd in, until one of them spotted James and lumbered over to see what he might be handing out.

James, who'd had his window down, quickly rolled it up and honked his horn to let the idiots in front of him know he was there.

The car, an old Chevy with Montana plates, was probably a local this time of year. Its driver honked back and didn't budge.

Even more irritably, James backed up a few feet and prepared to ease his way around the idiot and the moochers. Hoping with all he had he wasn't about to knock anything, including the Lincoln, off into the river thirty feet below, he crept around the Chevy and the bears. The bears ignored him. The driver threw him a rude gesture. James shook his head and drove on.

Fortunately, he didn't run into any more obstacles after that, but passed the campground and a new cluster of house trailers tucked behind a rise, and arrived at Mammoth a few minutes later all in one piece.

It hadn't changed much, either. The stolid stone buildings of what had been Fort Yellowstone in his childhood still stood, and probably would until someone decided to tear them down and build something better suited to their current purpose of park administration and housing.

Jo was waiting on the steps of the visitor center, wearing almost the same clothing he'd last seen her in, jeans and a pale blue oxford cloth shirt. Both looked like she'd bought them in the men's department. James hadn't realized how glad he was going to be to see her, but her smile made his resentment at being here vanish. A charming sensation.

"You made it!" Before he could get out and open the door for her, she'd opened it herself and climbed in.

"Where's your suitcase?" he inquired.

"Oh, it's back at my quarters. We can pick it up when we're ready to go."

James frowned. "I thought we were heading out immediately."

"Not quite." She gave him a quick, obviously teasing, scowl back, then laughed. "Are you in that big a hurry to hit the highway again? How long did it take you to get here?"

She had a point. "Too long." But now he didn't know what to do, sitting there in front of the visitor center with the engine running.

"Park the car, James," she said patiently.

"Where?" Back at her quarters?

She rolled her eyes at him and gestured at the long row of parking spaces, empty this late in the season. He supposed he deserved that. "Where are we going?"

"For a walk. It's a beautiful day, and there aren't going to be many more of those before winter sets in."

Sighing, James did as he was told. He'd forgotten how bossy Jo could be, somehow, and he wasn't sure – no, he was quite sure he didn't like being reminded.

When they were out of the car, she looked him up and down and nodded in approval. "No suit?"

He glanced down at his sensible khaki trousers and plaid shirt, and the brand-new boots he'd bought for this trip as if he'd known he'd be doing a lot of walking even in Helena, and he couldn't help but smile back at her. "I had time to plan this go round."

Her smile dimmed. "I'm sorry."

That puzzled him. "For what?"

"Reminding you."

Everything about this trip was going to remind him of things he didn't want to remember. It was the whole point, why he was, well, not here, but Helena. To find out more about what had happened to his son, his grandfather. To himself. "Isn't that why you asked me to come?"

She had the grace to look sheepish. James wondered, not for the first time, if she didn't, as Pritchard would have said, have an ulterior motive for inviting him along. He rather desperately hoped she didn't.

"It's all right. If I wanted to forget, I wouldn't have come back."

She was silent for a moment after that, and James wished he'd kept his mouth shut. Then she shook herself. "Come on."

* * *

They strolled down the sidewalk in front of the old stone buildings. Past the visitor center and on. James didn't say anything. Obviously that wasn't her destination, at least not now. The sidewalk was rough and broken from the roots of the cottonwood trees spearing up under it, and he was glad to have his footing to concentrate on instead of the memories.

"You grew up in the park, didn't you?" Her question startled him and he almost tripped. She reached out as if to take his arm, then dropped her hand back to her side.

"I spent my summers here as a kid."

"I envy you that."

"Don't. I hated it."

She stopped and stared at him, then shook her head again and moved on. "Why on earth are you here?"

"You tell me. I thought we were going to Helena."

"I thought – I'm sorry, I didn't realize –"

"You can quit apologizing," James told her flatly. "If it bothered me that much, I'd get back in my car and go home."

She raised an unplucked eyebrow. "Well, I guess you told me. Do you want to?"

James glanced up. He supposed it was a coincidence they were standing in front of a particular old officer's quarters building. Talk about memories. He glanced up at the window of the bedroom where he'd camped out for weeks after he'd come back from the war, trying to regroup, to get his spirit back. To forget what he'd seen so he could move on. His mother, worried about him, trying to talk him into staying longer before he went back to Denver. Trying to talk him into not going to Denver at all, to going back to Helena or Bozeman or somewhere closer to the home that wasn't home, period. Of how he'd told her he couldn't do that even for her, how he'd only wished he'd had anywhere to go but here. How he'd hurt her feelings over it. More than her feelings. But she'd always forgiven him. Always. More than he deserved. "Want to what?"

"Get back in your car and go home."

"I've driven far enough in the last two days. No."

"Are you sorry you came?"

James let out his breath on a huff. "No." He put a hand on Jo's arm. Her skin, through the thin cloth of her shirt, felt sturdier than he did just then. "I'm sorry. I'm not very good company here."

She tilted her head up at him. "Are you better company elsewhere?"

That startled a laugh out of him. "God, I hope so."

"Well, let's see what we can do to improve your mood." She pulled her arm back, and his hand slid down, to be grasped firmly in hers. She pulled him along the sidewalk, through the gold coins of cottonwood leaves mounded in windswept windrows. She scuffed her foot through one pile, aiming the dusty leaves at him.

"Hey," he protested as they drifted down. He brushed one off that had managed to stick to his shirt.

"You're too perfect looking. Had to mess you up somehow. See that pile of leaves? If I thought I could get away with it, I'd give you a shove and see if I could knock you into it."

"Well, thank you." Perfect-looking? He wished he knew what she meant by that. She probably thought he looked like a city man. Well, he was a city man. And he wanted to stay that way.

"Quit scowling. I didn't mean it in a bad way. You're a pretty good-looking guy." She paused. "For your age."

He couldn't believe he was doing it, but he reached down and scooped up a handful of leaves with his free hand. She was ducking, unsuccessfully trying to yank her hand from his grip, when he dropped them squarely on top of her untidy head.

* * *

"My parents lived in that house every winter for years after my dad started working for the park service," he volunteered, surprising himself, after they'd both dusted cottonwood coins off their clothing and out of their hair. James knew he wasn't as tidy as he had been, but if she preferred him that way, he would manage, for now. They ambled down the sidewalk. "He was one of the very first rangers here." And proud of it, he thought. His dad had been nothing but proud, and his grandfather even prouder. Everyone in his family had loved this place to distraction. Everyone but him.

"Not you?"

He glanced at her, puzzled at first, then light dawned. "Lived here, you mean? No. My father was still working for the Wylie tent camp people in the summers and teaching school in Helena during the rest of the year when I left home."

She looked at him curiously as she brushed one last stray leaf off his shoulder." When was that?"

"1911. I was eighteen." Or so he'd thought. He supposed his grandmother's choice of birthday for him couldn't have made much difference.

"Did you come visit them here?"

"Not in that house, not then. It was still part of the fort. Officers' quarters. In the park, every summer while I was in college. After college, not for a few years."

"Busy setting the world on fire?"

"No."

"Then why not?"

He knew his tone was flat, forbidding. "I was in France."

"Oh." He watched her do the math. "Fighting the Kaiser?"

"Something like that."

She was silent for a moment, but he knew it was too much to ask for it to last. He wondered how many questions he'd have to answer about the War before her curiosity was satisfied. He started walking again, and Jo kept pace. "I'm glad you made it back in one piece."

After a fashion, James thought. But he'd been so much luckier than many of the men he'd fought with. A little mustard gas went a long way, though. "Thanks. So am I." And that was it?

But she had something else on her mind, apparently. He should have known. "Did you come back to visit much after that? I know your parents missed their grandson. You'd just taken Chuck back to Denver for the first time when I met them at one of their end of the summer shindigs."

Yes, and annoyed them greatly because he hadn't stayed for the party. Where he might have met the woman standing in front of him now. Now it was his turn to be curious. "Just how well did you know them?"

"Oh, everybody loved Ranger McManis. And your mother." Her tone was light. "I've eaten your mother's *lefse*," she added. "I hadn't been here very long, but your mother and I hit it off right away, and I visited them quite a bit at their house in West after he retired, too."

"Lucky you." His mouth watered just a bit, thinking about the potato pancakes spread with blackberry jam that had been a treat of his childhood. "She brought that recipe back with her from the Klondike."

"So she told me. Sourdough instead of yeast."

James cocked his head at her. "That recipe was a closely-guarded secret."

Her voice was smug. "She gave it to me."

"Really? Why?"

"Yes, really. She liked me. And I wheedled." Her eyes were sparkling at him. They were lovely, really. Dark. Not quite brown, not quite hazel. "Mine are almost as good as hers."

"Almost?" His mouth *was* watering now.

"The older the sourdough, the better the *lefse*."

That made him smile. "That sounds like a direct quote."

"It is." She was looking very pleased with herself. And with him.

"I don't suppose –" He couldn't keep the wistfulness out of his voice.

"I'd make you some? It'll be too late to hit the road tonight, anyway." She gave him a challenging look.

He stared at her. "I'd been planning to get a room at the hotel."

"No, you weren't."

No, he'd figured they'd be halfway to Helena by now. James wished they were with all his heart. He tried to think of a way to back out gracefully. After two days cooped up in the car, the last thing he needed was to sleep on a lumpy old government-issue couch. "I wouldn't want to cause you any trouble."

"Oh, James." She was laughing now. "Don't be such a prude. After all, you've slept with me already. In the strictest sense of the term, that is."

He backed up a full two steps. "I appreciate the offer," he told her stiffly. "But I think I would be more comfortable at the hotel."

Her face fell. "Of course."

What *had* she been thinking, he wondered, astonished. Yes, he was attracted to her, as inexplicable as it was, and now, he supposed, he knew she was attracted to him, even if he had to be fifteen years her senior. But did she really expect him to fall into bed with her? He could hear Catherine's ghost all but laughing at him. *She won't bite, darling.*

"I'm sorry. I didn't mean –"

He didn't like seeing Jo ill at ease, he decided abruptly. She deserved the benefit of the doubt. Maybe she had just been offering him the couch. "But I'll still take you up on the *lefse*. I haven't had any in years."

Her lips quirked, but the discomfort in her eyes vanished, and that was what mattered. "Of course."

* * *

They wandered over to the hotel, where James discovered had he been even one day later he'd have been sleeping on Jo's couch whether he liked it or not. He'd forgotten what it was like to be in a place where everything was seasonal and the world shut down for the winter. But the hotel wasn't closing down until tomorrow, and he signed for a room with a sigh of relief.

He was more than ready to head back to his car and get his suitcase, but Jo led off again, this time in the other direction toward the springs, and James found himself following her up the wooden stairs, past the water flowing over smooth stone the color of orange sherbet. "Wait," he told her as she continued to climb. "Where are you going?"

"To watch the sunset, of course." But she did wait until he caught up before striding off again.

"From here?" The springs faced east. And he really did not want to have to pick his way back down the path in the dark. Never mind he'd done it any number of times, and back in the days before boardwalks. He'd been much younger then. And more foolish.

"It's pretty up here this time of day."

"We could have taken the car. Up around the loop." His throat was dry, and his breath was coming faster. The boards creaked under his feet.

"The exercise is good for you." But she stopped near the top and sat down on a wooden bench built into the railing. James sank down beside her. He leaned back and let out his breath.

The view *was* beautiful, whether he wanted to admit it or not. Down the travertine-covered mountainside glistening in the beginning of dusk, across the valley to the snow-capped mountains still gleaming pink with alpenglow, to the darkening sky above. Lights were just beginning to come on in the hotel and the store, far below. The old Fort Yellowstone buildings looked empty and dark by comparison. Not how he remembered them from his youth, when they'd been bustling with soldiers and the sound of taps floated across the parade ground this time of day.

"My grandfather worked for the army," he said.

"He was a soldier, too?" Jo asked, and confused James briefly, until he realized she was referring to his stint in World War I. He hadn't thought of himself as a soldier in so long it felt odd.

"No. He was a civilian scout here in the park. Chased poachers and fought fires, mostly."

Jo gave him a puzzled look. "I thought he and your grandmother ran Calfee's photo shop."

"That was later, after my grandmother persuaded him he was getting too old to tramp around in the wilderness when it was fifty below. And after the Panic in the early 1890s, when the army's budget was slashed and they let him go."

"But they —"

James grimaced. "You read the letter."

"Yes. They were winterkeeping the Fountain Hotel in 1897."

"That would have been just like my grandfather, to take a job putting the two of them out in the middle of nowhere, snowed in for months. Just like Chuck, too. Funny, that. I can't think of a single thing my grandfather would have enjoyed that my son wouldn't have reveled in. Or vice versa. And God knows I've tried." He shrugged. "But at least my grandmother was out there with him so she wouldn't have to worry."

The lights in the hotel were getting brighter in the gathering gloom. The first stars began to gleam, faintly. The rim of the moon rose over the now barely discernable mountains.

It was all very lovely and very romantic, but James was in no mood to appreciate it. "It's getting late. And windy. I want to get an early start in the morning." The 'and get out of this benighted place' was given, James thought. He hoped she thought it was.

The breeze was more pleasant than not, wafting the steam from the springs to and fro, but Jo rose. "You're right. Come on."

CHAPTER 11

Picking their way back down turned out to be every bit as precarious as James had feared. He wished he'd brought a flashlight. But they made it back to his car without any turned ankles or falling off the boardwalks, and he let Jo drive them back to her quarters, one of that cluster of house trailers across the road from the campground.

They could have been much worse for government housing, at least as he remembered it. They didn't look like much on the outside, tucked into a hollow mostly out of sight of the road, but inside it appeared to contain all the necessities. And hers, at least, smelled wonderful when they stepped inside.

"Goulash," she told him when she caught him sniffing. "*My* mother's recipe. So you're going to be eating memories from start to finish tonight."

"You don't look Hungarian."

"I'm not." She didn't elaborate, but went straight to the kitchen.

James wandered around her tiny living room, divided from the equally tiny kitchen only by a long, tall counter. The room suited her: practical and efficient. More colorful than he'd have expected, with bright throw pillows on the mud-brown sofa and vivid, scenic photographs on the plain white walls. Not just local subjects, either, although the park was well-represented by a shot of a geyser he didn't recognize offhand and a classic view of the lower falls in the canyon. Red-rock cliffs, a hillside sweeping with trees turned a thousand shades in autumn, an ocean at dusk with a lighthouse beaming welcome.

"Who's the photographer?"

Jo turned from her preparations. "I am."

"You're good." He wondered if there was anything she didn't do well. A career, maybe. He glanced around again, baffled at the incongruity.

"I'm full of surprises." But she didn't sound offended.

"Yes, you are. Most of them quite wonderful."

There. He'd surprised *her* for a change. After a moment her mouth quirked up. "I like to think so." She strolled over and handed him a wineglass. It was half full of a garnet-colored liquid.

"Thank you." James took a sip, and was pleasantly surprised yet again. "And here's another."

"We're not all hicks out here in the wilderness. There's a nice wine shop in Bozeman. All those college professors, you know." She went back in the kitchen.

James leaned an elbow on the tall counter dividing the kitchen and the living area. "How did a seasonal fry cook rate a place of her own instead of a bunk?"

She smiled. "I wondered when you'd catch on."

James waited, but she didn't say anything more as she dished up the goulash and brought it and a large bowl of salad to the table built into the corner. It was set with placemats that looked hand-woven and vividly-colored stoneware dishes. "Are we playing twenty questions?"

She laughed. "No. I was filling in for the regular fountain manager. Her daughter had a baby, and she took a week to go down to Salt Lake to be with her after the birth. She came back even after the earthquake, though. We don't normally allow the ninety-day-wonders to take time off in the middle of the season, but she'd been working for us every summer for years, and she wanted it in her contract just this once, so we made an exception. It was easier –" she shrugged "– no, I was looking for an excuse to get down to Old Faithful for a change. So I just took the hours myself."

James noted the 'us' and the 'we' and shook his head. So, on top of everything else, he'd misjudged her on that front, too. And she'd known he was behaving like a snob, and let him get away with it. *I'm not a snob,* he thought defiantly. Then what *did* he call it? And how else could he put a foot wrong with her? "What do you do normally?"

"Onsite manager for Hamilton Stores." She set the goulash bowl down, where it steamed gently, and handed him the ladle. "Let's eat before it gets cold."

James, bemused and honestly rather embarrassed, scooped out beef and noodles and thick, reddish-brown gravy into the stoneware bowl on his plate. He should have known something was up, but he'd had more important things to worry about at the time. So what was his excuse now? "You were enjoying what I thought of you, weren't you?" He handed her the ladle.

She scooped up a serving for herself. "I suppose I was. It wasn't fair of me, but I have to say I'm glad to find out you're only stuffy when you're upset."

And again she explained his bad behavior away as if it were perfectly normal. Maybe it was. But he didn't need to be a jerk, as Chuck would have said. "That figures." He took a bite and what remained of his indignation or embarrassment or whatever this mishmash of feelings was utterly vanished as every taste bud in his mouth went into ecstasy. He tried not to let her see how his tongue was melting, but when he glanced up at her, she looked very pleased with herself. "I'm glad, though. You were completely wasted as a fry cook."

"Hey, I make the best hamburgers in the park."

"As I said, wasted. Although I don't suppose you get to cook much in your current position, either." He took another bite, savoring it. Mrs. May was more than adequate in the kitchen, and he'd been in his share of sophisticated restaurants, but this was the last meal he'd expected to find in a place like this. "No wonder my mother trusted her recipes with you."

They ate in companionable silence. When Jo got up to get the *lefse* dough out of her tiny refrigerator, James followed her and leaned on the end of the counter to watch as she began shaping the pancakes. This brought back memories, too. Ones he hadn't thought he'd want to remember. But his mother – he couldn't think of Karin McManis any other way, no matter where or when he'd come from – had been gone for five years now, and they were comforting, not so sad anymore. And the smell of the *lefse* frying took him right back to his childhood, here and in the little house in Bozeman.

"I have lingonberry, too, if you'd like it," Jo told him as she spread blackberry jam on the first one, rolled it, and handed it to him in a napkin. "It's supposed to be more traditional." James supposed he couldn't blame her for not making him wait till they were all cooked. He was practically hanging over her like a vulture.

He took the first bite, quite conscious of her watching him as his tongue threatened to melt away again as he chewed. He swallowed and said, "Not in our house. But thank you." He took another bite.

"So I understand." She kept at it until the plate nearby was stacked nicely with rolls of potato pancakes, spread neatly with thick, dark blackberry jam. "Here, take this to the table."

He took the plate from her outstretched hand. "Thanks. But where's yours?"

She shook her head, obviously amused as he'd intended, and followed him.

* * *

It was later than he'd realized when he finally stepped out into the star-crusted dark. The moon, less than half full, was almost directly overhead. So much for getting back to the hotel at a decent hour to make an early start in the morning. James shrugged into the jacket he was glad he'd brought in with him. The temperature had definitely dropped from the shirt-sleeve warmth of earlier in the day.

"Thank you," he told Jo. "I had a wonderful evening." And he had. He refused to feel surprised by that fact any more.

"You're quite welcome. "She held out her hand.

James took it. "I'll pick you up tomorrow morning?"

She looked sheepish. James braced himself for God knew what.

"I meant to mention this earlier, but –" she stopped.

Being hesitant again, too. He didn't want to ask. "But what?" he prompted her.

"I have to run down into the park for a bit before we leave town. It shouldn't take long." She was talking faster now. "I'd love the company if you'd like to come with me, but I understand if you don't want to. I'm sorry. I really should have done it this afternoon, but –"

"But you were expecting me." James sighed. "I could wait here, I suppose. If you won't be gone long."

She looked crestfallen. Also cold, standing there in shirtsleeves." I can give you a house key," she said doubtfully, "since you'll have to check out of the hotel tomorrow. I'm sorry. If you want to go on to Helena without me, I understand." She looked like she meant it, her expression sincere, not teasing. And very disappointed, for some reason.

"How long do you think you'll be gone?" The closest 'down into the park' place she could conceivably need to go for her job was the Roosevelt Lodge, but he suspected that wasn't where she was headed. If she needed to go as far as Old Faithful or the Lake Hotel, it would be an all day trip at least, if she spent any time at all at her destination.

"I'm not sure. One thing about my job, I never know if the 'little' problem really is, or if it's a gasoline fire waiting to blow up in my face. This late in the season, though, it can't be that bad."

Right. Of course. Going down into the park was the very last thing he wanted to do. He'd had enough memory lane today to last him a good long time, and he didn't want more. He was ready, more than ready, to leave for Helena bright and early in the morning. But he found himself reluctant to disappoint her, too. Or to leave her behind. "Let me think about it, all right?"

She brightened, as if it was more than she'd expected of him. And as if it really mattered. Why it would baffled him. "That's fine." She shivered.

"Get in the house before you freeze to death," he told her.

"Yes, sir." Still holding his hand, she leaned forward and kissed him. Just a peck on the lips, was all. But it startled him. More than startled him.

When she drew back, he could tell it showed on his face, because the look in her dark eyes was obviously amused. How much more embarrassment was he going to have to deal with around her? "See you in the morning."

"What time?"

"As early as you can manage."

"All right. Good night, Jo."

He turned away and headed for the Lincoln, his back stiff. Her voice wafted behind him. "Good night, James." Yes. Definitely amused. James gritted his teeth and climbed in.

* * *

Some time later, having settled himself into his room and his bed and fallen asleep almost too easily, he awoke with a start, and leaned over to peer through the dark. The alarm clock, provided since the otherwise very nice rooms lacked telephones for wake-up calls, read a quarter past three in the confounded morning. *Not* the alarm, then. So what the – There it went again. And again. It sounded like someone was strangling a trumpet underneath his second-story window.

James threw his head back on the pillow, so puffy it almost bounced back, and groaned. He knew that noise. He'd grown up with it, associated it with going back to civilization every fall. He hadn't heard it in decades, but it wasn't something he was likely to forget. He closed his eyes. Tried to ignore it, but he knew from long experience it wasn't ignorable. It was about as persistent as persistent got, even in the middle of the night. Especially in the middle of the night.

He finally pulled a second pillow over his head. Better to almost suffocate than listen to that particular racket for the rest of the night. But it still took him the better part of an hour to get back to sleep.

* * *

As a result, James was not at his best when he pulled up in front of Jo's house trailer at seven-thirty the next morning. She'd evidently been waiting for him, because the door opened before he could get the key out of the ignition. She strode toward the car, swinging an obviously loaded duffel bag. Was she planning on spending the night down in the park, or being optimistic about getting on the road toward Helena quickly? James fervently hoped it was the latter, as he climbed out of the car.

"Hi!" She looked and sounded far more pleased to see him than the situation warranted. "So are you staying here or coming with me?"

"Good morning." James hesitated. "If I don't go with you, how are you going to get there?" No vehicle sat in her gravel driveway. That was odd, come to think of it. "Where's your car?" She had to have one.

"My personal car went to the great parking lot in the sky. A buffalo got too friendly with it last July."

She sounded too nonchalant about it, James thought. *Far* too nonchalant. "You weren't hurt, were you?"

"Oh, I wasn't in it at the time. I've been cadging rides or using the company truck when I need one since. But I thought I'd wait and see if you wanted to go with me before I made other arrangements this time."

132

"Oh."

"I was hoping I might talk you into hitting a car lot or two while we're in Helena."

James heard himself say, "Of course." Being around her was like being sucked into a whirlwind. Or getting lost in a maze. Either way things just felt more and more out of his control.

"So?"

He stared at her. "So what?" Wait, he hadn't meant to sound rude –

Before he could apologize, she asked, "So are you going with me, waiting here, going on by yourself, or what?"

He felt like throwing up his hands, but he didn't. Instead he found himself opening the Lincoln's trunk. She plopped the duffel in next to his suitcase. The two items of luggage looked about as mismatched as James suspected their owners did.

"Good." He had to give her credit, she did sound genuinely pleased. "Have you had breakfast?"

"No."

Something in his voice must have given him away, because she straightened and gave him the once-over, obviously not approving of what she saw. Well, and was that *his* fault? "Wasn't the hotel up to your standards?"

As if she didn't know. "Elk," he said flatly.

At least she didn't laugh, although she looked like she wanted to. "I'm sorry. It is that time of year."

"I know." It didn't mean he had to like it. In the fall, when they were in rut, no bull elk was going to take no for an answer from any of the cows, whether she belonged to another bull or not. And if it took all night for them to hash their differences out, well, that was just too bad for anyone else. Including any hotel guests trying to sleep in the rooms directly above the battleground.

"Come on in and we'll eat before we hit the road. I've got coffee," she added when he hesitated.

He wasn't hungry. "The sooner we get going, the sooner we'll be back."

"And more *lefse*."

James gave in. Might as well fortify himself. He suspected he was going to need it.

* * *

She talked him into letting her drive, and James was tired enough it didn't take much for her to do so, although it did mean she didn't have to tell him where they were going. When they reached Mammoth, she turned east instead of south, raising his spirits a little. Maybe they were just going to the Roosevelt Lodge and back after all.

The elk herd was grazing on the old parade ground, its grass dry and tan this time of year. A couple of dozen cows meandered about, and the bull with his full rack of antlers sat posed in their midst, looking smug. He must have won whatever argument he'd had last night, because he was the only male elk in sight. James threw him a mental rude gesture. The bull raised his head as they passed. Stared as if he knew exactly what James had just done. Well, it wasn't as if *he'd* challenged the stupid creature. He'd just wanted him to shut up.

On the other side of the road, the old stone fort dozed in the early morning shadows. That view was much more peaceful, ironically enough. The little chapel was the last building in the row.

"Stop here for a minute," said James, and added, "Please."

Jo raised an eyebrow at him, but she pulled over willingly enough. As soon as the car stopped, James climbed out and went to the door. It swung open easily enough in spite of its weight. Apparently the tradition was still in force of keeping it unlocked for anyone who wanted, or needed, to go in. He stepped inside, not looking back to see if Jo would follow him or wait in the car.

It was chilly and quiet inside. James shoved his hands in his pockets and stared up at the cross at the front. He'd never been a very religious man. When he was growing up, his parents hadn't been, either, but his grandmother had brought him here occasionally. She'd said he shouldn't grow up a heathen entirely.

This was the first place he'd ever attended church services. It was a far cry from the Episcopal cathedral in Denver he attended now, more because it was where the movers and shakers went than from any personal attraction to what was preached there. He certainly hadn't felt any solace there after Catherine died. And he hadn't even bothered to go there since August.

He wasn't about to appeal to a God, if he existed, to bring his son back when, if He did exist, He'd been the one to take him away in the first place. And where did the bizarre tale his life had become fit into a religion he wasn't sure he'd ever believed in, anyway?

Obviously, being here wasn't telling him. Thinking it was only a stupid whim. James turned, to find Jo standing just inside watching him. Embarrassed again, a state he found extremely annoying especially around her, he strode up and past her. He shoved open the door. Held it for her with an exaggerated politeness he didn't feel.

She didn't say anything as he led the way back to the Lincoln, but slid into the driver's seat before he had a chance to reclaim it. He couldn't blame her. He'd be dubious about riding with him behind the wheel right now, too.

They rode on down the valley in silence. After a bit Jo said, "I'm sorry I disturbed you back there."

James lifted one shoulder, let it fall. He really didn't want to talk about it. "I shouldn't have stopped. It was a waste of time."

More silence, then she completely changed the subject. "This is the way Charley, Eliza, and Anna came to Mammoth after they escaped the Indians, isn't it? According to the story?" And not for the better, so far as James was concerned.

After a moment, he found his voice. "I suppose it is."

"Only to find nothing but a dead body when they got there. That must have been pretty scary."

"The way he described it, I guess so. The young fool was lucky he didn't get shot himself."

Silence, then , "You really don't think much of your son, do you?"

He loved his son. He missed his son. He was still grieving his son. "How dare you say that."

"I'm sorry."

She darned well ought to be. "This was a bad idea. I suppose it's too late to turn back now?"

"Hang on." She kept going. A few minutes later he saw a sign reading "Lava Creek Campground," with an arrow pointing off to the right. She swung the car off the road and stopped. Not that it would have mattered if she'd stopped in the middle of the road. They hadn't passed a single car since they'd left Mammoth.

James stared straight ahead as she turned toward him in her seat. "If you really want to go back, I'll take you back. I just thought – oh, look at me."

Slowly he turned his head. God knew what she was seeing.

"On second thought – No. James, I am sorry. And pushy. I can see you think the world of Chuck." She hesitated. "In spite of everything. Forgive me?" She put a hand on his arm.

After a moment, he put his free hand over hers. "Yes." She let her breath out in a whoosh. "But I don't know if I can do what you seem to want of me."

"If I quit being such a pushy broad, will you go on with me?"

He wanted to. He wanted to stay with her. He suddenly wondered how she'd react if he told her he was beginning to fall for her. In spite of everything. "Yes. Let's go on."

CHAPTER 12

She beamed at him. James basked in the warmth of her smile as she pulled back out on the highway. He supposed she was trying to 'not be a pushy broad' as she drove on without saying another word. But it was a peaceful silence, and as he watched her handle the Lincoln competently on the narrow, winding road, he relaxed. Let her be in charge. Quit caring about where they were going and how long it would take them to get there. Even if he actively disliked the place, it didn't mean he had to ruin things for her.

Besides, he was too tired to be obnoxious. He leaned his head on the seat back and closed his eyes. Odd, how Jo Bennett, of all people, made him think of Catherine. They were different as two women could be. Catherine had been feminine and elegant, always appropriate and dignified. Aloof, he'd have said if he hadn't loved her so much. And if she'd ever behaved that way with him. But she hadn't, not from the beginning. And he could almost hear her now, that silvery laughter pealing out of her, pleased with him. He knew she hadn't been pleased with him very often since she'd left him.

She's gone, he reminded himself. She hasn't been able to be pleased or displeased with me for a long time. But he knew that for the lie it was. Even if she only lived on in his mind, she lived on. And somehow he knew she was glad he was finally climbing back out of the shell he'd crawled into when she died.

Which, he supposed, was what he was doing. And it pleased him, just for a moment Then James remembered the circumstances which had introduced him to this woman in the first place, and the weight settled back down onto his shoulders like an anvil. It was so heavy. But it felt so good for a few seconds while it was gone. And it was so wrong to feel that way.

"Wake up, sleeping beauty."

The car had come to a stop again, he realized. He opened his eyes. "I wasn't asleep."

"Then why were you snoring?"

Surely he hadn't been – "Where are we?" But he knew, as he looked around at the low-slung, rustic building, a porch stretched across the full length of the front. The cabins around it, their shutters closed and latched, looked as if a giant had scattered them like a handful of dice. The Lincoln was the only car he could see.

"Roosevelt. I need to stop here for a bit, check on a few things. Why don't you go for a walk? Wake yourself up?"

What he wanted to do was go back to sleep. Stretch out on the wide, comfortable back seat and just –

"Go on, lazy bones."

So he did.

He watched her as she strode off toward the lodge, which looked closed up for the winter, too, pulled a key out of her pocket and let herself in. After she'd disappeared inside, he headed in the opposite direction, on the trail up the hill toward the petrified tree. It was as good a destination as any other, he supposed. Better than wandering aimlessly. Anything was better than wandering aimlessly.

What he'd forgotten was the view from the hillside where the lone trunk stood, long since surrounded by a wrought-iron fence to protect it from the vandals and souvenir hunters who'd gradually made its twin disappear. He could almost imagine Chuck – no, according to his account, Eliza'd started calling him Charley by then – standing somewhere not far from here, and the utter relief he must have felt seeing the soldiers' campfires down below. Only to turn around and see that mama bear, well, bearing down on them, murder in her eyes for threatening the cub he hadn't even known was in the tree over their heads.

It wasn't that he hadn't heard the stories all his life. His mother in particular had been most impressed with his great-aunt Anna's version, in which his grandfather had performed like a hero on the proportions of Superman in Chuck's childhood comics. Saving not only his own life from everything from Indians to snowstorms, but that of the woman and the girl under his care.

His grandfather, according to Great-aunt Anna, could do anything. His father, too, for that matter, according to his mother, whose tales of the Klondike Gold Rush included Will's rescue of her at least twice, once when he was still recovering from an accident that according to her would have killed anyone else.

James shook his head. They'd never told him he'd have to live up to their exploits. They'd never had to. Which was why he'd always known if he didn't become someone completely different he was doomed to failure. His war experiences had certainly taught him heroism was decidedly not his cup of tea. He supposed it should have been a relief to know now his grandfather hadn't thought he was all he'd been cracked up to be, either, but all he could think was it was all the more impressive knowing he'd been – who he was.

A throwback, in the most literal sense of the term. I shouldn't resent my own son, James thought. But he did. Oh, he did.

He started back down the trail, Charley's shadow following him all the way.

* * *

Jo was waiting for him at the car. James began to apologize for keeping her, but she waved it away." It's a gorgeous day. I'm glad you got out in it."

He had to admit it was. Clear bright blue mountain sky, aspens in full golden glory. Even the pines didn't look as dark and forbidding as they usually did. The dry grass crackled under his feet.

"Ready to hit the road again?" he asked.

"I'd like to stretch my own legs first. Do you mind?"

He wondered if she wanted him to wait here. But no, she hung onto his keys." Come on."

James sighed. Well, it wasn't quite noon yet. Maybe they'd make it as far as Bozeman tonight. A man could hope, at any rate.

She headed in a completely different direction than he had, back down the little spur road toward the highway, and across the highway to the huge meadow he'd been imagining Schofield's command into a few minutes ago.

It smelled of sagebrush and dust, and even that innocuous odor was evocative to him. He imagined stumbling down that hill in the dark into an armed camp, hoping the soldiers would ask questions first and shoot later.

"They were lucky not to be mistaken for Indians."

"What?"

He hadn't realized he'd spoken aloud. "Never mind."

"Your granddad and company?" She held out a hand to him. Bemused, he took it. "I bet. I'm glad they weren't."

"Me, too." And another thing. Where would it have left him if this seemingly endless loop had been broken? So many ways it could have happened. He shivered in spite of the sun beaming down on them. He was not going to be grateful his forebears were foolhardy or heroic or whatever their admiring womenfolk wanted to call them. Or that what had happened to his son had happened.

"So what are we doing out here?" And when can we leave? he added silently.

"There's not going to be many more days like this before the snow starts to fall."

And? he thought. She'd been using the weather as an excuse for dragging him around since he'd gotten here.

She turned to look at him and pursed her lips, as if she could read his question in his expression. "Don't you wonder what it must have been like, being here in the early days?"

"I don't have to."

"I know, and I envy you that." She sighed. "I guess I keep hoping you'll thaw out. Come on." She dropped his hand and headed back to the car.

James didn't move. Thaw out? She didn't want him to thaw out. He could guarantee it with the same amount of accuracy as he guaranteed the books he kept. But that's what Catherine had told him, too. Maybe not in so many words. Let go. Trust. And he had. And look what that had gotten him.

Jo turned back, as if suddenly realizing he wasn't with her. "Come on."

"I don't know what you want from me."

"Right now I want you to go back to the car." She smiled, but it didn't reach her eyes.

"Yes, ma'am." He caught up with her, and she fell into step beside him.

They retraced their steps, but after they'd climbed back in the car and driven up to the main road, Jo turned the car to the right, instead of left back toward Mammoth.

She kept glancing over at him as if she expected him to object, or at least say something, and looked disappointed when he didn't. Or maybe that he didn't say anything at all. But anything he wanted to say would have been the wrong thing.

He certainly wasn't going to ask her to turn around again. So he sat, and stared unseeing at the scenery, and hoped she'd turn around on her own. But she didn't.

* * *

Jo made another stop at Tower Falls. She didn't urge him to get out this time, and James waited in the comfort of his car while she strode toward the small building. He'd done his walking for this morning, so far as he was concerned. The Lincoln wasn't the only vehicle here this time, and a man approached Jo, his family nearby looking hopeful, as she unlocked the door to the place. He could see her shake her head and gesture, and the family slumped their shoulders as they went back to their car. He supposed they'd been hoping the lunch stand would be open soon.

She went inside. She took longer this time, and she wasn't smiling when she came back to the car.

"Something wrong?" James asked.

"Nothing I hadn't expected." She started the car and backed out, apparently having said all she had in mind to say.

Well, he had a right to know, he thought, since she'd dragged him down here. "What are you doing, anyway?"

She glanced over at him, as if surprised he cared. It was better than her silence, but not much. "Checking to see things are being shut down properly for the season. Water and power, shutters battened down, everything cleaned up and shut up tight against the snow and the critters."

"Weren't they?" And was this part of her job? It sounded more routine than what he'd been led to believe she'd be doing today.

"They are now."

"By who?" Surely she didn't do it all herself in an hour.

"The crew. Or the two kids who're what's left of the crew at this point, anyway. Not every site's got a supervisor at this stage of the game. Especially not this year."

He'd thought the buildings were empty, that the other car in the mostly empty parking lot belonged to tourists who'd gone for a hike. "Oh," he said inanely, and fell silent.

She'd turned away from Mammoth again, headed south. Good grief, James thought, are we going clear around the entire park? But he didn't ask out loud.

* * *

The road climbed as they headed south, toward Dunraven Pass. James couldn't help thinking of his son's account of stumbling down the mountainside in the snow turned to rain, the first of their worn-out horses giving out completely. Of his great-aunt Anna's much more embellished account of how he'd kept them going, and how he'd comforted Eliza and taken care of them both.

"I wonder if we're all that far from the way they went," James said suddenly.

Jo glanced over at him, and, unsurprisingly, knew exactly what he meant. "I wouldn't be surprised if we're driving on it. There's not a lot of options going over these mountains." She pulled over and stopped the car. "Do you want to get out and look around?"

He did. He didn't. It was stupid to dither about it, and the sooner they got going the sooner they'd be back. "Yes, for a minute if you have the time."

"I've got the time."

It was immensely quiet outside, so still the ticking of the Lincoln's cooling engine sounded like a metronome. Warm in the sun, almost cold in the shade of a small cluster of firs at the edge of the road. James walked to the edge of the pullout and looked across the mountainside falling in front of him, making him want to lean back away from it. He resisted the urge. The landscape before him was tundra, he supposed, at this elevation, but it felt more like the rangeland he'd driven across so much of to get here. The Beartooth Mountains loomed in the distance, autumn snow already making them shine white.

"Must have been some hike," Jo commented, coming to stand beside him.

"So he wrote. And," he added, because even he knew he sounded snippy, "so my great-aunt Anna says. She was there."

"Really?" Jo's voice perked up. "Is she still alive?"

He couldn't help responding to her interest. Besides, he loved his great-aunt Anna. She was, she was – another great joy of his childhood. Just like his mother, with whom she'd been great friends. "Yes, the last I heard. She's in her nineties now. I was hoping to see her on this trip. She lives in Helena."

"Oh, I'd like that."

Well, why not? He knew Aunt Anna would be tickled to meet Jo. And if she made unwarranted assumptions about their friendship, well, what she didn't know wouldn't hurt him. Jo would obviously be in hog heaven, as his grandfather would have said. James found himself smiling at the image and decided he wanted to see it in reality. "I bet she would, too."

And it might get her through the park more quickly if she had that to look forward to. Or possibly not, since it looked like Jo really did have work to do here first.

"You know, I've hiked all over this place. I've backpacked for days at a time. But it's just not the same thing."

That startled a laugh out of him. "I certainly hope not."

"You know what I mean." She was gazing out over the landscape with an almost proprietary pride.

"I mean I hope you took a tent and a sleeping bag and plenty of food, and didn't have to sleep out in the rain with your stomach growling."

"You take all the romance out of it."

"Taking turns sleeping, at that, to keep watch for Indians."

"But it must have been so exciting." She sounded positively wistful.

"That kind of exciting I can do without," he told her.

She gave him a reproachful look. A gust of wind, colder than the rest, buffeted them both. James reached out and put an arm around her shoulders. He'd only been meaning to nudge her back to the car or so he told himself, but she turned to him inside the circle of that arm. Her eyes were laughing as she tilted her head back.

"Very smooth, sweetie, but don't stop there."

He shook his head and led her back to the car, but he wondered what she'd have done if he'd called her bluff and kissed her.

* * *

They stopped again at the top of the pass itself, "just to look around," Jo said. "I don't suppose this car could handle the road up to the top of Mt. Washburn."

The words slipped out of his mouth. "It's been to the top of Pike's Peak."

"You don't say. When was that?" She sounded like she didn't believe him. He supposed she had no good reason to. Maybe he should give her one.

"Chuck talked me into the trip, just after I bought the car last year." And what a memory that was. Wheels spinning, gravel flying, more sharp turns than an entire package of bobby pins, grades so steep he'd thought they were going to flip over backward like a turtle more than once. The boy had loved every minute of it. And so had he, James thought, even if the only reason he'd agreed to go in the first place was to keep Chuck from following through on a threat to take his motorcycle up the unpaved road to the top of the fourteen thousand foot peak. Well, not the *only* reason. "I think it can handle Mt. Washburn."

"Really?" Jo grinned at him.

He couldn't help but grin back. She looked so pleased. And so surprised. "Really. Would you mind if I took the wheel?"

"Don't you trust me?" But she was still grinning.

He was beginning to, he thought. "It's my turn to have some of the fun."

She opened her mouth, closed it, and handed him the keys.

Like a gentleman, he helped her scoot over before walking around the car and letting himself back in. Like a gentleman, he drove sedately to the turn-off and made the turn. Then he let the Lincoln loose.

Mt. Washburn was no Pike's Peak, James thought a little while later as he pulled up in front of the fire lookout at the top in one last rooster tail of gravel, but it hadn't been half bad. He missed that sort of thing, missed having someone along for the ride to egg him on. Catherine had been an expert at such things, her hair tied back in a scarf, her eyes shining. And Chuck hadn't needed to learn to love it, either. James's exhilaration faded, but not from sadness this time. He'd gotten his love for machinery and the speed it could create from his grandfather. Who'd gotten it from him. Who'd given it to him. Suddenly he felt dizzy, but in a good way.

"Holy cat!" Actually, it wasn't the first time Jo'd said that. She'd been more or less chanting it ever since he'd swung the car off the highway. "Good grief!"

She *sounded* pleased. . . James shut the engine off and slid around in the seat to face her.

She looked as exhilarated as he'd felt. "You didn't tell me you drove the Indy 500 in your spare time."

He couldn't help feeling smug. "Hardly. Did I scare you?"

She rolled her eyes at him. "Of course not."

"Darn."

"You mean to tell me you *wanted* to scare me?"

James pursed his lips judiciously. "I thought you could use a little excitement in your life. After all, here you are, stuck all day with an old stick in the mud."

She laughed. "After what you just did, that's the last thing I'd ever call you."

"Good. My new goal in life is achieved." But he said it lightly.

And she took it in the spirit in which it was intended, putting a cool, strong-fingered hand on his and squeezing it before she let go and said, "Come on. Last one up the fire tower's a rotten egg."

CHAPTER 13

James snatched both their jackets from the back seat and followed her up the stairs. He couldn't remember the last time he'd been up here, but he didn't think he'd ever been here on such a clear day.

They were greeted by the lookout, who said, "You're not supposed – Oh, hi, Jo. What's up?" Once again, James thought, Jo was ignoring the rules as if they didn't apply to her, which was evidently the case. Rules were a good thing most of the time, but he had to say he was enjoying her cavalier approach to them right now. His heart was still pounding. Exhilarating.

He acknowledged her introduction to "Henry, the fire lookout," and left them chatting while he strolled around the catwalk, gazing out into what even he had to admit was a gorgeous view. Views, actually. One in every direction. The canyon cut a swath to the east which looked like a giant had taken a knife and begun to peel the earth's surface back, then thought better of the idea. Glorious mountains rolled away in every other direction, some far across the wide, flat crater marking the dying volcano, some right at his feet. To the immediate west he could see clearly what Jo had meant about 'not many choices' for Charley, Eliza, and Anna to escape over those mountains. The thin gray stripe of the Grand Loop road followed what looked like literally the only option. He supposed taking the path of least resistance would have found it for them, but even he knew it wasn't that easy. James stared down at the road, trying to imagine what the trek had really been like. His grandfather's notebooks had described it, and Aunt Anna had talked more about the adventure of their escape than anything else. His grandmother – well, he couldn't blame her now for not wanting to talk about the days just after her first husband had been shot and they'd thought he was dead. According to Charley's version, she'd been mind, body, and soul grieving at that point. And for some time afterward. For all the stories he'd heard growing up, he knew far too little about his own family – yes, *his* family, James thought stubbornly, even if he hadn't been born to them.

"James!" Jo's voice startled him out of his reverie. "Come here!"

James strode around to the other side of the fire tower, to find Jo peering through a pair of binoculars and Henry pointing and gesturing. As soon as James came near, Jo shoved the field glasses at him and pointed. "There's a mama bear and her cubs down there."

James took the binoculars and held them to his eyes. He widened the two halves of the thing at the hinge until he could see through them clearly, and scanned the forest below.

"Farther out. In that open spot," Jo told him. "Hurry before they disappear into the trees."

He wasn't quite sure why he was bothering. Animals were her interest, not his. But he kept scanning – There they were. A big furry blob trailed by two smaller ones. He adjusted the focus, and suddenly they leaped into clarity.

"That's a big one," he commented. "I'd forgotten." But he was remembering now, the time his father had taken him hiking up the Mary Mountain trail one summer while he took a bear census. They'd counted rubbed trees and scat and, finally, seen one lone grizzly. It had been an enormous old male, and it hadn't liked seeing them. Chuck – Charley – Granddad – son, James was beginning to realize he no longer knew what to call the man he'd known at both ends of his life – had seen a mama with cubs like this on his escape over the mountains, too. And been smart about it. The boy wasn't a fool. He just wanted to be someone James didn't want him to be. It was a punch to his gut, even though he realized he'd known it all along.

"She's a grizzly," Henry was saying. "I've seen her a few times over the summer. The cubs had to have been born last winter."

James watched the trio a little longer, then handed the field glasses to Henry. "Thanks."

"You're lucky," Jo said. At first James wasn't sure who she was talking to, then he realized she was actually jealous of the fire lookout's job.

James couldn't imagine being envious of the man, stuck out here on his own for months on end, dealing with the endless flow of tourists in the summer while trying to get his own work done, only to face the stark, lonely side of it every night. But then he apparently hadn't understood his own son at all, either.

"I've seen bighorn sheep and mountain goats over on the cliffs there, too. And I get elk in the meadow. Buffalo don't get up to this part of the park much, though."

"Someday I'm going to come and spend a week up here," Jo said.

"Any time," Henry told her.

The fellow had to be young enough to be her son, James told himself. No reason to think she was interested in him. She'd probably want to spend time up here even if it meant sharing living quarters with an axe murderer.

"Well, I suppose we'd better get going. Work to do," she added.

The boy looked genuinely sorry to see them go. "There always is."

"How much longer will he be here?" James asked as they climbed back in the car. He didn't give Jo the keys back. She didn't ask for them, either.

"The fire season officially ends with the first solid snowfall. He gets the forecast on his shortwave, so he'll have time to get down before it hits."

James concentrated on getting the Lincoln back down the steep, curving, gravel track to the main road. It was easier to drive like a madman going up than down, as he knew from experience. "Would you really want his job, or were you just trying to make him feel better about being stuck up there all summer?"

When she didn't answer right away, he stole a glance over at her. Evidently he'd put his foot in it again.

"You're determined to think we're all nuts for liking it here," she said eventually." Aren't you?"

He hadn't meant it quite that way. "No." But his voice sounded weak, even to him. Still, he didn't know how to answer her in a way she would approve of and stay truthful at the same time. He wanted to, though. Then he realized he could. "The view was spectacular from up there. In every direction. It's wonderful to be able to see so far."

"I'm glad there's something about the park you can like." She sounded almost petulant.

James sighed. They'd reached the main road. The way back north beckoned to him, but he asked her, anyway. "Where do you need to go next?"

* * *

"This is new," James said a few miles later when they reached a cluster of oddly modern-looking buildings. "What happened to the old hotel?"

"Oh, it's still there, down the road apiece. But they've closed it down. It's got structural problems." She opened the car door. "I'm going to be a while here." And climbed out.

She could have picked a worse spot to take time. "Which way to the canyon?" The new development had him rather turned around, but it couldn't be that far.

She leaned back in and pointed. "That way."

"I'll swing back and get you."

"All right." She looked pleased with him, which didn't surprise him. It didn't even bother him as much as it should have.

James waited until she'd let herself into the building and disappeared before he started the car back up again.

The side road was obviously newly-paved, and much smoother than the Grand Loop. It curved through the trees, past the campground on one side and an enormous grouping of modern cabins on the other, the land looking raw and scraped around the few trees left standing. Both cabins and campground looked deserted as well, and he supposed they were closed for the season like everything else.

When he reached a T he turned left, toward Inspiration Point, or so the sign read. The small parking lot was empty, the path to the viewpoint likewise. Peaceful. He took a deep inhalation flavored with pine, and gazed out across the slash in the earth below. The canyon had been his favorite part of the park as a boy. He wondered if this trip would be the last time he saw it. *Probably.* The thought disconcerted him, briefly, catching him by surprise. He hadn't seen the place in decades, so what, as Chuck would have said, was the big deal? It had always been here. It always would be. If he wasn't, it was by his own choice. He leaned out over the iron pipe railing and gazed over the canyon below, bright in the noonday sunlight.

He seemed to be doomed to reminiscences today, but he supposed it was to be expected, given the time and the place. At least here he wasn't reminded of his son's/grandfather's harrowing story . He wished he knew what to call him now – the one man he'd always thought were two, and two he'd have thought to be so different from each other – he was my *son*, James thought. Whatever else he became, he was *my* son first.

A movement down by the river caught his wandering attention. A bird, and a big one, too. It hovered, then stooped down into the river and came up with something silver-shining in its claws. An osprey, James supposed, although even with the fire lookout's binoculars he wouldn't know for sure. He watched as the bird flew up to a spot on the cliff where it landed, then let his gaze wander up and down the canyon.

He couldn't see the falls from here. He wondered if he had the time to drive around to Artist Point on the other side before Jo would be ready to go on to wherever she had in mind to go next.

James decided he didn't care whether he did or not.

* * *

He'd been watching the falls from Artist Point for some time when a familiar voice behind him said, "You do like views."

James turned around. "How did you get here?"

Jo shrugged. "Got tired of waiting. One of the rangers saw your car headed this way, and gave me a lift."

"I'm sorry."

She waved his half-hearted apology away. "I'm just glad to see you do like something here."

James wished she'd quit automatically assuming – well. It wasn't as if he'd not given her every excuse. "My office is on the twenty-third floor of a high-rise in downtown Denver. I can see almost the whole Front Range from my windows."

She leaned back on the railing. "Is that why you chose it?"

Yes, he thought. "Mostly I chose it because it's a prestigious address, and that's good for business."

"Of course." And he'd just given her another excuse. Suddenly James realized he didn't want her thinking that way.

"But I could have chosen an office on a lower floor. The rent would have been less, and it would have been more practical."

"But you didn't."

"No."

She turned, her back to the view they'd come there to admire, and watched him curiously.

He shrugged. "Catherine talked me into it." When Jo just kept looking at him, James explained. "My late wife. She said I needed to see beyond my own nose." Suddenly he'd had enough of the view. More than enough. "Come on. I'm sure you've got better things to do."

"Not right this minute." But she followed him back to the car. "Are you hungry?"

He'd been wondering about that for some time now. "Yes."

"How about a picnic?"

A couple of tables perched near the parking area, and the weather was still cooperating. "What are we going to eat?" Then he noticed the brown paper sack sitting on top of the Lincoln's trunk. It bulged promisingly. "Where did that come from?"

She grinned. "I have my ways. It came from the Canyon store. Just packaged sandwiches and bottled soda, but they'll fill you up."

"Still making sure I get fed?" But he was smiling as he asked her.

"Somebody has to."

She was right, the sandwiches weren't much better than filling, but they got the job done. James resolved that tonight, wherever they were, he would buy her the best meal available.

"Now where?" he asked, mostly for form, since he'd given up on any chance whatsoever she was going to tell him she was done and they could head back to Mammoth now.

"I'm hoping you'll humor me," was all she said, and she waggled her fingers at him when he pulled the keys out of his pocket.

"I'll take us where you tell me to go."

She sighed. "Men and their cars. All right. Turn left at the main road."

South again. James shrugged and made the turn.

* * *

They passed the big dark hulk of the Canyon Hotel, looming at the side of the road. "I remember when that was new," James commented." It was fancier than the Old Faithful Inn. It's too bad they've let it go like that."

"Mission 66 has been good for a lot of things, but there's some things the government got dead wrong. One of them was the planners thinking people were going to want to stay in those little cabins instead of that beautiful old place. But the ground's unstable under it, and now after the earthquake, well, if they hadn't been planning to try to fix it before, they certainly aren't now. They're going to tear it down this fall."

James shrugged. "Things have to change, even here."

"This is the one place things should never have to change." Her tone was vehement.

James didn't think she'd thought that one quite through. "What? You think people should still be riding around in stagecoaches on dirt roads? Or on horseback with no roads at all?" He was forcibly reminded they were following his son's escape route from the Indians again. "Give me my car any day."

"You sound like Charley and his motorcycle. Every time he mentioned it he sounded like he was whining. "She was amused at him. Again.

James gritted his teeth. "Remind me again why I'm humoring you?"

Instead of answering him, she pointed. "I wondered where the herd was."

They had just rounded a bend into the widening valley. James hit the brakes. It wasn't as if he could do anything else. They were all over the road. Buffalo. Most of them bigger than the Lincoln. They didn't look like they were in any hurry to get out of the way, either. He glanced around and behind. The road was too narrow here to turn around, and no pullout anywhere. "Great. Just great." He nudged the car forward a foot or two, hoping forlornly that the enormous animals would get the hint.

"Don't. They'll charge if they feel threatened," Jo cautioned him, unnecessarily, he could have told her.

"So are we going to sit here all day?"

She settled back in her seat. "They'll move on in a bit. Just turn the engine off. We're not in that big a hurry."

Maybe she wasn't. But James shrugged and did as she suggested. It wasn't as if the animals were allowing him much of a choice. But with the engine off, he could hear them, too, snuffling and snorting, the thunk of their hooves on the pavement sounding like the pounding of a hammer. When one of them plunked itself down on the edge of the road, he swore he could feel the ground shake. He shuddered and closed his eyes.

When he opened them again a moment later, it was to see Jo turned in her seat, watching him curiously. "What's the matter?"

What wasn't the matter? He didn't want to be here, he didn't want to look like a fool in front of her again, he didn't want to *remember*. He shook his head. He was too busy watching one big creature eyeing them, he could swear, with evil intent to answer her. She followed his gaze. "Maybe you should back the car up a bit."

Maybe he should back the car up all the way to the nearest pullout, turn it around and bug out. But he started the engine. The evil-eyed beast all but shrugged and meandered away. So instead of backing up, he edged the car forward a bit more. Another few feet opened up, and a few more, and a few more. Some of the buffalo were close enough that if he and Jo had been stupid, they could have rolled down the windows, reached out, and touched their filthy hides. But none of them charged the car, and in a few moments the herd was behind them.

James realized he'd been holding his breath, and let it loose in a whoosh. He let loose his white-knuckled grip on the steering wheel, too, and flexed his fingers, one hand at a time. Before he could put his right hand back on the wheel, Jo grasped it.

"You're shaking," she said, sounding as if she couldn't believe it. "It's all right."

"I need both hands to drive safely."

"Then stop."

James shook his head. "Not till we're safe."

She let go, reluctantly, and he drove another mile before he felt like he'd put enough space between the car and those monstrous beasts. Reluctantly, he pulled over and turned to face her.

She was turned in her own seat, staring at him. "What just happened back there?" she demanded.

"I don't like buffalo."

"Why?"

He gazed at her helplessly. "They scare the liver out of me."

She didn't look amused anymore. "Oh, James."

What was he supposed to say to that? But she didn't give him a chance to answer. Instead, she reached out with both hands and laid them one to each side of his face.

Her palms felt cool against his overheated skin. He reached up and laid his own hands on top of hers, not to remove them, but to keep them there. He could feel himself leaning in, see her leaning toward him, too. Until they were so close he could see her eyes weren't black, but the deepest, darkest, richest brown he'd ever seen. Until they were so close he was kissing her.

CHAPTER 14

James had a brief moment, a second, no more, of awkwardness, of "this isn't Catherine" – ness before he let himself quit feeling guilty, even after all these years, over feeling pleasure with another woman. Because kissing Jo was a pleasure. He'd have thought she'd want control of the encounter, and while he knew if she didn't want this it wouldn't be happening, he was the one taking the lead, guiding her where they both, he hoped, wanted to go. And she was letting him, in a way Catherine, or the few women he'd gotten close enough to for intimate contact over the long years since she'd left him, never had.

It was heady. And suddenly, the feeling of betrayal, of him being betrayed by his own feelings, not by Jo, never by Jo, caused him to pull back.

"My apologies." He knew he sounded brusque. He didn't dare look at her, but turned to face forward again and start the car.

Jo didn't say anything, although he could hear her quickened breathing, along with his own, over the Lincoln's engine. They were a mile or more further along before she said anything. "Why are you scared of buffalo?"

That wasn't what he'd expected. He wasn't sure if the question wasn't worse than the one he had expected. "Had a run-in with one when I was young and foolish." He hoped she wouldn't pursue –

"What happened?"

So much for that hope. He'd known it would be forlorn, but he tried again, anyway. "It's a long story."

"I've got all afternoon."

"Another 'old days' story for your files?" he asked, trying to sound as if he asked lightly and knowing he failed. She should have been demanding to know why he'd kissed her, not dredging up ancient history. "It wasn't that exciting." Except to him at the time. He remembered it vividly, staring mesmerized at the huge animal from at an arm's reach away. "I was about eight and curious. I went too close to it. The buffalo got annoyed. But Granddad —" his breath caught, but he forced himself to go on. "Granddad rescued me." Just before the monster charged both of them. James concentrated on his driving even though there wasn't an animal in sight for once, and the road itself curved lazily alongside the wide, deep, smoothly-flowing river, hardly demanding such intense attention.

Perhaps she kissed men all the time, and it was of little consequence to her. Perhaps she didn't think much of his kissing ability. He had to admit he was rusty at it. More than rusty. The thought unsteadied him.

Suddenly she said, "Let's stop here."

They'd reached the place called the Mud Volcano. Obediently James turned into the little side loop and parked the car.

The stench hit him as soon as he opened the door. Rotten eggs, although James had never smelled any eggs that reeked that badly, and hoped he never would. "Do you really want to get out here?"

"It's one of the places Charley mentioned," was all Jo said as she climbed out.

James followed her, his nose wrinkling. Jo lifted an eyebrow at him, but all she said was, "Come on."

He followed her up the slope past a set of mud pots, plopping thickly this late in the season. He dodged a flying blob of steaming muck as he trailed her toward a cavern filled with gray, dirt and debris-filled water churning and splashing as if a demon was taking a bath in it. It was, aptly-enough, called the Dragon's Mouth, according to the sign.

But she didn't stop there. Instead, she went past it, into its evil-smelling steam, and disappeared. James took a breath, held it, and plunged in after her.

The ground rang hollow under his feet at first, disconcerting him, but became more solid as he went on. The hot fog cleared a little, and he caught a glimpse of Jo disappearing around a curve, apparently following a steep-walled stream bed, dry this time of year.

James let his breath out. "Wait up, will you?" he called out, and hurried on. What she was trying to accomplish he had no idea, but she had no business wandering, or striding, around by herself.

She'd probably hiked this alone a hundred times. Well, not with him here to protect her. James almost laughed at that. At himself. As if she needed protecting. Or he was capable of protecting her from the kinds of dangers she was likely to find here. He wanted to drag her back to the safety of the Lincoln. Or did he?

He was watching his feet, careful not to stumble over the rough excuse for a trail, when he ran headlong into her.

"It's about time you caught up," Jo told him as he reached out to steady her. To steady them both.

"Where –" James deleted the *do you think you're* "are we going?"

"This must have been the way they came down to the river," Jo said. She sounded positively excited.

"We're not hiking clear across the park," James said flatly.

"Of course not, silly." She patted him on the shoulder. It could have been an almost sisterly gesture, except it did not make him feel in the least brotherly. He grasped her hand. She didn't pull away, but tugged him along with her. "Just a bit farther."

He had no idea what she was looking for. He was pretty sure she didn't, either, but this was her idea of fun, he reminded himself. Not his.

But now that they were out of the reach of the mudpot stench, his own curiosity was piqued, a little. The stream bed leveled out a bit, and the little canyon it occupied widened out, and the whole thing was rather picturesque, tawny grass with a scattering of evergreens and aspens.

Chuck certainly hadn't thought it picturesque when he'd been here, but then he'd been sitting on a horse with his hands tied to the saddle horn all day. Getting rained on and windblown and dragged along against his will. With no idea how he was going to escape, and worried about the two women he'd gotten himself into that mess trying to rescue. He supposed he couldn't blame the boy. No, he couldn't. Not for trying to rescue Eliza and Anna. And Chuck was no longer a boy by that point, James had to admit. He was a man, and taking on a man's responsibilities for rescuing the women who, for all he knew, were in worse shape than he was.

He wouldn't have changed any of his experiences for the world, the letter had said. All the hardships he'd gone through, all the horrors he'd seen – He'd seen a man shot, a man die from infection he'd known could have been cured now but not then, he'd been kidnapped, hurt, attacked by bears, lost in the wilderness and left to die. And he wouldn't have changed any of that.

Because it gave him a chance to prove himself. To be who he wanted to be.

James realized he still held Jo's hand. And that he'd gone on ahead of her and pulled her behind him instead of the other way around. He stopped and tugged her to him. Let go of her hand and wrapped his arms around her instead. Muttered "thank you" into the top of her head.

She pulled back slightly, just enough to look up into his face. She tilted her head at him. "What for?"

"Never mind." He could feel the smile on her lips as he kissed her, lightly this time. He kept an arm around her shoulders as they continued up the now almost-level stream bed. Instead of objecting, she put her own arm around his waist.

"Chuck must have been scared to death right about here," Jo commented.

"He knew the Nez Perce were going to be captured," James replied.

"But he didn't know what would happen to him and the women before that."

"No, he didn't. You're right, he must have been terrified." And James couldn't have done anything to save him. Chuck had rescued himself. The helplessness he'd been feeling ever since Chuck disappeared overwhelmed him. Again.

Jo's arm tightened around him. "But he survived. And he made sure Eliza and Anna did, too." She stopped again, and gazed up at him. "I'd be proud of him."

"I am." And, James thought in amazement, he was. "It's been a while since I've been proud of him," he admitted. "I'd forgotten how."

He gazed around, noticing the deepening shadows for the first time. "We'd better get back before the sun goes down."

Jo nodded, and he let go of her so she could precede him down the trail. His arm felt empty with an almost palpable loss, and he almost reached out to pull her to him again.

"Where are we spending the night, by the way?"

"At the Lake Hotel."

"Isn't it closed for the winter?"

"Yes." She smiled over her shoulder at him. "So don't expect anything fancy."

James snorted. "Don't worry. I won't."

* * *

The gleaming expanse of Lake Yellowstone glimmered in the starlight by the time they arrived at the hotel. It, too, was unlit, although hardly dark with its coat of pale yellow paint looking almost luminous against the night sky. At her instruction, however, he drove past the hulking building, and fetched up at one of the cabins behind it.

"I'll be back in a bit," she told him, and strode off in the dark.

She obviously didn't want him to go with her, whether he thought he ought to or not. James leaned his head back on the seat and closed his eyes. What felt like less than a minute later, something thumped on the hood, startling him out of his doze so suddenly he nearly put a dent in the roof of the car. When he looked out, Jo was standing there, her arms full of bedding and a key in her hand.

"I'm sorry." She didn't sound nearly apologetic enough, however. "Come on, let's get inside."

James gave in and levered himself out of the car.

Inside, the cabin was dark and cold. The windows were shuttered tightly and the beds were bare.

"The electricity's shut off for the season, so we'll have to make do with the flashlight," Jo told him. "That means no heat, too, but –" she dumped her load on the bed "– there's plenty of blankets."

"I'll be right back," James said, and stepped out to the car. Unlike hers, the square six volt flashlight he carried for emergencies was big enough he wouldn't have to prop it on anything. He turned it on and went back inside.

"Oh. That's better." She smiled at him. "You must have been a Boy Scout."

"Always prepared?" He made a point of leaving as little as possible to chance, but this was the first time since he'd arrived he felt he had something solid to contribute, even if it was just a flashlight.

James glanced around at the space. It was almost the identical twin of the cabin he'd slept in at Old Faithful, and the reminder wasn't pleasant. Off-white walls, a clothes rod with hangers in one corner, a tiny pine dresser, a white porcelain sink next to the door, the bed taking up most of the space. The only bed. James swallowed and glanced sidelong over at Jo, who shrugged and turned away from him. Was she expecting –

"The water's turned off, too," she said quickly.

"Oh."

"We'll have to go inside the hotel for the facilities."

He couldn't care less about the facilities just then. "All right."

"I know it's not what you're used to."

"It's fine," he told her impatiently. "Jo –"

"The only reason we're in this cabin is because it's the closest one to –"

"Jo."

"What?"

"I know this isn't what it looks like." He dared to look at her now. He couldn't read her expression, in the sharp, overlapping shadows cast by the two flashlights, but he could have sworn her shoulders slumped. He strode over to her, a matter of two steps. "Unless you want it to be." He put a hand under her chin and tilted it up so she was forced to look at him. "Do you want this to be what it looks like?"

She wrenched her face away from his. He couldn't tell in the poor light if she was blushing. No, she wouldn't be. But she was obviously uncomfortable because of him. James discovered he very much didn't like Jo being uncomfortable because of him. But what could he say?

Maybe he didn't need to say anything. He put his arms around her. And held on until she relaxed. It wasn't a hardship at all right now, being here with her. And then he did know what to say. "I hope you do want it to be what it looks like."

She tilted her head back. Her eyes shone in the dark. "Really?"

He smiled down at her. "Yes."

* * *

It wasn't, however, as if they were going to strip down and do the deed on the spot. Neither one of them was ready for that, James thought ruefully as they strolled hand in hand to the hotel, where, Jo told him, the hotel's winterkeeper, who was a friend of hers – of course– had invited them for supper.

The winterkeeper's quarters were what they were. Cramped and crowded. He supposed the cave-like atmosphere was a deliberate affectation, given the purpose of the place. Like everything else in the park, they brought back memories for him. James tried not to let them overwhelm him. Not that he'd ever been in this particular set of rooms, but all places like this had more in common than expected at first glance, and they were far more like the ones he'd spent a couple of winters in as a boy than he would have preferred.

Shelves of books lined one entire wall, for instance, and a wood stove glowed with heat. More modern conveniences than he remembered. He was sure they were appreciated by the cheerful, bearded man somewhere in his thirties who welcomed them into his home.

Supper at the trestle table was plain but tasty, and the company good. When the winterkeeper, who'd been introduced by Jo as Larry, obviously relishing their company, suggested a game of Scrabble after supper, James, who was beginning to worry about his audacity earlier, agreed enthusiastically.

Jo quirked an eyebrow at him, so briefly he wasn't sure he'd really seen it, but went along with the suggestion as well, and James discovered another of her hidden talents. She almost beat him. But not quite. Poor Larry was quite out of his league, but he didn't seem to mind.

At last, however, they took turns in the tiny bathroom and bid their host good night. A chill breeze blew in off the lake, and James put his arm around Jo's shoulders. She began to pull away, disconcerting him, and he tightened his hold. "Just trying to keep you from freezing to death," he said lightly, and she relaxed. So did he. The last thing he wanted to do, he discovered, was ruin their friendship. And if being intimate would do that for her, then it wasn't worth it.

"I know." She sounded normal.

James let his breath out in relief. "I had a good time."

He could hear the smile in her voice. That was even better. "I could tell. Nobody told me you were a cutthroat Scrabble fiend."

"It's my deep, dark secret."

"Not any more. Now Larry knows, you'll be famous all over the park. Nobody'll dare play with you again."

"Except you."

"That goes without saying."

They reached the cabin door. Jo rummaged in her pocket for the key. James took it from her, and unlocked the door. She stumbled on the threshold in the dark, and James caught her. "Here, watch out."

"We should have taken the flashlight with us." She slipped out of his arms, picked it up off the little desk and turned it on. Shadows sprang to life, and the bed confronted him, seeming to take up the entire room. Jo turned to him and smiled. "That's better." She came back to him.

He had to ask. "Are you sure you want this?"

"If I didn't we wouldn't be here."

* * *

The cabin was pitch black when James awoke. And colder than a son of a gun, or so his face told him. It was the only body part he possessed not smothered under blankets. Or under Jo, who, still fast asleep, was sprawled over him as if she thought he would try to escape during the night.

He had no idea what time it was. Nor did he care. So that part of him hadn't died, altogether. Not at all. His sexual experiences since Catherine's passing had been few and far between, and had finally become unworthy of the effort it took to engineer them.

He hadn't – He hadn't felt that good since the last time he and Catherine had made love. James waited for the guilt to seize him up as it always had before. Instead he could have sworn he heard her laughter, fading away into the distance. *It's about time, love.*

Jo stirred, then lifted her head. James almost lifted a hand to press it back down to his chest, but didn't. It was murky enough he'd be lucky to make out her expression, even at this close range.

"Good morning."

"Is it?" She glanced around in the darkness. "How can you tell?"

"Good point."

"I'm not ready for it to be morning," she told him flatly, then went about showing him what she *was* ready for it to be. James had no objections, although he wondered if she realized that at his age – well, never mind. Apparently with the right encouragement, it didn't matter that much after all.

* * *

When he finally pushed the cabin door open, the sun was higher than he'd expected. The air was warmer outside than in, too.

"I hope Larry's still around," Jo commented as they headed across the pine needle covered asphalt to the hotel.

"Why wouldn't he be?"

"He's got work to do, you know." She smiled up at him.

But when they reached the door, there was a note tacked onto it. *Go on in*, it read. *Door's unlocked.*

"Well, that was nice of him." She started to shove the door open in her usual style, but James beat her to it. The smell of coffee wafted out and took precedence over everything else.

Less than an hour later, leaving a thank-you note on Larry's kitchen table – they'd raided his pantry as well as his coffeepot, Jo assuring James the winterkeeper wouldn't mind – they were on the road again.

"Which way?" he asked.

"Back the way we came, please."

"All right." Almost against his will, he turned the Lincoln to the north.

It was ridiculous, he thought, but now they were headed back, he didn't want their little adventure to end. Jo was uncharacteristically silent this morning, which bothered him, although otherwise she seemed her usual cheerful self. He hoped last night wasn't why they were headed back now.

He started to say something himself several times, then thought better of it. What could he say? Thank you seemed right out, somehow. "I don't want this trip to end," seemed disingenuous, too, after the night they'd just spent. Especially after he'd spent most of the previous day making it quite clear he'd wanted to be just about anywhere else but here.

She had him stop briefly at the Fishing Bridge store, and he strolled out onto the bridge while she did whatever it was she was doing at each stop along the way. He watched the clear green water flowing briskly under his feet for a few moments, then strode back to the car. The wind was colder than the day before, a reminder it was October, after all. They could get snowed on any time now.

It could snow any day of the year here, he reminded himself. He had chains in the trunk if worse came to worst, and wondered if Jo would call him a Boy Scout again if he had to pull them out. Even if she did, he thought, it was better than being stuck. He thought about being stuck here with her, spending more nights in that cabin, alone with her, and he almost wished it would snow.

* * *

She was waiting by the car when he got back. "I'm sorry," he said as he hurried up and unlocked her door for her.

"It's all right." She was smiling, as usual, but it seemed opaque, somehow. As if it didn't go all the way to the heart of her.

He closed her door for her and went around to the driver's side, hoping against hope she'd tell him they needed to go on instead of back, but she directed him back north again, and they drove on in silence for a while, until she said suddenly, "turn here."

The road certainly wasn't much. James wasn't sure it was a road at all, actually, but obediently he eased the Lincoln down onto the dirt track. They passed one picnic table, then another and another, but she didn't tell him to stop until they were almost to the river, then climbed out.

"Come on," she said, and James followed her obediently.

She went down to the water, and stared out at it, across the swiftly-flowing river to the thick lodgepole pine woods on the other side. James waited, watching her.

"Do you know where we are?" she asked him at last.

James shook his head. "No."

"This is where your son almost drowned."

CHAPTER 15

And what was he supposed to say to that? "I'm glad he didn't."

"So am I." She paused. "So many things could have happened."

"So many things did."

"That's not what I meant." She turned to face him. "You still don't realize how special what happened to him was, do you?"

"Special? That's not what I'd call it." Special was what had happened the previous night. But she didn't seem to think it was.

"You wouldn't be here if he hadn't been there to rescue you. Seems like a habit he couldn't get out of."

"You don't know that." He still didn't want to believe that part, those little red high-top sneakers buried in the bottom of his suitcase notwithstanding.

"I do. I think, down deep you do, too."

"No." And he didn't want to be standing here arguing with her, either. Last night had been wonderful, but he couldn't have felt farther away from her now had he driven straight home to Denver. "It's cold out here." It was chillier today, and the breeze off the water was brisk, but it wasn't cold. Not really. It was an excuse and she knew it as well as he did, judging from her expression. "Where do you need to go next?"

He hoped, as they got back in the car, that she'd say it was time to head back to Mammoth, but he knew better. They did go back north, but when they got back to the Canyon junction, she had him turn west on a road he'd never been on before. It was narrower, and not nearly as well-maintained, and a sign read, "Service Road."

"Where does this go?"

"Across the park. It comes out near the Norris museum. You said you didn't want to hike that far, so we'll drive it instead." She grinned, as if the argument had never happened. "I bet Chuck would have given his eyeteeth for the choice."

James capitulated. "You'd have to find someone else to bet against. The boy said so himself, if not in so many words."

"'God, I missed my bike,'" Jo quoted, and James found himself laughing with her in spite of himself.

But after they'd sobered, he said, "It wasn't funny to him at the time. I still can't imagine what it must have been like."

"But he adapted, and, from what he wrote and what you remember of him, he adapted well."

"Better than I ever did."

She gave him a sharp glance. He knew what she was thinking, and wished he could take the words back, but she didn't say anything more. He concentrated on his driving. The road spun out across a thickly-grassed meadow and into the forest again. Before long, it wound its way up to a minor summit, then down along a tumbling creek – the same creek Chuck had drunk from? No, they were too far north from where he'd crossed. But James would have bet it looked almost the same, if he was a betting man.

It wasn't long at all before they arrived at a T-junction. James looked his query at her.

"South, please." Of course. Although there was still a chance they'd head out of the park's west entrance, somehow James didn't think it was their destination. Or maybe it would be, eventually. But not until after. After what, he didn't want to know.

Still. It was something that had eaten at him for a while now. She knew so much about him and he so little about her. "What happened to your husband?"

She gave him a startled glance. "My husband?"

"You said you'd had one, but he was gone."

"Oh." She laughed, a small huff of air which didn't sound as if she were amused at all. "I'm sure he's still right where I left him. Richard wasn't one to go gallivanting off if he could stay home."

And she wasn't one to stay home if she could go off gallivanting, James thought. It was best if he remembered that. "Where was home?"

"Richard's home, you mean?"

"I suppose." Since her home was obviously here.

"San Francisco."

James was feeling an inkling of what she must have felt toward him. He thought of Chuck's oft-used phrase about pulling words out with pliers. "What does he do for a living?"

"He's a lawyer."

"A lawyer?"

His astonishment obviously amused her. "Me, married to a lawyer? I suppose it does seem a bit odd. I was going through my 'attempting to be respectable' period at the time. I will say one thing for him. He was respectable. Rock solid. Still is, from what I hear."

"Are you still in touch with him?"

She turned and patted him on the shoulder. "Don't worry. He's not going to come after you for sleeping with me."

James could feel his face heating. "That's not what I meant."

"He knows how to contact me, and I know how to contact him, in case either one of us hears from Stacey. Not that we expect to by now. It's been four years since she vanished."

"Oh." An unusual choice of words. Vanished. Not left.

"He's remarried."

"Oh," James said again, feeling like he'd opened a box of chocolates and found it full of worms instead.

"Clara's as respectable as he is, from what I understand. Kind of like your Catherine, and from what I gather, he met her the same way. She was his secretary."

"How did you meet him?"

Jo shook her head. "You don't want to know."

James aimed the car into a pullout and stopped the engine. "Yes, I do."

"Right. Remember, you asked." He couldn't tell if she was embarrassed or proud. "My parents hired him. To defend me in court."

He could feel his eyes going wide. "What did you *do*?"

"Nothing."

He wouldn't bet on that. James waited.

"I didn't. People do get falsely accused sometimes, you know. Can we go on? I've got work to do."

The benefit of the doubt. James realized he should have given it to her in the first place. Too late now. Always too late. "I'm sorry."

"It's all right."

"No, it isn't." He reached out for her and brought her to him. She came, but reluctantly, he thought.

He wanted to ask again what she'd been accused of, but she'd obviously been acquitted, whatever it was. And ended up marrying her lawyer. He wondered what that had been like, if she'd really loved the fellow or just fell into it trying to be 'respectable.' Respectable. He couldn't imagine anything putting out Jo's fire more than trying to be respectable. He was genuinely glad she'd given up on it.

Jo pulled back. "I really do need to get where we're going."

Reluctantly he let her go. "Which is?"

She smiled, but a bit of anxiety lurked under her expression. "Old Faithful, of course."

"Of course."

And the opportunity to find out more about the woman he was beginning to think he didn't want to leave when the time came vanished, as Chuck would have said, puff of smoke optional.

* * *

Jo made him stop several times along the way, in spite of her professed hurry to get to where they were headed. All were what James was beginning to think of as "this is where your son did this" stops. At the bridge over Nez Perce Creek, named after the tribe who'd kidnapped Eliza and Anna, who Chuck had followed as they fled across the park with the army barely days behind them. He followed Jo up the creek bed a short way, the same way he had where Chuck had come out on the other side. The ground was marshy, even in the late season, and knee deep in grass.

James was finding it easier and easier to imagine his son's terror, and his bravery. And beginning to feel like he hadn't known the boy at all. Was this what it had taken for him to realize it? Part of him wanted to thank Jo for teaching him this. Part of him wished he'd figured it out long ago, so he could have told Chuck how proud he was of him.

His feelings for her, he realized, were far more wrapped up in this – pilgrimage, he supposed he had to call it, than he wanted them to be. And in his changing feelings about his son.

He had no idea what to do about it. And Catherine, he suspected, was laughing at him about it right then. No. She was pleased for him, he was sure of it, but she had never been so cruel as to laugh at such things. But he certainly wasn't getting any help from his memories of her.

Their next stop was at the Fountain Paint Pots. James didn't need Jo to tell him Chuck and his companions had spent their last night camped near here before the Indians captured them. He pulled over without comment and they strolled around the trail.

"Clepsydra's still going strong," Jo commented. "It started up during the earthquake, and it hasn't stopped since." She glanced over at him, and apparently saw more interest in geysers than he was actually feeling, because she told him far more than he wanted to know about what had happened in the geyser basins after the earthquake.

" – And the biggest surprise was Sapphire Pool down in Biscuit Basin, which only a few people knew was a geyser before the quake. It blew up like nobody's business, and it's been erupting off and on ever since." She sounded so enthusiastic. He couldn't help but smile at her.

"I've never understood why people get so excited over geysers," he confessed.

She stared at him, then shook her head. "I should have known. Another childhood incident like the buffalo?" She strode back toward the car. James followed.

"No, not really – Maybe."

"Well, which is it?" She was walking faster now, impatience emanating from her very pores.

"I just wondered – I don't remember being found, not really, not the way – Charley described it in the letter. But I wonder if something happened to me –"

She laughed. "Something obviously did." Then stopped, so suddenly he almost ran into her, and turned around, her impatience no match for her curiosity. "You mean other than the obvious."

"Or maybe the obvious was enough." He took her hand. "Come on."

"What's your hurry?" But she went with him willingly enough.

James hustled her back to the car and helped her in, then asked, "Where's Cliff Geyser?"

* * *

"It ought to look familiar," he said.

"Yes, it ought. You were here just a couple of months ago." Jo sounded amused.

James felt oddly angry. "You know what I mean." They stood on the edge of Iron Creek. James stared across at the peculiarly square basin on the opposite bank that was Cliff Geyser. It was empty and dry now, and obviously had been for some time. "But it doesn't. It just looks like a hole in the ground."

"Well, that's what it is. At least right now."

He wasn't going to think of it as some sort of idiotic metaphor. He wasn't. "Gone down the drain? Like the rest of my life?" James immediately wished he could take those words back. "I didn't mean that the way it sounded."

"You didn't?" She didn't sound amused anymore. He wouldn't have put that tone in her voice for all the world. He stepped toward her, some half-formed idea of kissing the hurt away in his head, but she backed away, and he wasn't so far gone he'd chase her into the creek.

"I'm sorry. It's just, well, frustrating. I was hoping for more, I guess." Oh, no. If he put his foot in his mouth any deeper he was going to choke on it. "I mean from being here," he added quickly.

"What were you hoping for?" Cool. Calm. Everything he wasn't feeling at the moment.

"Some sort of sign, I guess."

"I didn't think you believed in that sort of thing."

"I didn't believe in a lot of things until recently." For one thing, James had quite firmly not believed he'd ever fall in love again. Yet here he was, and maybe the reason he'd been so sure was he'd known if he did he'd bollix it up. Well, at least he'd been right about something. He took a deep breath, but the question that came out of his mouth wasn't what he thought he'd have asked. "How often does Cliff Geyser erupt?"

At least his query jerked her mind off of his stupidity. "I don't know."

He gave her a dry look." You don't know."

"I'm not the expert on everything you obviously think I am." She seemed to be considering something. "We could ask George."

"Who's George?"

"George Marler. He's a naturalist. Specializes in geysers. I know he's still around. Probably will be all winter." She shivered, in spite of her coat. The day had gotten colder as it went on. Or maybe the company she was keeping made her feel cold. He wanted to put an arm around her, but knew better than to try.

"Are we staying at Old Faithful tonight?"

"I'd – yes. If that's all right with you."

James raised an eyebrow at her. "You're concerned about that now?"

The look on her face was as familiar to him as Catherine's now. James waited for the guilt to hit. It didn't. He gestured. "Come on, then. Let's go find George."

* * *

"Cliff's dormant most of the time." The geyser specialist sat with them at one end of the long, Formica-topped table, employee cafeteria trays in front of them, and wiped his mouth with a napkin. "I can count the number of times I've seen it erupt in the last ten years on one hand, and I haven't seen evidence of an eruption more than a few times, either."

"Did the earthquake have any effect on it?" James asked.

"Not so I've been able to tell. But then there's been so much to observe. I can't keep up with all of it."

"A geologist's dream?" Jo asked lightly.

"It seems selfish to think of it that way," Marler admitted, "given what happened over at Hebgen Lake. But yes."

"Better that some good come out of something so awful," James said.

Marler and Jo both stared at him. Marler's expression was unadulterated surprise, but after a second Jo nodded firmly, looking pleased.

After a moment Marler asked, "Did you ever find your son, Mr. McManis?"

"I – heard from him."

"So he did run away?"

James looked helplessly over at Jo. He was going to have to figure out how to answer that query without arousing more questions one of these days.

"Not really," she said, apparently realizing he had no idea what to say, truthfully or otherwise. "It's a long story. But he is all right."

"I'm glad to hear it." At least Marler sounded sincere, but it was obvious he'd only asked to be polite, and went right back to his main interest. So perhaps James simply shouldn't worry about more questions. If people were curious, they could *stay* curious, her non-answer seemed to say. "So far, I've counted almost three hundred springs and geysers affected in some way by the earthquake. It's been an amazing couple of months."

And so it went for the rest of the meal. James let their conversation, full of "cracked wide open" and "you should have seen the Lion Group after the aftershock two weeks ago" and "Sapphire Pool erupted again last week," flow over him. Jo seemed to absorb every word the man said, though, which did not surprise James in the least.

Marler did not stay any longer than it took him to inhale his meal. "Got to get back to work," he said, looking, in spite of his years, rather like a child who couldn't wait to get back to his new toys at Christmas.

"Are you staying all winter?" Jo asked.

"Yes." He picked up his tray.

"Lucky you."

"And don't think I don't know it." Tray in one hand, he levered himself up from the table with the other. "See you around?"

"For a little while, anyway."

Marler nodded. "It was nice to meet you, Mr. McManis."

James tilted his head in return. "My pleasure." He watched Marler leave, then turned to Jo. "You really love this stuff, don't you?" Which meant she would not leave here and he would, and what would happen after this jaunt of theirs?

She didn't look surprised at his question. "I truly do. Everything about it." She smirked at him. "What's not to love?" And rose. "Are you done?"

He was. The cafeteria lunch sat heavy in his stomach, but the rest of him felt light as air. He wasn't about to examine why, not just then. "Now what?" he asked as they bussed their trays and headed out.

"Now you're on your own for the afternoon," Jo said regretfully. "This trip isn't solely for your benefit, you know. You've got your key?"

James patted his pocket. "Yes."

"Well, then, I'll see you for supper, unless I can wrangle myself loose before then."

"All right."

"Don't get yourself in trouble." She leaned closer to him. Was she going to kiss him here, where anyone could see?

Apparently so. It wasn't much more than a peck, but James still felt himself color. She reached up a hand and patted him on the cheek. "Have fun."

"You, too."

She trotted off, to go harangue delinquent employees or do whatever it was she'd been doing at every stop they'd made so far. James looked around at the all-but-deserted parking lot, and then at his watch, wondered what he was going to do for the rest of the day, and headed to their room.

* * *

Things weren't quite as rustic as they'd been at the Lake Hotel. They had electricity, and heat, even if the bathroom facilities were down the hall. Their room was in the shared employee dormitory where the year-round concessions staff lived in the winter, including the hotel and lodge winterkeepers. The décor reminded James of Chuck's college dorm room before the boy had moved in. Spartan was a kindly description. But it was clean, and the bed was comfortable, and James did not want to think how Jo had explained his presence, and why he was sharing her living quarters, to whoever was in charge of the place.

Fortunately, she'd sent him out for their luggage while she'd handled it earlier, and no one stopped him and asked him what he was doing there as he walked in, trying to look, and feel, like he belonged there. He didn't hear anyone snickering at him, at least.

He hadn't had a good night's sleep since he'd left Denver. Since long before he'd left Denver, if he wanted to be honest with himself. Since Chuck had vanished. And while at least last night he'd had the best of excuses, he suddenly realized just how tired he was.

Even as something nagged at the back of his brain, telling him he needed to be out there looking, finding – something – the plaid-blanketed double bed beckoned to him. Whatever it was, he wasn't sure he'd find it, anyway.

James toed off his shoes and fell onto the bed as if into a well. He was out in seconds.

* * *

He awoke with the feeling he'd been asleep for a very long time, but the clock on the nightstand told him it wasn't as late as he'd feared, just mid-afternoon. He rolled over and ran a hand over his hair as he sat up.

He'd had the strangest dream. He supposed he should have expected it, given where he was and what he'd been thinking about for the last two days. The last two months. The more time he spent here, the more it sucked him in. As if the place was trying to tell him something. And that was about as fanciful as time travel.

James yawned, and swung his legs over the edge of the bed. It had been good to see his mother again, though, even if it was only in a dream. Karin had been dressed oddly, in clothes that would have been unusual even now, and utterly scandalous when she'd been as young as she'd been in the dream. But it had been her. He was certain of that. And she'd been as glad to see him as he'd been to see her.

The location was painfully obvious, too. They'd been right where he and Jo had been this morning, standing on the path across the stream from Cliff Geyser. No, there'd been a boardwalk there, in his dream. And the geyser'd been erupting, its strange square basin full of water churning and splashing. He'd been vaguely aware of other people milling around, their voices muted by the noise of the geyser. Cameras clicking.

But his eyes had been only for his mother. Then she'd turned away from him, and walked away. Deliberately. He was certain of that, too.

Another voice had called his name. He knew that voice, too. No, not his name. His childhood nickname. He hadn't been Jim, or Jimmy, like most boys named James. No. He'd been Jem. His mother always said it was because he was a gem. And his father always added yeah, he was a diamond in the rough all right.

Suddenly James became aware tears were sliding down his cheeks. And he didn't want to remember anything more of that dream.

He needed to see the real place. To dispel it.

Less than five minutes later he was on his way.

CHAPTER 16

He didn't bother with the Lincoln. It wasn't a long hike from Old Faithful over to Black Sand Basin and Cliff Geyser, less than a mile, and he needed the time to clear his head. All the walking he'd been doing lately made the distance seem shorter now, too. He wasn't sure what he was going to find when he reached his destination, but now that he was headed there, the longer it took him to get there? The happier he'd be.

On the way there, between time and between places, that was the ticket, as his father would have said. It always had been. As a child, he'd always been happiest when they were on their way somewhere. Between the park, where his father spent the summers working for Mr. Wylie, and Bozeman, where he taught school in the winters. Between Mammoth Hot Springs, where his grandparents ran the photo shop they'd co-owned with Mr. Calfee, and Helena, where the relatives on his grandmother's side lived. Even a few times on the train to Seattle, where his Myre grandparents lived. The only time he hadn't felt that way was on the troop ship headed for France.

James had never thought to question the fact that he had no McManis relations besides his grandfather. Well, now he knew the answer to that one. In spades. And at least his son wasn't his own great-grandfather by blood. Every other way but blood, yes. Whose blood James had given him, well, wasn't that the sixty-four dollar question.

He snorted, and strode on.

The wind picked up, and swirled the white dust along the side of the road into little whirlwinds rising and dying only to rise again. The crickets leaped away from his feet with every step he took, as if they hadn't seen him coming from yards away. The tall tan grass waved in the wind, and sparks of blue from the few remaining harebells glinted between the stalks. The clouds poured in from over the looming dark cliffs, that he knew were part of the great volcano crater he was inside of.

Those clouds were much thicker now, and ominous. Snow clouds if he'd ever seen them. So the weather was to break. Finally.

As he approached Black Sand Basin, his steps slowed. Would Cliff Geyser's square basin be full of water, ready to erupt? What would he see if it did? Was he setting himself up as his son had, for something he couldn't explain? At least Chuck's – experience – had been an accident. It wasn't as if the boy had possessed a single suspicion as to what would happen to him, even if others had manipulated him into it. He hadn't realized *what* had happened to him for days after, for crying out loud. It wasn't his fault.

James stopped dead in the middle of the little parking area. It wasn't Chuck's fault. He hadn't asked to be transported through time. He hadn't known it was possible. All the boy wanted was the time to say good-bye to his beloved grandparents. To fulfill the request in his grandfather's will, which was well within reason. And James had been so stingy, so single-minded, he couldn't even allow the boy time to grieve in his own way. So angry. At who?

Did he really want to know? No, James thought, he didn't. Not that it mattered now.

Slowly he forced his feet forward, one step at a time, until he stood on the little viewing platform, across the stream from Cliff Geyser's basin.

It was still empty. Why had he been so sure it wouldn't be?

* * *

He'd been right about the snow, at least. The first flakes started falling as he passed the Inn, and were coming down thickly enough to soak his hair through to his scalp by the time he got back to the bunkhouse. The more fool him, for going out without a hat. Or a proper coat. Getting out of here tomorrow was going to require chains. At least he'd had the foresight to bring them with him.

Now what should he do? Maybe he'd missed something in the letter. Some hint that would make sense now.

James wished for a good strong cup of coffee, or at least something warm to drink, and settled down on the bed – it was either that or the only chair the room afforded, a straight-backed affair that did not lend itself to comfort. He took a deep breath, and opened the bundle for the first time in two months. The letter lay on top, just where he'd left it, the handwriting strong and square in spite of his grandfather's age.

June 1, 1939

Dear Jem,

Since you're reading this, August 17, 1959 has come and gone, and you must be in Yellowstone searching for me. I hope you weren't there for the earthquake. It was a humdinger and no mistake.

I know you don't believe this, but I'm not there. So you're going to need to figure out a way to stop whatever search the rangers have running. I guess you can tell them I did run away, after all. Chances are good they'll believe you by now.

But I want you to know, for the record. I wasn't running away.

James believed him now, with all his heart. He only wished he'd had the chance to tell Chuck so before he'd vanished. Water under the bridge, he knew, but if he had one regret he was going to take to his grave, that was going to be it. Having his last words to Chuck be in anger. If he'd only known, he thought sadly.

But it wasn't true, he realized suddenly. His last words to Chuck hadn't been his last words to his son. So to speak. His last words to Charley had been said in love to his grandfather, not long before he died.

James let his shoulders slump and leaned back against the headboard. Closed his eyes and remembered. He and Catherine had gone to Helena for Christmas in 1938. For some reason – for some reason, ha – his grandparents had insisted, and pregnant Catherine had also insisted – on humoring them, in spite of James's worries about travel in her condition. Even the weather had cooperated, waiting until after they'd made the long drive from Denver to dump a foot and a half of snow, stranding them there for four days longer than he'd planned. Four days he'd begrudged at the time, but which had become more precious to him than diamonds only a few months later. Thank you, Catherine, James thought. And thank God.

His grandfather had been hale and hearty, for all he'd been, what? Eighty years old. There'd been no indication of the stroke that had done him just before Chuck was born. He'd been so happy to find out he was going to be a great-grandfather. For more than the obvious reason, in hindsight. James wondered how hard Charley'd sweated the fact that James hadn't married until he was past forty, even though he'd known how it would work out.

Catherine had been so excited about their child, too. She'd wanted a big family, and since she'd been so much younger than he, he'd had no objections. James squeezed his eyes closed tightly in pain. Charley had known the agony James was going to go through, and hadn't told him. Even if it had been for his own reasons, James couldn't begrudge him now. He wouldn't have given up a minute with her even if he'd known. Now he could just be grateful for the time he'd had with her. No, he was glad. Glad. If he'd known, he might have tried to avoid the best thing that had ever happened to him.

He rubbed his eyes and picked the letter up again.

> I was mad at you for trying to run my life, but
> I wasn't running away. I just wanted to get away for
> a bit. Say good-bye to Grandmother and Granddad.
> And try to figure out how to get you to let me be who
> I wanted to be, not who you wanted me to be. You
> are a bulldozer, Jem, and no mistake. You've been one
> since the first day I met you.

He'd always felt like he'd had to be. As if he didn't push himself he'd never be anyone. And he'd pushed Chuck, too, to be someone he wasn't. As if only one definition of success ever existed. You're not here to feel guilty, James told himself. You're here to learn. Yes, he believed the whole story, which didn't even seem so crazy now. Now it was time to find out what had happened to himself.

> That's the other thing I need to tell you. I don't know how much you remember about how we found you.

He wished he could remember it at all. James stared at the letter, as if by holding the paper like a talisman he'd be able to. But his memory was frustratingly blank on that subject, and had been, even standing out there where the event had happened. He sat up again and read on.

> About how you came to live with us and how Will and Karin came to adopt you. We never talked about it when you first came to us because it upset you so much, and, well, it was easier not to. And later on, it seemed to make more sense to let sleeping dogs lie.
>
> I'm sorry about that now, in some ways. But I wonder how it would have changed things if we'd told you. If you'd have taken steps to break the loop or if you'd have understood and let me go, anyway.

He probably would have tried to stop it. What responsible parent wouldn't have? Charley had certainly known him better than he'd known Chuck.

> But you need to know. What happened to me, happened to you, too. I don't know where you came from, but if you look at the t-shirt, it's dated on the back.

James set the letter down. He pulled the carefully-folded little shirt out from under the stack of legal pads and shook it out. He supposed Jo was responsible for it not being thrown in helter-skelter. Or left behind.

The cotton knit fabric was worn thin and faded from black to a splotched dark gray. A hole marred one shoulder and another the hem.

The image on the front was appalling. A skull and crossbones, thick plastic blood still bright red if cracked 'dripping' down out of the eye sockets, and the words *Iron Maiden* in elaborate medieval-looking script above it. Who would put *that* on a four-year-old?

He turned the shirt over. *1983 World Tour*, the script said on the back, with a long list of cities and dates below it in regular type faded almost to invisibility. The cities ranged from Europe to Australia, and the dates from February through August. Had he really traveled all over the world that year? Why would someone take a child clear to Australia and back? And to Europe? And commemorate it with a t-shirt? One that looked like that? The only thing he knew about something called an iron maiden was a medieval torture device. He'd seen one in Paris in a museum after the war, while he was waiting his turn on the troopship to come home.

According to the t-shirt he'd been in Nice in March, and Adelaide in April, and in San Francisco in July, among all the other places. Why wasn't Yellowstone on the list? He'd obviously been here, too. He ran his finger over the numbers. 1983. It must have been a whirlwind year, but he couldn't *remember* any of it. James tossed the t-shirt down and picked the letter up again. The shirt wasn't telling him anything, except by its very existence.

> I can tell you I first saw you on October 23,
> 1897. I took a job winterkeeping at the Fountain Hotel
> that year after your dad headed for the Klondike, and
> Eliza and I just happened to decide to go exploring that
> day before the snow set in.

James looked up at the window, which was now a whirl of white. Exploring. Just as he had. But unlike Charley and Eliza, *he* hadn't found anything. And if he had? What would *he* have done, in his grandparents' place? Not knowing the possibilities?

A child is a child, he thought firmly. No matter when he comes from.

> We were the only people for miles in any
> direction. I don't want to think about what would have
> happened, to you or to me, if we hadn't gone out, but

I guess it was fate, or destiny, or part of what was meant to be. Thank God.

We found you sitting on the ledge above Iron Creek, next to the geyser they call Cliff nowadays. You were all by yourself, shivering and crying. You were wearing that t-shirt, shorts, and those little red sneakers. Mind you, it was just beginning to snow at the time. After we took you back to the hotel and got you calmed down and warmed up and fed, Eliza asked you your name and how old you were. You told us it was Jem Whitehorse, and held up four fingers. And that's everything I know about where you came from.

Asking you to explain how you'd got there, especially when you were only four years old and scared to death at the time, was pretty much impossible. But from that moment on you were ours, our family's, and you still are. No matter what.

He'd been so lucky. So far as he could tell, he'd have died of exposure out there. Even giving whoever'd had charge of him the day he'd disappeared – and he wondered what *they'd* thought, and how long they'd searched for *him* – the benefit of the doubt, he couldn't feel kindly toward them. Whoever they were. He shook his head. Read the last bit, and smiled wryly.

Don't miss me. If you've read my story, you know things turned out all right for me. I hope they turn out all right for you, too, Dad.
Love,
Chuck

So. He wasn't who he'd thought himself to be all his life. He'd come to terms with the knowledge, after a fashion. It wasn't as if he'd had a choice. Or as if it would have made a difference in who he'd made himself to be.

But he wanted to know who he'd been. Charley, at least, had known. Envy snaked through him. He had no way to find out. No way to look up the future in order to find his own past.

* * *

Jo found him there, the t-shirt in his lap, his head tilted back and his eyes closed, when she came looking for him for supper.

"Asleep again?" she asked lightly.

"No. Thinking."

"About what?"

Mutely he held up the letter.

"Ah." But she still sounded puzzled.

"I was trying to figure out how to look into the future," he said wryly.

At least he'd succeeded in startling her, but not for long. She leaned over and picked up the t-shirt, her knuckles brushing his lap. "It's a puzzle, isn't it? I can't believe you were ever small enough to wear this."

That stung, for some reason, as if she thought he'd always been old and stuffy. "I didn't spring full-blown from the head of Zeus," he told her stiffly, and rose from the bed. "Is it time to go eat?" His stomach certainly thought it was.

"Yes. That's why I came back, to get you." She folded the shirt and put it back in the box. "I bet you were an adorable little boy. All that black hair and those eyes. How on earth did you end up with a blond, blue-eyed son?"

And just like that, once again she defused his annoyance. He could feel it melt away. "Chuck had – has his mother's coloring."

"And your features, at least according to the picture you showed me. But certainly not your build. How old was he the first time he could look down at you?"

"Fourteen." James grinned in spite of himself, remembering his son's consternation. "'Dad, you shrank!' That's what he told me when I came to pick him up that September. We hadn't seen each other for three months. He'd had a growth spurt, and my mother told me it was all she'd been able to do to keep him in clothes that summer. She finally just told him to wear shorts, but then he grew out of those, too. He was two inches shorter than I am when he left home that spring, and three inches taller when he came back. His voice changed that summer, too. I delivered a child to my parents in May, and –" James shook his head, unable to go on with that particular thought.

"Where did he get the height?"

James sobered." I don't know. Not from Catherine's side, I don't think. Her father was shorter than I am, and she was petite." His frustration returned in force. "I just don't know."

"From his great-grandfather, no doubt." Jo headed for the door, but James grabbed his coat and hat and beat her to it. She raised her eyebrows as he swung it open for her, but stepped through without comment about his insistence on manners. "Come on. If you're as hungry as I am, you must be starving."

* * *

Another aftershock rattled dinner. James was, he thought, almost getting used to them. The only reaction from the others in the room was to hang onto their trays, except for George Marler, who jumped up and strode out, leaving his half-eaten meal on the table. James looked inquiringly at Jo, who commented, "That wasn't fear, that was wanting to find out if any new geysers were jarred loose."

Several people sitting nearby overheard the comment and laughed, and one of them said, "At least we know he won't freeze to death out there."

Which was true. While he'd squirreled himself away for the afternoon, the snow had turned to rain and amazingly enough the temperature started to rise. He almost found himself feeling disappointed. It was as if he'd been counting on the snow to keep them there long enough for him to find out – something. Anything. Although he hadn't the first clue how to go about doing it.

James realized Jo was speaking to him again. "I'm sorry. What did you say?"

She was sounding apologetic again. "Is it okay if we don't leave yet? I'm not quite ready to go."

"I wasn't expecting us to leave tonight – wait. What?"

"I've got at least another day's worth of work here, maybe two."

He shouldn't feel this relieved, he told himself. "That's all right."

"Are you sure? When did you say you had to be back in Denver? Will we still have time to go on to Helena?"

Fine time for her to start worrying about it now. But he wasn't complaining about it anymore. He'd lost track of the time, but really, he'd only been gone, what? Five days? Six? Less than a week, at any

185

rate. And here it was, only the 22nd. He could call Sally and tell her he was extending his trip – The 22nd. Tomorrow was October 23rd. His head began to buzz, like static on a television. No, he couldn't leave tomorrow. He had to stay. Had to. Had to. Had to –

Gradually he became aware someone – Jo? was shaking him, and saying his name, over and over. Gradually he realized he was lying on the floor, and tried to sit up, but she put a hand on his chest and held him down. Far too easily.

"James? Are you all right?" She sounded worried. He tried to tell her it was all right, he was all right, but he couldn't quite get his mouth around the words.

Another voice. James realized his eyes were closed and, after some effort, got them open. Two faces were peering down at him, one Jo's and the other a man's. Behind and around them, more faces were a blurry backdrop.

"He's awake." The man's voice sounded far too authoritative for his apparent age.

"James?" Jo sounded almost plaintive

James put all his effort into it, and managed to say, "What happened?"

"You keeled over, you fool." Her tone was sharp, but with relief, James was sure, not with anger. "Right into your lasagna."

Now that she mentioned it, he did feel something odd on his right cheek. He reached up and wiped something red off onto his fingers. "Blood?"

She grinned. "Tomato sauce."

"Oh." He tried to sit up again, and this time they not only let him, but the man helped him.

"I think he just fainted, Jo," the man told him. "Nothing more serious."

"But why?"

"Well, he probably should get his doctor to check him out when he gets home, just as a precaution, but really, sometimes it just happens."

The man helped James to his feet. "Thank you."

But Jo still looked worried as she watched him wipe sauce and cheese from his cheek. "Maybe we ought to get you back to Denver tomorrow after all."

James didn't quite know how to convince her, but he wasn't going anywhere now. Not till after tomorrow, at least.

If he'd tried to explain to himself what he was about, even this morning, he'd have thought himself crazy. He was quite sure she was more open-minded than he'd ever been until now, but he still didn't want to get into what he was about to try. Not with her, not with anyone. Not till it was over.

"I'm fine," he told her with as much conviction as he could muster. "Honestly I am."

He'd never seen her look quite so dubious before, but she only shook her head as he sat down to finish his squashed lasagna. It wasn't bad, really, and he was still hungry.

CHAPTER 17

Jo insisted they go back to their room immediately after supper, and then that he lie down and rest. James, feeling more antsy than he had since he'd arrived here, did not feel in the least like resting, but he humored her.

And tried to reassure her. "I'm fine, really."

She obviously wasn't reassured. "I thought you'd had a heart attack or a stroke or something even worse. You're not a young man, you know."

He knew. And he didn't need her to remind him. "I feel better than I have in years," he told her.

"And that's why you fainted?" she demanded incredulously.

He didn't know how to tell her what really happened. He shrugged, wondering what she saw in the face she was watching so closely.

"Is the altitude bothering you?"

Now she was just getting silly. "Jo, I've spent all my life at altitude. Denver's the mile-high city, remember?"

She did have the grace to look sheepish at that. "I suppose."

James crooked an arm at her. "Come here." He had better ways of convincing her of his health than talking at her, especially when she wasn't inclined to listen to him.

She sat down gingerly on the edge of the bed. James tugged her to him, but she resisted. "You shouldn't be –"

He kissed her. She relaxed a bit, but then pulled away. Reluctantly, James didn't fight her on it. "Honey, what's it going to take to get you to quit worrying about me?"

She gave him an odd glance, probably for the endearment, which had just slipped out, and ran a finger down his cheek. Had he missed a bit of lasagna sauce? He could see where that would be off-putting – But no. She slid her hand back along his scalp. Her palm felt wonderfully warm. The rest of him wanted that warmth, too. "Were you out in the snow this afternoon? Your hair's damp."

"Yes."

"Please don't give yourself pneumonia."

"Yes, Mother." That didn't just slip out. He didn't want her worrying about his health, he wanted her thinking about them. Or not thinking at all.

She winced. "Sorry."

"I can think of a better way for you to apologize," he told her, and winked.

She laughed. But she came into his arms again, and this time she didn't leave them.

* * *

By the time they were done making love, James was pretty sure she'd forgotten all about his nosedive into the lasagna. Another aftershock hit just as he was beginning to drift off to sleep, jarring him awake again, and wasn't that awfully soon after the one at dinner? They seemed to be getting more frequent, not less, as time went on, and he didn't think that was the way it was supposed to work.

The jolt was enough to bang the headboard against the wall and elicit a "hey, not again!" from whoever was in the room next to them.

Jo laughed. "The cabin was better, even if it didn't have electricity. More privacy."

"I feel like a teenager," James confessed. "Not that I'm complaining." He paused, half afraid to put words to the other conundrum he'd been facing for the last couple of days. But now, in the dark, alone together if you didn't count the young lout next door, cocooned under their blankets, it seemed at least halfway safe to ask the question. "Have you given any thought as to what we'll do after this trip?" Did she see their relationship going anywhere, or was he just a fling? If the latter, he was very sure he didn't want to know, even though he knew he needed to.

She didn't say anything at first, just snuggled into him, her head on his shoulder, increasing his nervousness. But at last her breath whooshed out, ruffling his chest hair. "I've been afraid to think about it."

James almost laughed at the two of them. "What I'm afraid of is that we've both been so scared to say anything about it we're going to let this slip away from us." His hands roamed up and down her back. "If you weren't afraid, what would you want?"

She kissed his collarbone, her lips warm and soft. "I'd want to hang onto you for all I'm worth." But even as he nearly sank through the bed in relief, she added, "But I can't give up my life here, not even for you."

And there was the other sixty-four dollar question, to go with the one he'd finally faced this afternoon. The irony of the situation did not escape him. Was he willing to come back to this place he'd hated for most of his life? Where he'd lost his grandfather, and his son? Where he'd almost lost – even now, James shied back away from that one. In some ways it was easier to think about the incredible things he'd learned about his family and himself in the last months than it was to think about – that.

He'd been quiet too long. Jo was trying to pull away. He held on and didn't let her go. At least at this stage in their lives he wasn't about to lose her the way he'd almost lost – "I know you couldn't," he told her, pulling himself back to the conversation by main force. "And I wouldn't want you to."

"But if I don't, I can't have you." She almost sounded as if she were pouting, as if he, or their relationship, was a possession she didn't want to give up. As if she wanted to have her cake and eat it, too.

That sounded promising, once he thought about it. He wondered if now was when he was truly going crazy. "I'm selling my business," he told her. "Now Chuck's gone, there's no real reason to hang onto it, and I can retire on the proceeds."

Her head popped up, narrowly missing his chin, and she stared at him. "And you'd move here? For me?"

"Would you want me to?" He waited, absolutely still.

"Would you want to?"

And let go with a whoosh. "Christ. Maybe it's too soon." It was decidedly too soon. He'd known her, what? Two months? And the amount of time he'd spent with her could be tallied in days. Most of which had been when he was too upset and angry to think straight about anything. "It *is* far too soon. But if we don't settle things one way or the other now, I don't think we ever will. I'll go back to Denver, you'll stay here, and that'll be the end of it." It was the last thing he wanted. But she'd stopped snuggling up to him. He inhaled deeply. It didn't help his nerves. "I don't want that to happen."

Her voice was so small he could barely hear it. "I don't, either."

He leaned back, trying to peer at her in the dark. "You don't?"

Her eyes gleamed at him, black shining on brown. "No, I don't. So we agree we won't let that happen. Whatever else does happen, we'll make sure that doesn't. Okay?"

James let the relief sweep through him, tightening his arms around her as if to prevent her from escaping. "Okay."

"And now," Jo said decisively, "We need to get to sleep."

* * *

The snow was all but gone in the morning, the sky a brilliant cloudless blue. So much for needing the chains to get out of here. With his one excuse gone, James was very grateful Jo had her own reasons for wanting to prolong their visit.

She seemed reassured as to his health, at any rate, although he got the distinct impression as they parted ways after an early breakfast she'd have vastly preferred to stay with him, or drag him off with her to wherever she was doing whatever it was she *was* doing.

Much as James enjoyed her company, it was all he could do to not seem overeager to get her out of the way today. Today. October 23rd. Happy birthday to me, he thought wryly. Or whatever it was. No. Birthday. If nothing else, this day was the birth of his life as it had become. The way August 19th had been for Charley. And now he understood why his grandparents had thrown a barbecue every August and invited everyone they knew. He'd never even thought to question the date. It was just something that happened every year, like Christmas and the first day of school. James shook his head and went back to their room to gather what he needed for, for whatever it was he was expecting to happen. He wasn't sure what he was expecting to happen, but he was definitely expecting something.

First, he rummaged through his suitcase and found Chuck's brownie camera at the very bottom corner. He hadn't known what prompted him to bring it on this trip, but he'd followed the impulse and now he was glad he had. Apparently Chuck had filled it with a fresh roll of film before he'd left, and hadn't taken any photos before he'd been flung back in time. In a way, James wished he'd had. Or, better yet, that he'd had it with him when it happened. It and the photos would have made quite the family heirloom. Charley had never mentioned wishing he'd had his camera, not the way he'd longed for his motorcycle. But photography had played a big part in his subsequent life. James glanced over at the photo of Grand Geyser, sitting on the desk where he'd left it yesterday afternoon, its proof of the impossible tucked away behind the brown paper backing. He thought about taking Chuck's report card out, taking it with him, too, but left it where it was. He still didn't know what he thought was going to happen out there, simply because today was today. He just wanted to see. Maybe take a few pictures.

Of what? James snorted and jammed the little folded camera in its embossed brown leather case into his jacket pocket, almost ripping the seam. What else did he need? He was dressed warmly enough.

But he didn't intend to come back until he'd seen something. He didn't know why he was so sure he would. But it was October 23rd. *October 23rd.* He wondered briefly when his real birthday was. He'd probably never know.

Well, he was going to find out as much as he could, or die trying – *no.* He was *not* going to die trying. He was going to find out as much as he could, period. And then he was going to live.

* * *

The walk back to Cliff Geyser was beginning to feel comfortable, the exercise normal. He hadn't spent enough time in the real outdoors in years. In decades, a little voice corrected. He was beginning to feel good here, the way it had when he was a boy. Before he'd almost lost his mother. Lost Karin. His mother in all but blood.

They, but especially she, had never made any secret about him being adopted, and they'd made sure it never mattered. She'd taken his instant attachment to her and built on it, encouraged it, loving him like the child they'd never had. Like the child she'd almost had. Like the child she'd lost. This place gave, but took away more.

James wanted to shy away from thinking about that time, but the place brought it back to him. If he wanted to come back here, be happy here again, then something was going to have to give, and he knew it would have to be him. So face it, he thought, suddenly grim. You've faced the rest of it. Now? Yes, now.

He'd been fourteen. The same age Chuck had been when he sprouted like a weed. Far more responsible than his son – no. He'd been as typical a teenage boy as his own son that winter, and he had to give them credit, neither of his parents had realized his mother was pregnant. They'd given up on having children of their own by then, after ten years of marriage.

James couldn't remember why his father wasn't teaching that year. He only remembered the Inn's regular winterkeeper had died that summer, and his father – Will – no, Will had been his father in every sense but the literal one – had been in the right place at the wrong time, needing work.

They'd talked it up as if it were an adventure. James, who'd started refusing to answer to the childish nickname Jem a few years before, had been as excited as either of them. Charley wanted to take the job himself, but by that point his wife's father had become ill, and Eliza'd been reluctant to leave him for any length of time, so they'd stayed in Helena that winter to be near him. John Cooper had died the following spring, as a matter of fact. The three of them had gotten back to Helena barely in time for the funeral, his mother just well enough to travel at that point, and he and his father worrying over her in spite of her insistence on making the trip.

Cautiously, James pushed himself to remember the excitement, the anticipation of their arrival here that fall, not the sadness and anxiety of the following spring. When he was young, this place had always felt like home. Bozeman, where they spent most of their time while he was growing up, was only the place they lived when they couldn't be here. Unlike Charley, Will hadn't ever been able to earn a full-time living here, at least not until 1916, when the National Park Service had come into being and he'd been hired as one of the first rangers. But James left home long before that. Went off to college. Escaped from this place that had betrayed him by almost killing the one person who understood him. His mother, who'd miscarried out in the middle of nowhere. James had found her on the floor of the winterkeeper's quarters, blood everywhere. Snow outside deeper than he was tall. . .

At least it was the first, last, and only winterkeeper's job Will had ever taken. His father learned from his mistakes. But the damage had been done.

James realized his feet had carried him on while his thoughts were otherwise occupied. He stared across Iron Creek at Cliff Geyser's dry, empty crater, his mind suddenly wiped blank. Why wouldn't the stupid thing *fill?* Why wasn't it erupting? Why wasn't there an earthquake? There'd been aftershock after aftershock ever since he'd arrived in the park. They'd become more and more frequent and stronger and stronger, and now, today, it was as if the whole thing had shut down.

Well, he wasn't going anywhere. Not until he had at least one answer. He could be as stubborn as it was. James looked around, saw the log separating the pathway from the edge of the parking area. It didn't look very comfortable, but it was better than sitting on the ground. He walked over and sat. Yes, he could still see that idiotic dry geyser hole from here. He shifted in a futile effort to get more comfortable, and unzipped his jacket. The sun was beaming down. Yesterday's snow might well have never fallen. Even the pavement was dry.

He resigned himself, closed his eyes briefly, and settled in for the duration. Whatever that was.

* * *

His backside had long since gone numb, and James was beginning to feel an utter fool. The sun was high and the sky was clear and he could feel the beginning of a sunburn on his face and arms. His jacket, removed several hours ago, lay draped across his awkwardly-angled lap like a blanket. It was hot there, but not as hot as it had been while he was wearing it.

He still couldn't bring himself to leave his self-inflicted post. When a car pulled up into the parking area, he creaked to his feet, snagging his jacket by the collar and throwing it over his shoulder, trying to look casual. It was only the second time he'd done so this morning, traffic in the park this late in October being almost non-existent and all official. But he recognized this car as his own. Jo must have found his keys where he'd left them on the bed. He hadn't questioned that thought, almost as if he'd wanted her to come find him in spite of the fact that he hadn't left her a note.

Sure enough, she climbed out. "Thought I'd find you here." She didn't ask him what he was doing or why. Instead, she went to the trunk of the car and opened it. James strolled over, still trying to look casual, as if spending an entire morning sitting out in the sun waiting for an empty geyser hole to fill and erupt was a completely normal thing to do.

"Where did you find those?" he asked, fighting the urge to grab one of the two folding lawn chairs that had miraculously appeared in the trunk of his car and plunk his aching backside in one of them.

"We sell 'em," she said smugly. "In the Upper Ham store."

"How much do I owe you for one?"

"We'll just borrow them for the afternoon." She pulled them out and handed them to him. "Go on. I'll be there in a minute." Instead, James watched as she pulled a basket out of the recesses of the trunk.

"You're not planning on staying here with me?"

"Why not?" She reached into the trunk a third time and pulled out two wide-brimmed hats. One of them, a well-worn, once-white straw with a feather stuck in the band, she plunked on her own head. The other was tan, woven of something looking rather like very fine, very finely woven wicker, shaped like a cowboy hat, with a brown leather band around the crown with the words "Yellowstone National Park" tooled into it. She reached out and the next thing James knew, his sunburned nose was shaded and his head was about ten degrees cooler. "There," she said with some satisfaction. "It suits you quite well."

James was equally sure it didn't, but it made being out in the sun so much more comfortable he couldn't quite bring himself to care what he looked like.

She took the basket, said, "Well, come on," and headed down the path.

James hefted the two lawn chairs and followed her.

As he expected, she stopped at the little overlook opposite Iron Creek from Cliff Geyser's barren hole. James glanced over at it, then stared. Not so barren now. A small pool of water lapped at the very bottom, barely visible from this side of the creek. He could just hear the soft sloshing noise above the flow of the creek.

Jo glanced over at it, too. "Well, that's encouraging."

James wanted to pretend he didn't know what she meant, but –
"Yes, it is. Do you think the earthquakes had something to do with it?"

"It's possible." She gestured at him, and he unfolded the two chairs next to each other. She plunked the basket down between them. "Hungry?"

* * *

She left an hour later with an empty basket, without a protest or an awkward question. She left him his lawn chair and hat, too, for which he was more grateful than he had been for the food.

James sat with the little Brownie camera on his lap watching the water rise almost imperceptibly in Cliff Geyser's pool. He couldn't remember the last time he'd had such peace and quiet, and even yesterday he couldn't have imagined finding it here, of all places. Small, white, puffy clouds came and went, their shadows cooling him as they passed. Crickets bounced. The stream splashed over the rocks. The quiet lulled him, weighted his eyelids. He leaned back in the chair, his new hat tipped over his forehead. And simply breathed the tension away.

A splash woke him. James sat up, pushed his hat back, and stared around. The afternoon sun had almost disappeared behind the cliffs to his west, the sky a deep, deep blue edged with fire. The crickets had vanished, as had the clouds. A breeze had picked up, just enough to swirl the finely-ground dirt into dust devils. Cliff Geyser's pool was full, pulsing from its center, sending water splashing over the sides of its basin into Iron Creek, but not quite erupting. Not yet.

New voices behind him made him jump. More nervous than he wanted to admit, James turned to see who they were.

CHAPTER 18

Half a dozen people, at least; some appearing out of nowhere, some piling out of a decrepit Volkswagen minibus with the most leprous paint job he'd ever seen on anything, let alone a vehicle appearing as if the paint was the only thing holding it together. Once-vivid yellow and pink daisies on a faded olive green background were half-obliterated by dull gray patches of putty and bright orange lines of rust. James watched as it took two of the car's passengers several tries to get the side door slid shut with a slam.

It was a wonder the vehicle was legal. Even from this distance the tires looked bald.

The people matched their minibus: their jeans ripped, their shirts in equal condition, the men's hair as long, and as lank, as the women's. At least, James thought wildly, Chuck's jeans and t-shirt had been clean, his motorcycle gear in good condition, his hair always tidy even in the buzz cut he'd insisted on sporting. These people looked as if they hadn't seen the inside of a bathtub or a laundromat, let alone a barber, in days, if not weeks.

Three park service vehicles, one an ambulance and two park police cars, pulled in behind the bus, and rangers started climbing out.

One of the rangers, an older man who looked strangely familiar, began questioning one of the people who'd appeared from nowhere, a young man with black hair in a braid hanging down his back, wearing a familiar-looking t-shirt. Very familiar. The words "Iron Maiden" and the skull and crossbones were printed on a once-black shirt even more tattered than the small version back in James's room. He wore it with an equally disreputable pair of blue jeans. Scuffed leather sandals covered his dirty feet. But he looked concerned. Genuinely worried, as he gesticulated at the ranger.

James tried to get up from his lawn chair, but found he couldn't. He should have been panicking, he thought vaguely, but he was too mesmerized by the scene in front of him.

As they approached, he began to hear what they were saying. "– about so tall," the man with the braid said, gesturing about hip-high. "Black hair. Wearing a t-shirt like mine, shorts, and red hi-tops."

A woman from the minibus ran up with a photograph. "Here." She handed it to the officer. James strained to see it, and now the fact that he literally could not move finally sank in. It wasn't just that he was stuck to the chair, although it felt like he'd been glued to it, it was that he literally couldn't get up. He could breathe, and he could blink, and he could turn his head. But he couldn't open his mouth to even try to speak.

In any other situation, he'd have thought he was having a nightmare. But somehow he knew he was awake, and seeing, and what if he was dying? What if he was stuck halfway between his own time and now? Because it didn't take looking at the back of the young man's t-shirt for him to know this was not 1959 anymore.

The young woman, dressed in jeans shortened to indecency and a shirt that tied at the nape of her neck and her waist, leaving her back and shoulders completely bare, her blonde hair streaked with a red not found in nature and her feet in Japanese sandals, of all things, was crying as she brandished the photograph at the ranger, who took it from her.

James saw why he'd mistaken Karin for her, back when he was four. Put the two women side by side, and he'd have been able to see this young woman's eyes were a more aqua blue than Karin's almost violet, and that her nose was longer and not quite so turned up at the end. But their heights and builds and, red streaks notwithstanding, hair colors were almost identical. Then the young woman looked past the ranger, and James's breath caught. She stared right into his eyes. She could see him. He knew she could see him. But he watched helplessly as her eyes rolled back up in her head and she collapsed.

The young man caught her before she hit the ground. "Shannon! Shannon, are you all right?" He turned to the ranger, his arms full of her limp body. "I'll be back." But he strode off to the bus, not the ambulance.

The ranger said, "All right, let's do this in an orderly fashion," and all of the other rangers, half a dozen of them, gathered around him. So did the motley crew from the minibus. "Everyone fan out. Cover your assigned area thoroughly. He's small enough he could be hiding, or even have fallen behind a rock or a tree." The rangers nodded, and headed off, each in a different direction. Some went across the road. Some went out on the trail. Some went in between, stepping carefully, James saw, to avoid thin spots in the sinter.

The people from the bus started to head out, too, but the ranger in charge stopped them with a held up hand and an authoritative, "No, you stay here." And James suddenly realized who he was. He was, what was his name? Pete. Pete Marshall, the young ranger at the station at Old Faithful who'd been so sympathetic during the search for Chuck. He'd apparently moved up in the world since then. James watched him curiously. He'd been competent then, even at such a young age. Now, in charge, he looked thoroughly comfortable as he – handled was the only accurate word – the distraught group. Family? No. James didn't think so.

For one thing, they all looked to be roughly the same age. The young woman, his – mother? dear God – who'd fainted, couldn't have been more than twenty. If any of the group was over twenty-five, he'd eat his brand-new hat. And they all looked like indigents, no better than the vehicle they rode in. Was that who he'd been? A vagrant, born to a teenage girl? A bastard? Did the girl even know who the father was? Perhaps traveling through time had saved his life. Was he supposed to be grateful?

The young man with the black braid rejoined the group, gesticulating and demanding to know why they weren't out searching. James watched him speculatively. Are you my father, he wondered? No. The answer came easily. Will was his father, and Karin was his mother. Eliza was his grandmother. Charley, who saved his life, was his grandfather as well as his son. These people cared, though, even if they were careless. Enough to be upset. Enough to do as much as James had done for Chuck. Enough to search and search and search. . .

The young woman who'd fainted got out of the bus, her face pale under her freckles but her entire demeanor making it very clear she was not going to be held down from doing what needed to be done unless it was by main force.

Then again, all six of them were radiating the same determination. Perhaps she just – James watched in shock as she lifted a *baby* from the back seat and came back to the group. Adjusting her halter top, right there in front of God and all of them, she put that baby to her breast.

James gaped, then looked away. Was that his brother? His sister? Against his will, he looked back to see the tiny shock of black hair resting against the woman's freckled skin.

He jerked himself back to the conversation. "– can't just stand here." The young man sounded half-desperate. "We've searched everywhere they're looking. Can't you do more?"

"What would you suggest? It's been how many hours since the boy disappeared? Why didn't you notify us right away?"

"We thought we could find him. Jem's never wandered far before."

"You should never have let him wander at all."

One of the others broke in. "He's a cop, Mike."

Another added, "I told you this wouldn't do any good."

The ranger ignored them. Instead he told the young man with the braid – Mike – "We're doing everything we can. We've got a helicopter coming in from the airport at West Yellowstone to do an aerial search. It should be here within the hour. In the meantime," he added hastily, as several of them spoke at once, "we're doing everything we can to find your little boy."

James cleared his throat, and discovered he could speak after all. "I'm right here," he said wryly, but with some sympathy. Or was that empathy? The young woman with the baby had moved over next to Mike, but she jerked and stared in his direction, then shook her head and bent to nuzzle the baby.

Mike put his arm around them both. James could feel the lump rising in his own throat, but the evidence the young woman could see? hear? him? Something, at any rate, had him watching her. He tried again. "I'm really sorry, but you're not going to find him – me."

Her head jerked up. The baby squawked. "We are, too! We're not going to stop looking until we do!"

The entire group stared at her. Ranger Marshall said soothingly, "Of course we aren't."

Mike said, "Shh, Shannon, we'll find him. We're not going to give up." He gave Marshall a direct glare. "And we're going to keep looking ourselves, too. You can't stop us."

Marshall glared right back. "If you step off the trails, I can. And will. The last thing that little boy needs is for one of you to get hurt looking for him. Or killed. That crust is mighty thin in places."

Shannon cried out. The others moved closer to her, and one of the men said, "Stop it. You're scaring her."

Marshall sighed, a world of resignation in the sound. "There's a reason for the rule to keep your children under your control at all times in the geyser basins."

James sighed, too. "It's true, you know."

"I *know*," Shannon cried, but whether in answer to him or the ranger, James couldn't tell. At any rate, Mike took her back to the minibus and urged her into the seat. The baby had apparently finished nursing, and Mike took him? her? from her and laid it in the back somewhere. Shannon put her head in her hands, and one of the other young women, a blackhaired girl in an equally skimpy outfit, came to sit with her.

"Go on, Mike," she said. "I'll stay with her. "She gestured at her obviously pregnant body, poking out from under her own loose top, and added, "I can't do much, anyway."

The ranger gave her an approving nod. "Thank you. Ms. –?"

The young woman rolled her eyes. "Sanders."

"Thank you, Ms. Sanders."

Mike nodded, too. "Thanks, Marie." He put a hand under Shannon's chin and lifted it. James watched, that lump in his throat growing, as the young man kissed her gently on the lips. Whatever else they'd done wrong, however irresponsible they were otherwise, there was love there. And when Mike lifted his head, James could see his features clearly for the first time. It was like looking in a mirror.

* * *

His parents. His *parents*. Or at least the people who'd given him life. James found he couldn't think of anyone but Will and Karin in those roles, even with the evidence looking right back at him. Right back past him. Apparently only the woman who'd given birth to him could actually see him. He wondered at that. Perhaps the resemblance was coincidental. Or maybe Mike was her brother. James thought back to the kiss Mike had given her. No, that hadn't been brotherly at all.

So far as he could tell, there was no rhyme or reason to how this whole insane thing worked. No way to predict who would be able to do what. Perhaps it only worked for the woman who'd given birth to him because only she had the gene. The time travel gene. Right.

James suddenly realized he was gripping Chuck's Brownie camera so hard his hands hurt. Quick, before they got away, before he went back – God, he hoped he wasn't stuck here in limbo forever – he lifted it to his face. Yes, he could lift it. Somehow he was becoming more and more here – No, he wouldn't think about that. He didn't want to *stay* here. He just wanted to see, then go back. Go back to where he belonged.

He put his finger on the button and peered through the viewfinder. And pressed it, moved, pressed it again, pressed it, pressed it, pressed it, until he had photos of everyone, his mother, his father, the other four ragamuffins. He took a couple of pictures of the minibus, for good measure. And Ranger Marshall. Why not? James clicked the shutter over and over until the film ran out, then dropped the camera to his lap.

He looked up from it to see Shannon sitting on the passenger seat of the minibus. Her female companion, Marie? was nowhere to be seen. Neither was anyone else, James realized, except Ranger Marshall, who'd gone back to his car and was talking on a radio.

Slowly, she stood, and turned to bend over something in the back seat. The baby, James guessed. He hadn't heard a peep out of it just then, but she puttered over it, pulling a diaper out of a bag on the floor next to it and dealing efficiently with it. Then she picked the baby up and cuddled it. "Oh, Joanna," he heard her say. "Oh, baby, my baby, where is he? My poor boy, what did I do?" Her voice trailed off into disconsolate weeping. James turned his head away, wished he could turn his ears away, too.

At last, a coo from the infant Joanna made the young woman gulp and stop crying. James was almost too distracted to note the baby's name. Almost. Surely it was a coincidence. Surely Jo wasn't wrapped up in all this. He didn't even know what Jo was short for. For all he knew it was Josephine, although that had been just a guess on Chuck's part. Oh, God, he hoped he'd get a chance to ask her, that this wasn't a one-way trip –

But he wanted, needed, to learn as much as he could, whether he was stuck in limbo here forever, or whether he did return to his own time – which was his own time, now? Was this the universe trying to rectify itself? Charley had never come back, but he'd never, to the best of James's knowledge, ever had a glimpse forward, either. Eliza had, but she was –

James realized he was hyperventilating, and deliberately slowed his breathing. It was, he thought, the only thing he had control over just then.

Slowly he turned his head. To find Shannon – Mother? – staring at him once more.

CHAPTER 19

At least she didn't faint this time, which was good, since she was holding the baby in her arms. Her eyes were wide and dark, the aqua a mere rim around her pupils. He'd never wondered where Chuck got his coloring, since Catherine had been blonde and blue-eyed, but now James realized Chuck's hadn't been the same as hers. He'd had his grandmother's coloring, not his mother's, even though James knew by all rights he couldn't have acquired it from her. The shape of her eyes was like his, too, but her lashes were thick and coated with mascara. She wore no other makeup he could see, and her hair, pale but for those insane red streaks, hung loosely to her waist. Even as he watched, she shoved one side of it behind her ear, behind her shoulder, as the baby gurgled and grabbed at it. A practiced motion, as she transferred the baby to her other arm and repeated the gesture on the other side. Then, still staring at him, she cradled the child in both arms, as if it – she – were her only salvation.

"Who *are* you?" she asked, her voice little more than a whisper.

James glanced around. Even Ranger Marshall was gone. They were alone, at least for now. "My name is James."

Her breath caught. "That's my little boy's name. But we call him Jem."

"That's what I was called as a little boy, too. My mother –" Breathe, girl, he thought, watching her breath stutter again. "My mother said it was because I was one. A gem, that is." He smiled self-consciously at her.

She did not smile back. "That's what I always tell Jem, too." She drew herself up. "Why are you just sitting there?"

And how to explain that? He opted for the literal truth. "I can't get up."

She stepped forward, then stopped as if thinking better of it. "Are you hurt?"

"No." Not, at least, in the way she meant. But he was hurting. For her, for himself, for everything.

"You look so sad."

"Do I?" That did not surprise him, but he tried to smile. From her expression, he gathered his effort wasn't having the effect he wanted. "Too many memories, I guess."

She didn't ask him about them. He supposed it wasn't important from her point of view. Instead she asked him, "Have you been here long?"

He supposed it depended on how you looked at it. 1959 to 1983? 24 years? He didn't think she'd get the joke, if joke it was and not just nonsense. "No."

"I don't suppose you saw my son. He's four. About so high –" she shifted the baby to one arm and gestured. "Black hair, dark brown eyes. Insatiably curious."

That made him wince. He'd never been insatiably curious, not that he could remember. Being curious had only gotten him into trouble – His own breath cut off. What a time to realize where this attitude had come from. "No." He added in utter sincerity, "I wish I had."

"I wish you had, too." She turned away.

"Wait."

She didn't turn back. "Why?"

"Why didn't you watch over him?" Over me, James thought. That little boy was me.

She whirled around, fire in her eyes. "You have no clue what I was doing."

James was quite sure he did. "Look at you, dressed like that, riding in that, that –" his anger was getting the best of him at last, but he couldn't stop it. "That excuse for a vehicle. With a bunch of derelicts and two small children. Do you even know who their father is? Or are? Do you even care?"

Her eyes widened even further now, as he suspected his were. He could not have cared less what her feelings were. All the pent-up fury from everything that had happened to him in the last four months, oh, who was he fooling, all the pent-up fury plaguing him all of his life, ever since he was four years old, was exploding through his head, and dear God, he wanted *answers*.

"Of course I care. Jem and Joanna are my life. So is their father. I love Mike with all my heart, and he loves me." She nuzzled the child briefly.

"Are you married to him?"

She glanced at him, then back to the child. Was she ashamed, or defiant? "Why do you care?"

She wasn't. James wished he hadn't asked. "I think you know."

"No, I don't know, and I don't care." But she didn't back away. He was quite sure she did care, and that it hadn't been her decision. What would he have done if Catherine hadn't agreed to marry him? Would he have lived in sin with her? Gotten her with child? Loved her the same? The answer to all three, he was quite sure, was yes. And, given those answers, how could he condemn his mother for making the same choice? His father, on the other hand. . .

"I'm sorry." He couldn't quite bring himself to say, it isn't any of my business.

She nodded tightly and hugged the child to herself again. "Apology accepted."

"I am sorry, but I'm also curious," he told her. "I feel like I know you, somehow."

That startled her. "I don't see how. I'm not even sure you're real."

"May I see the baby?"

She looked taken aback. And frightened. She clutched the child more tightly.

"I promise I'll just look." The baby was his sister, after all. His heart clutched. He had a sister. This young woman could apparently do with ease what his own mother – Karin – his real mother – had almost killed herself failing at. He glanced down at the camera in his lap and wished he hadn't used up all the film. He picked it up and clicked it forward in a forlorn hope. There *was* one last shot left. "May I take a picture of her? Please?"

"Why do you want – oh, never mind." Shannon leaned forward, not holding the child out, but keeping her close to her breast as she tilted Joanna so James could see her.

A shock of dense black hair, skin only a few shades lighter than his own. Her little red mouth was puckered, as if she still nursed. She was dressed in a brightly-striped terry-cloth romper with snaps up the insides of the short legs. Her tiny feet were bare. Her eyes were closed in sleep, and James wished she'd wake up, if only so he could see her, really see her. "She's beautiful." He held up the camera. "Do you mind?"

Shannon shrugged. "Sure."

James lifted the camera, but couldn't stand up to see through the viewfinder. He gestured. "Could you?"

She squatted down, went to lean one hand on the arm of his lawn chair – and her palm went right through it. She gasped and jerked back to her feet. "You aren't real!" She backed off several steps, still staring at him, but James had gotten his photo. He wondered rather wildly now if the film would actually show what he'd photographed, or if the whole roll would be blank. He'd give anything for it not to be blank.

"I'm real," he told her carefully. "I'm just not now."

She stopped, her entire body radiating wariness. But she *had* stopped, James told himself. It was more than he'd have done in her place.

"I don't understand."

Neither do I, he started to say, then stopped. He didn't want to make things worse. Then he realized what he wanted to ask her. "Has anything like this ever happened to you before?"

She started to shake her head, then looked as if she thought better of it. "I've had dreams like this." She looked away, then back at him, almost defiant again. "I always thought they were because of a bad trip."

She'd baffled him. "Trip?"

Now she really did look defiant. "You know."

No, actually, he didn't. He shook his head.

"Grass. I've never done crack or anything else, but sometimes the pot gets cut with weird sh – stuff."

James was pretty sure she was speaking a foreign language. "I don't understand."

She shook her head. "It doesn't matter. But I haven't ever seen you before."

Well, at least that made sense, insofar as any of it did, which wasn't saying much. "What have you seen?"

"Just the usual stuff." She didn't seem too interested in expanding on that tantalizing phrase. "Nothing this real, though." She started to reach out as if to touch him, then pulled back. "Why can't I touch you?"

"I don't know." Sighing, James gave up on that line of inquiry. "Tell me about yourself." He wanted to know, after all, even if he was afraid of what he would learn.

She shrugged again, a wary motion. "Can't hurt, I guess. It's not like you're real." She stepped forward, then plunked herself and the baby down on the ground in front of him, where she sat cross-legged. "Tell you what. You tell me something about you, and I'll tell you something about me. One for one, a fair trade."

James marveled at her change in attitude. And, worse, at how she seemed to have completely forgotten her son was missing. "What about Jem?"

"According to you, we're not going to find him." Her face crumpled, then she lifted her head, the defiance back in full force. "Tell me why."

She believed him? Was this the way it worked? James wished he'd kept his big mouth shut. But she was waiting. Maybe – Perhaps if he told her the truth, she'd think it was so farfetched she'd stop believing him. It was worth a shot. And if she stopped believing him? What would that change? Was he willing to try to find out? God, he wished he hadn't come out here. Not now, not ever. Insatiable curiosity. Apparently he hadn't rooted that out of himself as thoroughly as he'd thought.

She was waiting, her gaze up at him expectant. He took a deep breath. "Because I'm Jem."

Her expression didn't change, but Joanna squawked and she bent over the child, comforting her, singing a melody under her breath that sounded almost familiar. "What's that song?"

Her head jerked up. "Crocodile Rock. Mike laughs at me for using it as a lullaby, but I don't like heavy metal the way he does, and I do like Elton John, especially his old stuff."

211

James blinked. That made about as much sense as her comments about grass and pot.

"You look like him," she went on, the baby having relaxed in her arms once more. Because Shannon had relaxed, too, he realized. "And there's no reason for you to tell me if it wasn't true. Are you from the future?"

"No," James said, both aghast and strangely glad at how easily she was coming to terms with something that had taken him months to accept. "I'm from the past."

"Really? Cool!" She cocked her head at him. "How?"

And so he ended up telling her everything, figuring rather desperately that since she was in the future, she wouldn't be able to change anything that had happened to him up till now. He was here now, so he couldn't be found. He was very glad he hadn't been found, he realized as he primed her pump with questions and listened to the story of her life, too. And he didn't wonder why the hours seemed to tick by without any of the others coming back to check on her, or on the search, or each other. It was as if time was standing still, and he didn't want to wonder for fear of starting it up again.

Her story was, as he'd expected, the fuel of his worst nightmares. Her parents, from what little she was willing to say of them, were old-fashioned, "almost as old-fashioned as you," she said with an impish grin, "without the excuse." And stern, and religious, and unwilling to forgive her experiments with drugs and sex, especially after she'd wound up pregnant while still in high school. "I had an abortion that time," she said almost matter of factly as James tried to hide his horror. "It was horrible. And when they found out, they kicked me out of the house. I found out later they were claiming I'd refused to come back, but they never gave me the chance to."

She fell silent for a moment, then went on. "I met Mike while I was on the street, and he gave me a place to crash. Just as friends at first, but he's cute, and I wanted to give him something back, since I didn't have any money." She let out a puff of air. It could almost have been a laugh. "He wouldn't let me, though. Not for the longest time." She sighed. "He's so sweet."

"But you're not married," James felt compelled to say, and was surprised by a tinge of wistfulness in her eyes.

"No. His parents – well, they got divorced when he was about Jem's age," she closed her eyes for a moment, then went on almost as if she was pushing herself to do so, "and his dad's on his third wife, and his mother's on her fourth husband. He's afraid if we get married I'll leave him. Like I would."

James thought about his own lifelong wariness when it came to relationships. And his relationship with Jo. And, astonishing himself, decided he was in no position to say anything at all about the fact that he was a bastard.

"Where's home, then?"

She smiled and pointed at the minibus. "That's it, for now at least. We'll find a new place when we get back."

"Where's back?"

"Denver." She looked amused at him again, apparently at the expression on his face. "It's funny how you and I both ended up there. I wonder if we were looking for each other." She added, her mood mercurially swinging back to sad, for which he couldn't blame her in the least, "I'm really never going to see my little boy again, am I?"

"No," he told her, sad, too, in spite of himself. He didn't have to wonder what his childhood would have been like now, James thought. But for the first time he was wondering what he might have missed. "You really loved him, didn't you? In spite of everything?"

"With all my heart." She glanced up at him through a bright red lock of her hair, which had fallen in her face again. "You have no idea how much."

"Oh, I think I do."

She smiled at him then, but her eyes were still miserable. James smiled back at her, suspecting his didn't look much better.

"I'm sorry, Jem."

His childhood nickname, coming from her, sounded so familiar. "Me, too." Then he thought to ask. "What's your last name?"

"Nilsson."

"Not Whitehorse?"

Her lips quirked. "No, that's Mike. He's Native American. Part Lakota, part Nez Perce. How did you know?"

"That's the name I gave the people who found me," James told her. "My name is James Whitehorse McManis now."

"He'll like that," she said, then jerked her head around and scrambled to her feet. The baby squawked again and began to make sounds James recognized dimly as the precursor to crying. "They're coming. Will that make you go away?"

"It didn't before." But James stared down at his hands. He could almost see through them to the metal arms of the lawn chair. "But I think it is now."

Shannon swallowed. She looked fuzzy, as she hadn't before. Like a picture going out of focus. "I guess this is good-bye, Jem," she said, her voice catching at his name. "I'm going to miss you, and I love you very much." Her voice faded away on the last words, so he could barely hear them.

"Good-bye, Mother," James said, not sure she could hear him still. He tilted his head back and leaned it on the metal rim of the lawn chair. He closed his eyes, and wondered where – when – he would be when he opened them again. "I love you, too." He rested there in quiet limbo, waiting for he knew not what, he knew not when. Hoping, wanting to go home again. Home to 1959, and Jo.

* * *

"James! James!" A hand shook his shoulder roughly and he opened his eyes, looked up into a pair of beautiful deep brown eyes. Familiar deep brown eyes. Jo's eyes. He reached up and grabbed her by the shoulders and pulled her down to his lap, then simply wrapped his arms around her, burying his face in her hair. Relishing the solidity of her, of them, of being back in his own time.

She laughed. "Don't tip the chair over."

"You're here. I'm here." He murmured it into her hair, her warm, sweet scent filling his nostrils. He hadn't realized just how constrained he'd been in his visit to the future, how all he could do was see, and hear. No touch, no smell. He wondered vaguely, as he filled those senses with Jo, if she was what had held enough of him here to bring him back. Whatever had done the job, he was so very glad it had.

"Hey, it's all right. I just came to get you for supper."

"Okay." He breathed, kept breathing. "Okay."

She tilted her head back. He put a hand to the back of her neck and nudged it forward again. He wasn't quite ready to face her, not just yet. "Give me a minute."

"Sure." Her voice was muffled, but her arms had gone around him almost as quickly as his had wrapped around her. She was warm and solid and everything he'd been looking for ever since he'd lost Catherine. And, as much as he'd loved Catherine, and he'd loved her with all his heart, since long before he'd lost Catherine. Or found her.

"I love you."

He could feel her smile, he swore he could. "And I love you." This time, when she leaned back, he let her, although with palpable difficulty. "What brought that on?"

"Everything."

She raised an eyebrow. "That's fairly all-encompassing." Then she glanced over across the stream. "Cliff went off. Did you see it?"

"No, I missed it somehow." He let go of her, but just so they could get up and walk back to the car. His shining-new gray Lincoln, the only car in sight. No park service cars, and, most importantly, no rattletrap VW minibuses. Reluctantly he let her go. Even more reluctantly, he handed her the Brownie camera so he could fold the lawn chair and stow it in the Lincoln's trunk.

"I want to tell you," he told her as he opened the passenger door for her. "I want to tell you everything."

"And I want to hear what finally got you to admit it." She slid in and he closed the door behind her. She smiled at him through the windshield as he strode around to the other side of the car and let himself in.

"I've been pretty stubborn about it, haven't I?"

"As opposed to not being stubborn about anything else?"

James rested his hands on the smooth leather-covered steering wheel, then reached for the ignition. "You're not going to believe what I saw, Jo. It was the most amazing thing. I still can't believe it myself." The car started up with the wonderful vibration of a well-tuned engine. He could *feel* it. "They were looking for me."

"Who was?"

"My mother. My father. Their friends." He aimed the car back toward Old Faithful and their quarters. And the cafeteria. Now that he realized it, he was starving.

"*Who?*"

"I saw them, Jo. I *talked* with my mother."

"*What?*"

James pulled the car into its parking slot behind the employee dorm and killed the engine. He turned in the seat to face her. "You of all people ought to know what I mean."

She sounded breathless. "But –"

He picked the camera up and held it out to her. "And I have proof."

Jo laughed, loud and raucous and *her*, and that was when James knew everything was going to be all right. "Really?" she said, sounding so like Shannon it made his breath catch.

"Where's the nearest place we can get this film developed?"

"This late in the season? Probably Bozeman." Then as she watched his face fall, she added, "I'm done here. We can head out in the morning."

CHAPTER 20

They couldn't discuss anything over supper, not with a roomful of people around them, but it wasn't easy to keep the conversation light. James ate quickly but ravenously. Apparently time travel, even of the temporary, non-corporeal sort, took it out of a man. But he wasn't tired, oh, no. He wished they could leave here right this moment. Not because he hated the place, because he could never, ever hate this place again, not after what it had finally given him back. No, it was because that Brownie camera was burning a hole in his pocket.

Figuratively speaking, of course. It was too big to fit in any of his pockets except the one in his jacket, but it sat on the table as they ate, since James had discovered he was constitutionally unable to let it out of his sight. Jo kept glancing over at it and away as if she expected it to explode at any moment. James wondered if his own behavior toward the little brown leather case appeared as obvious as hers did. It did to her, he was sure, but there was no reason for anyone else to think so.

Ranger Marler plopped himself down beside them at the long table. James carefully moved the little camera out of the way. " So, did you see anything unusual out there this today?" James almost choked, but Marler kept going, giving him, thank God, the opportunity to collect himself. "Jo said you were going to spend some time out at Black Sand Basin while she finished her work here. I haven't had much time to observe out there lately."

Jo cleared her throat. James did not dare look up at her. "Nothing in particular," he lied through his teeth, his only comfort about it the fact that what he'd seen wasn't the kind of report the ranger was looking for. Not in the least, actually. James suppressed a very Chuck-like snicker. He'd hated those snickers, but now he understood how they could relieve stress. Rather like letting air out of a balloon, they were. James cast around for something to tell the man. "Cliff Geyser erupted."

"It did! That's the first time it's gone off since the earthquake, at least so far as I know. How long did it take for the pool to fill? Did you note the time? How long did the eruption last?"

James couldn't help himself. He glanced over at Jo, whose lips were pursed and eyes were alight with a glee he couldn't help sharing. It was all James could do not to hurt the man's feelings by breaking out into entirely inappropriate laughter. "I'm sorry. It was so wonderful to watch, I didn't think to keep notes."

Marler nodded resigned understanding. "Most visitors don't."

James sneaked another peek at Jo. She nodded, her eyes still gleaming. James checked their plates. Both empty, thank goodness. "It was nice talking with you again." He rose and picked up their trays. Jo, he saw out of the corner of his eye, had risen, too. "I'm sorry I couldn't be more help."

Marler shrugged. "One data point is better than nothing. Have a good evening."

"You, too."

* * *

They barely made it out of the employee cafeteria before taking one look at each other and bursting into laughter. It felt so good. What the snicker had started, the laughter finished. James had never felt this relaxed in his life.

"Can we go back to our room now?" Jo asked, still catching her breath.

"I think that might be advisable." James held his arm out for her, and after yet another chuckle, Jo took it. They strolled arm in arm under the stars, but when Jo tried to steer him toward their quarters, James tugged lightly and aimed their steps toward the benches at Old Faithful. It was a beautiful evening with a light breeze, warmer than it had any business being this late in October. It was the last evening he'd have here till spring, he thought, and he wasn't ready to go inside quite yet.

"Do you mind?" he asked as he led her to one of the array of wooden benches, looking for all the world like bleachers at a ball field, only with no grassy sward in front of them. Just a large, shallow mound with a hole at its epicenter, gently steaming white into the dark night air.

She sat, then pulled him down beside her. "No, of course not. It won't be long," she said, echoing his own thoughts, "before we won't be able to do this."

"I have to go back to Denver," he told her, and felt her slump a little. He wrapped an arm around her. "Just for a bit, to wrap up all my loose ends."

"I know."

"I don't suppose you could come with me."

She glanced up at him. Did she see the relief in his eyes? Yes, she did, and he shouldn't doubt it anymore, he thought happily. "I might. I haven't been to the big city in a long time."

"You might enjoy it."

"I might."

"A few weeks ought to do it."

She smiled up at him. "Ready to let go, are you?"

He let out his breath. "Yes."

After a long moment, she said, "This is probably more privacy than we'll have in our room, what with the thin walls and all."

"I know."

Another long moment. "If you don't want to talk about it –"

James let his breath out in a whoosh. "It's not that I don't want to talk about it, Jo, it's that I don't know where to begin." He inhaled. "She was everything I dreaded she would be, but somehow it didn't matter. You should have seen her. I hope you will see her." He gestured at the camera, lying on the bench next to them. "She had a baby with her. She nursed that child, right out there in front of God and everyone, tugged her excuse for a shirt out of the way and put my sister to her breast. When I asked her where home was, she pointed at the most rattletrap vehicle I've ever seen, and said that was it. She's not married to the father of her children. She's not married at all. But she looked so like my – like Karin. She made me want to weep. And she was so sweet. And young. God, she was young. And she said she loved me – him. And she was so sad when I told her she'd never see him again."

Jo's arm had slipped around him, too. He could feel himself shaking, feel her hold him, steadying him. "Isn't that all that matters? That she loved you?"

James shook his head. "Yes. No. I wish I could help her. I wonder what's going to happen to her. I wish I knew she was going to be all right."

Thankfully, Jo didn't reassure him of course she would be. Instead her arm tightened around him. "Did you ask her name?"

"Yes. Shannon Nilssen."

"That's pretty. Did you ask her about yours?"

"Yes. She called me Jem. Because I was her gem, she said. My – Karin used to say that, too."

"What about Whitehorse?"

James cleared his throat. "That was my – that was his name. The fellow who wouldn't marry her. His name is Mike Whitehorse. He's an Indian. I'd always wondered about it, given my coloring. She told me he was half Lakota, whatever that is, and half Nez Perce. Nez Perce like the Indians who kidnapped my grandmother." He let out a rueful chuckle. "I don't know if that's a coincidence, but I bet Charley would have thought it was hilarious. He was a pretty fierce-looking fellow. Wore his hair in a braid down his back, though." James grimaced. "And I thought Chuck's butch looked ridiculous."

"She must have loved him, to give you his name."

James snorted. "Oh, she did. And I think he loved her, even if he wasn't willing to step up and take responsibility."

"You saw him."

"Yes."

Her tone was serious now. "Was he searching for you?"

"Oh, yes."

"Did he look like he cared for her?"

James thought back to the way Mike Whitehorse had kissed the mother of his children. "Yes."

"Perhaps things are different in the future, then."

James snorted again. "She wanted to be married to him. He wouldn't because he was scared. She said so. What kind of man is afraid of getting married?"

Jo reached up with her free hand and turned his face toward her. "How old were you when you married Catherine?"

James twisted himself free of her fingers, even though he didn't want to. "Forty-two."

"How old do you think Mike was?"

"He couldn't have been more than twenty-five." James shifted uncomfortably on the hard wooden bench.

"Perhaps he wasn't ready yet. Like you."

"I didn't get some girl pregnant! Twice, no less."

Jo leaned up and kissed him. "Yes, you were perfect, weren't you?"

He'd never claimed to be, contrary to popular opinion. "Hardly."

"If he hadn't gotten her pregnant, you wouldn't be here."

"I know." He rested his chin on her head.

"Forgive him, James." Her voice was soft.

"I'm trying."

The breeze was picking up a bit, and the temperature dropping now that the sun was gone. Clouds blew across the sky, blurring the stars. Old Faithful let out a splash, then another, and another, before the water streamed into the sky, puffing billows of steam.

Two months ago Chuck had been here, wandering across the boardwalks in the middle of the night without the slightest idea his life was about to change forever. Now James was here, too, but this time he had the chance to change his own life.

"I do love you," he told Jo.

"I know," she said, smiling up at him.

He rose, and pulled her to her feet. "Come on."

"Where are we going?"

"To find our bed."

* * *

He couldn't ask her to marry him, not yet, James thought some time later as Jo slept in his arms. No sensible woman would take him on just now, especially on such short acquaintance. Good grief, the short acquaintance was the least of it, given his baggage. And he wanted to be sure she'd say yes when he did ask. Then he thought about his birth father, and how as far as James knew he'd made Shannon wait all her life, and wished he could know they had finally made it legal. Never mind he'd obviously committed himself to her as much as he thought he could.

It could be enough. Jo obviously wasn't as, what was the phrase Chuck had used? Hung up, that was it. Jo obviously wasn't as hung up on tradition as he, James, was.

James yawned, fighting sleep, even though his pleasantly tired body wanted it in the worst way. He wondered if he'd see anything in his dreams. If that would mean anything. If it mattered. If he would believe anything he saw in a dream. He rather thought he would, now.

He yawned again, and gave up the fight. They had a long drive ahead of them tomorrow, all the way to Denver. He supposed the original purpose of the trip to Helena was a moot point now.

* * *

"No, it's not," Jo told him. "We still need to poke around."

"What on earth are we going to find there that's more than what I found yesterday?" James heaved his suitcase into the Lincoln's trunk, then her duffel.

"You can't expect miracles every day."

"I've had enough miracles to last me a lifetime. Now all I want to do is get back to Denver, sell the house, and finish the paperwork on the business so we can come back home." He'd never have thought he'd say that, but now he could, and he was looking at the reason, dressed in jeans and a flannel shirt against the cool morning, standing stubbornly square in front of him. "You know," and he leaned forward to kiss her, which she returned with interest, almost sidetracking him from his point, "I never did say thank you."

"What for this time?" She cocked her head. "It seems to me you've done nothing but thank me for the most trivial nonsense ever since I met you." She paused. "Well, that and argue with me. Like you're doing now."

"Jo. By the way, what is Jo short for? Did my son get it right when he guessed Josephine that night in the soda fountain?"

"No. It's Joanna. Joanna Marie, if you want to get technical, but only my mother was allowed to call me that, and she's long gone, rest her soul."

"Joanna's my sister's name."

"I'd noticed that."

James realized he'd gotten sidetracked again. He slammed the trunk closed and went to the passenger door to open it for her, but she'd headed for the driver's side and let herself in. When he opened the passenger door, anyway, she held her hand out for the keys. James let his shoulders slump, just for show, and handed them to her.

"We're getting out just in time," she told him. "Did you see the weather report in the cafeteria this morning?"

"It seems hard to believe." He waved his hand at the sunshine beaming down on the car.

"Not when you've lived here as long as I have, it doesn't," she said cheerfully, and started the engine. James quickly climbed in and shut the door before she left him behind. "And we've already had two snowfalls so far this fall." She whipped the Lincoln out of the parking area and out onto the road.

"You're distracting me again." James settled himself into the leather comfort. His backside was still protesting the day before spent perched, first on a log, then in the webbed aluminum lawn chair, and it was a decided relief to be sitting on something that actually fit the contours of his body the way the Lincoln did. With difficulty, he brought himself back to the point. "I wanted to thank you for dragging me here. Without you I'd never have seen her." Never have learned where he came from and who he was. He could have wished for better circumstances for his birth and early childhood, but he would never again doubt he'd been loved the best his parents knew how to love.

"Well, it's not as if I knew what was going to happen." She slowed the car as they passed through a steam cloud blowing across the river from two enormous hot springs – what was that one called? Grand Prismatic, that was right. "But I'm so glad it did. I hope you are."

"Yes. I needed to know. I'm just sorry I couldn't do anything for her." He'd wanted to do something for her, so badly.

"She seemed happy, didn't she? Except for the fact that she'd just lost you."

"I suppose. She seemed wistful."

"She did, or you did?"

James chuckled wryly. "I don't know."

"You know there's no reason why she wasn't."

"Except for losing her child? I was given, she was taken away. Why does the one always have to result in the other?"

Jo let up on the gas again, this time to pass a lone buffalo settled on the edge of the road. As they passed, it opened its eyes briefly, then closed them again. "Now there's a question for the ages."

"I suppose. Doesn't mean I have to like it, though."

They came up on Madison Junction, and turned west. The Lincoln glided over the river and bumped over the patchwork of pavement and gravel the road crews had put together to get the road open after the earthquake, and before James realized it, they were back in the forest and heading out of the park.

The little tourist town of West Yellowstone was all shuttered up for the winter. When James commented on it, Jo said, "It's been all but shut down since the earthquake. It's going to take things a while to recover, but they'll be all right again next spring."

One gas station was open, thank goodness, and the attendant, who knew Jo, naturally, was glad to see them. They didn't waste time, but once the tank was full, headed north again.

They finally had that nice meal in Bozeman James had thought they were going to have a week before, but as lunch instead of supper, and they didn't dawdle over it. And the sun had just set over the Continental Divide to their west by the time they came over the last rise and saw the lights of Helena spread out below them.

James had taken over the driving after lunch, protesting he needed the stimulation to keep him awake after the luxurious meal. Now he pulled over and stared down at Montana's capital's earnest little attempt at urban sprawl.

Beside him, Jo stirred and raised her head. She'd long since scooted over and put her head on his shoulder, where it had rested comfortably for the last hour or so. "Are we there yet?"

"You sound like Chuck when he was a boy. Not quite." He pointed. "I haven't been here in years. Not since he was small. I haven't heard from the relatives here in years."

"Did you tell them you were coming?"

"No."

Jo raised her eyebrows at him, and a tractor-trailer blew past them, causing the Lincoln to rock in its wake. "This probably isn't the safest place to stop."

"Catherine told me that once, too. Right about here, if I remember correctly."

"Your Catherine sounds like a sensible person."

"Oh, she was." Carefully, watching for lights behind him, James pulled back out onto the highway and drove on down into town.

CHAPTER 21

Several modern motels had sprouted along the highway just outside of Helena since James's last visit, and he was inclined to stop at the best-looking of them and be done with it, but Jo insisted they see what they could find downtown.

"It will be more convenient," she insisted, although James had his doubts. The big old brick building where they wound up sat in the oldest part of town, along Main Street. The street had been called Last Chance Gulch in Charley's time. So had the whole town until a few years before that. But the hotel itself was clean, and even elegant in an old-fashioned sort of way. Their room, the desk clerk told them proudly, had just been remodeled a few months ago, and now boasted a private bath. Jo obviously, to James, anyway, had a hard time keeping her face straight as James registered them, using Mr. and Mrs. McManis to avoid any snide remarks on the young clerk's part. But she managed the feat with only her eyes gleaming her amusement.

The place even kept a bellhop on staff who took their luggage up, and once James had tipped the boy, the first thing he did was start looking for a telephone book. He found one, under the Gideon Bible in the dresser drawer and pulled it out.

"What are you looking for?" Jo inquired.

"You have to ask?" He thumbed his way to the "P"s.

She came to peer over his shoulder. "No, I suppose I don't."

"The modern world does seem to have come to Helena," James commented. "Here's a place saying they'll process photos overnight, and they're –" he glanced at his watch "– open for another half an hour. Come on."

He dragged Jo back down the stairs, noticing he wasn't having to tug very hard. They received directions from the clerk, and learned the place was only two blocks down from the hotel. "I told you this would be more convenient," Jo said, keeping step with him.

James didn't answer, but merely rolled his eyes at her and walked faster. He'd always thought, if anything, children inherited their mannerisms from their parents, but it seemed he was acquiring his from his son.

The store was empty of customers, but the lights were still on. James plunked the camera down on the counter. The young clerk said, "May I help you?"

"We need the pictures in this camera developed. As soon as possible."

The clerk picked the camera up, popped the back, and pulled the roll out. "There's an extra charge for overnight service."

"That's fine." A few more dollars were a moot point at this stage.

"All righty, then," the clerk told him, and handed him a form to fill out. "Your photos will be ready at 11 am tomorrow."

James thought about the hours looming ahead of them." Is that absolutely the earliest they can be done?"

"'Fraid so, sir." The clerk looked genuinely sympathetic. Well, if it was the best he could do, then it was the best he could do, even if James felt like stamping his foot with impatience. He wasn't sure how he was going to sleep that night.

"All right," he heard himself say, even though it wasn't. "We'll be back at eleven tomorrow. Please have them ready by then."

As they left the shop, Jo said, "You didn't have to intimidate the poor fellow to death."

James glanced over at her, surprised. "Did I?"

"The kid was shaking in his shoes. I won't ask you if that's your normal way of getting things done because I've seen you in action before, but I have to say it's no wonder you're a good accountant."

"Why on earth would you say that?"

One corner of her mouth quirked up. "Because I bet even the IRS cowers when they deal with you."

Incredulous, James stared at her for a moment, then the guffaw rose up out of his belly and out without any volition whatsoever on his part. He couldn't help it, was more than aware the few people walking along the street were staring at him, knew he was making a spectacle of himself, but he simply couldn't help it.

At last he caught his breath, and looked sheepishly over at Jo. She was grinning at him, that impish expression that had so caught his attention even through the grief and worry over Chuck's disappearance – only two months before. James sobered quickly at the thought, but it couldn't last long, not under the onslaught of that grin. He took her hand and headed toward the lights of a restaurant a few doors down. "You realize you've made yourself indispensable," he said, much more lightly than he felt.

She chuckled. "I told you, that's what I do."

James stopped right there in the middle of the sidewalk and looked her straight in the eye. "You know what you just said about me and the IRS?" Not that he could intimidate them, *nobody* intimidated the IRS, he just, well, he just worked with them. And was persistent. And knew how to get what his clients needed from them. That wasn't intimidation, that was his job.

She was waiting, patiently, for him to get back from his sidetrack. "Yes."

"What you're good at is making sure you're needed."

Her face fell. "I don't mean –

"That's not how I meant it and you know it. You have no idea how glad I am I find you indispensable." He started off down the sidewalk again, the scent of broiling Montana steak wafting out from the restaurant, making his stomach growl. "Absolutely no idea," he reiterated firmly, and determined, right then and there, to start showing her. Properly.

However, Jo sidetracked him again almost immediately. "You should call your relatives."

"What? Not now."

"When, then? After supper?"

James wasn't sure he wanted to call them at all. After yesterday, it was hard to think of them as his relatives, however unfair it might be. "I'll get to it."

But, in what James had long since quit trying to assign to coincidence, the pretty young hostess at the entrance to the steakhouse took one look at him, then stared, then exclaimed, "Uncle James! What are you doing here?"

* * *

The child – not a child now, although the last time James had seen her she hadn't started school yet – was not, strictly speaking, his niece. He had no siblings to give him any, of course. At least not in this time, he thought with a pang, and wondered how many he would have in the future he wouldn't ever see. But Isobel – Bella, her name tag read – was named after her great-great-grandmother, and was more of a distant cousin at least once removed than anything else. Very, very removed. She was the great-granddaughter of James's second cousin Alice, who was in turn the daughter of Eliza's brother Martin and his wife, Lucy. James tried to fumble through the strings of the relationship for Jo's sake, as they wound through the tables following their young guide.

Bella laughed as she settled them at their booth. "Uncle James is trying to make it sound more complicated than it is," she told Jo. "Family's family."

Jo gave her an approving nod. "I agree."

Bella smiled at her. "Are you – ?"

"I'm a friend of your uncle's." Jo answered the unfinished question. "Jo Bennett." She stuck out her hand. Bella juggled menus to one hand and tentatively shook it.

"Oh." Bella looked from Jo to James and back again, and grinned. "Nice to meet you." But then Bella turned to James. "Speaking of family, Aunt Beth's been trying to get hold of you."

That startled him. Beth was a second cousin from yet another branch of the family; his great-aunt Anna's youngest daughter, she was a year younger than he was.

"She called your house in Denver a bunch of times, and you never answered."

"I – I've been out of town for a couple of weeks."

"Well, call her." She set the menus down in front of them. "Your waitress will be here to take your order in just a minute. Have a nice meal." She paused. "And I mean it. Call her. It's important." She headed back toward the front of the restaurant.

James picked up his menu. Using it as a shield? Although why he was avoiding Jo's gaze was not something he really wanted to think about.

Jo's finger appeared on the top of his menu at the crease and pulled down on it. "She seems like a nice young lady."

"I haven't seen her since she was small. I'm surprised she recognized me." He tried, unsuccessfully, to slip his menu out of her grasp. "If it hadn't been for her name tag, I wouldn't have known which one she was."

"Are there that many?"

James snorted, startling the waitress who had appeared at his elbow. "Are you ready to order, sir?"

James was, and, as he glanced at her and she nodded, so was Jo. A rib eye with all the trimmings didn't require a menu, in his opinion. But as soon as the waitress trotted off, Jo asked him again. "So how much of the population of Helena is related to you?"

"None of them, apparently."

She was silent for a moment, while the muted clatter of the restaurant went on around them, silver and glass and conversation. At last she said, "Are you really going to renounce the family who took you in?"

"No. It's just, well, I didn't come here for a family reunion."

"But you are going to call – Beth, was it?"

"Will you lay off if I tell you I will?" This *wasn't* how he'd planned for the evening to go.

Jo's gaze fell.

James reached for her hand. "I'm sorry." He cast about for anything to set things right." Did I tell you how beautiful you are tonight?"

She had changed her clothing in the bathroom at the hotel, and done something with her face and her long black hair. Jo smiled, but she looked uncomfortable. Uncomfortable was the last thing James wanted her to be. But if she hadn't wanted him to notice how she looked, why had she – Oh.

Before he could say anything, their meals were set before them.

"That was fast," she commented, obviously relieved.

He picked up his steak knife. "Yes, it was." He wondered how much of it was his 'niece' trying to push them along. She'd been so insistent about him calling Cousin Beth. At least she didn't come back to their table and drag him to a phone.

James was careful for the rest of the meal to stick with small talk, and so was Jo. If he hadn't known better, he'd have said she was grateful to him for it.

* * *

They strolled back to their hotel after the meal, James for one feeling comfortably stuffed, and very ready to go back to their room. Jo acquiesced, but only, she said, "because it's finally starting to feel like fall." And, yes, it was chilly, with a breeze scooting the crisp leaves down the street between the tall brick buildings.

"I keep thinking Helena should look like Fort Yellowstone, with stone buildings instead of brick," she commented.

"My great-grandfather – Eliza's father," James corrected himself, "was responsible for most of those bricks. He owned a brick manufactory here, and another one in Butte, and after the big fire in the 1870s, not long before Charley got here, as a matter of fact, he provided most of the building material for rebuilding the town."

"Your family's been here a long time."

"According to my father – according to Will, practically since the town was founded. His grandfather Cooper was a carpetbagger who fell in love with a Southern girl during Reconstruction, and according to family history things got too uncomfortable for them back East, so they emigrated. They arrived here just after the first wave of gold miners and stayed." James opened the hotel door and waited for Jo to enter.

"It must be nice to have roots like that."

"It was."

She simply shook her head at him.

A sleepy elevator operator took them up to the fourth floor, and James unlocked the door to their room. Jo immediately went to the phone book. "What's your cousin Beth's last name?"

"It's too late to call tonight. I'll get hold of her tomorrow." If he decided to call at all. It wasn't as if they knew where he was. Whatever his now-putative cousin Beth was so hot to have him know, it couldn't be that important, or young Isobel would have told him.

"Aren't you curious in the least?"

James tried to laugh it off, but knew it was a mistake. "I'm more anxious about the photographs."

She shrugged, and headed off to the bathroom. It should have felt like a reprieve, but it didn't.

* * *

He did sleep that night, after all, in spite of everything, and given all the concerns running through his brain to distract him from sleep, he felt it was quite the accomplishment when he woke up to sun streaming in the window.

Jo was curled up, the position usual for her except this time she was facing away from him. James checked the alarm clock on the nightstand. Eight-fifteen. Still almost three hours until they could go get the photographs. He wished he hadn't woken up yet. The more time he could have spent asleep, the less time he'd have to be anxious.

"Jo?" he said softly, and set a hand on her shoulder.

She didn't respond for a moment, then rolled over. She hadn't been asleep. James leaned down and kissed her. "Good morning."

"'Morning." But when he would have said more, done more, she rolled out of bed and headed for the bathroom again.

She stayed in there an awfully long time, and when she came out, she wore an outfit he wouldn't have thought she'd own, it looked so proper. It wasn't the first time he'd seen her in a skirt, last night having taken that honor, but the blue dress, oddly, made her look her actual age, for the first time since he'd met her. The bodice buttoned up to a pointed collar, and the full sleeves ended at equally tightly-buttoned cuffs. The skirt billowed out to just below her knees, and she wore stockings, and black pumps with heels.

James's gaze made its inevitable way back up to her face. Her beautiful lips were covered in red, and her hair – "What did you do to your hair?"

It wasn't the right thing to say. James wished he could snatch the words back the moment they were out of his mouth. "Bundled it up." She turned around. The bun sat at the nape of her neck, a few long straight strands already coming loose. It looked – matronly,

James thought helplessly. Not like his Jo at all.

"The dress is pretty." It wasn't a lie. The color suited her more than he would have expected. "What's the occasion?"

She turned back to him, her face worried." I thought we'd be meeting your family today."

Dear God. As if she thought they needed to approve of her? "Jo." He went to her, put his arms around her. Rested his face in her hair, and nearly got a bobby pin in the eye.

Her arms came up tentatively to wrap around his waist. Tentative wasn't in the least what he wanted from her. He hugged her more tightly.

But she backed away. "I've got lipstick on your shirt. I hope you've got a clean one. And a more decent one than that to begin with." She went to open his suitcase, then stopped and looked up at him, embarrassed. Her lipstick was smudged. Privately, James thought it looked more like her this way than when it was perfect.

"Go on," he told her. It looked as if he was going to visit with the relatives today whether he wanted to or not. But he really did wonder if, knowing what he knew now, how awkward it was going to be

* * *

Cousin Beth was in the phone book, or rather, her husband Jack was. It wasn't as if they were one of a bunch of Smiths, James thought, amused. They were the only Sensanbaughers in the Helena phone book, and probably the only Sensanbaughers in all of Montana. The phone rang and rang, and James was about to hang up when he heard a firm "Hello?"

"Cousin Beth? This is James."

"Oh, my goodness! Where are you?"

"I'm in Helena, on, on —" on what? Certainly not business. "I'm doing some research."

"Were you going to let us know you were here? Bella called me last night and said you'd come into the restaurant."

Now he felt ashamed for even considering it. "I am now," he said apologetically." We just got in last night."

"We?" A pause, then a mollified-sounding "Well. Mother's been asking after you."

After last night he'd been expecting this, but it still seemed odd. "Aunt Anna? Did she say why?"

A few seconds of silence, then, "She's not doing very well, James. I know we all thought she'd go on forever, but she is ninety-five."

"Oh. I'm sorry." And he was, he realized.

"Do you have time to come by and see her while you're here?"

She sounded far more tentative than she should have. Did she think he'd refuse? "Of course I do. When and where?" He had just pulled the credenza drawer open looking for a pen when Jo pushed one into his hand. He gave her a grateful glance and took down the directions.

After he hung up, she took the paper from him and put it into the handbag which matched the shoes she'd produced from the bottom of her duffel bag. James had never seen it before, either, but he didn't comment. "What time?"

"She's in a nursing home." He was having a very hard time picturing his lively aunt Anna in a nursing home. A painfully hard time. "Visiting hours start at two."

Jo nodded decisively. "All right. We've got a few hours to kill before we pick up the photos and go there. We might as well go to the historical society."

It was where he'd intended to go when he'd left Denver less than two weeks before. Now he knew what had really happened, the research seemed like an exercise in futility, and that was pretty much what it turned out to be. Still, it was a pleasant place, on the top floor of the state historical museum, and as good a place as any to pass a couple of hours.

But when eleven o'clock finally rolled around, James took a firm hold of Jo's arm and not quite literally dragged her away from her perusal of the microfilmed headlines of 1897 and down the stairs, barely stopping long enough to help her with her coat.

They arrived at the camera store on the stroke of eleven. The young man from last evening was gone, replaced by a woman about Jo's age who sorted through a file drawer of envelopes. "M-Mc-McMan-McManis," she muttered under her breath as she searched, and only James's sense of dignity kept him from dancing from foot to foot as they waited.

At last she pulled it out. "Dratted boy doesn't know his alphabet." James handed over the money, and finally she handed over the envelope.

He wanted to rip it open then and there. But no, they'd be better off doing this back in their hotel room. Once there, however, the door was barely shut behind them before he tore at it, then, of all the stupid things, he couldn't quite bring himself to pull the photos out.

"Go on," Jo urged.

"What if they're blank?"

"What if they are? Being too much of a coward to look at them won't change that."

"Smart aleck," James said, but he took a deep breath and, delicately, between thumb and forefinger, as if his touch would damage them, he pulled the photos out.

CHAPTER 22

Even though he'd been waiting for hours to see them, part of him wanted to avert his eyes. But James took a look at the first photo, anyway. And sagged in disappointment. The photo depicted a slightly blurry view of Cliff Geyser. Nothing else. "Oh, no."

"Let me see." Jo held out her hand and James put the photo into it, then steeled himself to look at the second one. This view was of the parking lot, and was equally empty – No. It wasn't. "Look." And then he made it impossible for her to do so because he lifted it so close to his eyes she couldn't possibly see.

"What?"

"In front of that tree." Far more reluctantly than he would have liked, James handed the second photo to her.

She peered at it. "Are you sure? It looks like a smudge."

"No, it's not." He pointed at the 'smudge' in question. "The edges are far too sharp."

She shrugged, and reached for the third photo, but James wasn't ready to let it go yet. It wasn't a smudge. He was more than sure it was the outline of his parents' rattletrap vehicle. And those shapes surrounding it – they had to be people.

Then, when Jo practically snatched the photo out of his hand, he got a good look at the fourth photo, and he froze. "There, dammit," he said, completely forgetting himself. "There they are."

And there they were. Six people and a Volkswagen bus.

"Those are *not* smudges." With an effort, he handed the photo to

Jo, whose caught breath he barely noticed, and perused the next one.

Those were people. And, furthermore, he recognized them. There were his mother, and his father, and the others who'd been with them. He handed that one to her, and looked at the next one. And the next, and the next.

Each one was clearer than the one before, as if they'd gradually materialized to the point where the camera could pick their existence up and capture it. After a few moments the rangers' vehicles arrived and those men started piling out. There was Ranger Marshall, caught in the act of giving orders. And the other rangers in their uniforms, taking those orders, spreading out.

There was his father, arguing with Marshall. James could almost hear his voice. His mother came back with his baby sister. He hadn't realized he'd gotten a shot of her nursing the child.

The last photo was the one he'd taken of little Joanna, grinning and waving her fists at him. James stared at her, and wondered what would become of her. He'd never know. Somehow he knew he'd never live long enough to know.

Charley had known when he would die, and now James realized, so did he. Before the earthquake that had taken him back from 1983 to 1897. Sometime between now and then –

Jo's muffled exclamation brought him out of his ruminations. It was probably just as well, given where they'd been headed. "What?"

She held out one of the photos. It was probably the best one of the group Shannon and Mike had been traveling with, James thought, gathered around the bus, obviously trying to figure out what to do.

"Yes," James said, still marveling. "That's the whole bunch."

But Jo was pointing at one particular figure. Her hands were shaking, to the point where he almost wasn't sure which one. "Who is that?" Her voice was shaking, too.

James took the photo from her and peered at it. "She told the ranger her name was Marie Sanders. Why?"

Jo cleared her throat. "She's the spitting image of my daughter."

* * *

The silence after that lasted far too long.

"She's too young," James said at last. "Isn't she?"

"If what I'm looking at is 1983, she's far too young to be Stacey," Jo said slowly. "But she's not too young to be my granddaughter." She went silent again, examining every photo including the young woman. James watched her, the rest of the photos sitting in his lap. At last she surfaced again, her eyes wet as they met his. "I never met my granddaughter. I suspected Stacey was pregnant when she ran away, but I never knew for sure."

James hated to rain on her parade, but it had to be said. "You don't know for sure she's your granddaughter."

"Yes, I do." She held up one, the clearest shot of the young woman, although she was partly turned away. On her left shoulder blade, left bare by her skimpy top, was a mark of some kind. James couldn't tell what it was, but it looked oddly familiar. He looked up at Jo, knowing he looked as baffled as he felt. She smiled, wistfully, James thought. "Yes, I thought you might recognize that."

"A birth mark?" Now that was a bit of a cliché. And just a little too good to be true, from Jo's point of view. But somehow he knew there was going to be no going back for her, no renunciation.

"Yes. My mother had it, and her mother, and her mother before her. And my daughter had it, too."

"It's not positive proof," James said carefully.

"It's proof enough for me." She held up several of the photos. "May I have copies made of these?"

"Of course." James glanced at his watch. "But we'll barely have enough time to get something to eat before we –" he faltered "– before I go see my aunt."

She hadn't even noticed his hesitation, her gaze glued to the image on the photo. "Oh. Yes. Then we can head back home."

So much for research, James thought. But he'd done his. And the sooner they arrived in Denver, the sooner they'd be able to leave. So he didn't say anything, even if he suspected later he'd have wished he had.

They grabbed hamburgers at a diner on their way. Jo made as if to take the photos into the restaurant, but then reluctantly left them behind. She barely ate, and James had to admit his stomach was a bit unsettled, too. She went on out to the car while he paid the bill, and when he got there he saw she had the photos out again, and was tracing Marie's outline with one finger.

James shook his head, but he was too concerned about seeing Aunt Anna to give Jo's new obsession any thought.

* * *

The nursing home was a big, broad-shouldered, red-brick building in an incongruously colonial style, with black shutters and white trim. The cupola on top looked like an undersized party hat. The lawns, too, were an out-of-season bright green. James parked the Lincoln in the semi-circular driveway out front where several other cars already sat and killed the engine. He glanced over at Jo, who, so far as he could tell, would have been better off alone with the photos back in their hotel room. "I don't know how long I'll be," he told her. "Will you be all right here?"

She shook herself and her eyes met his for the first time since they'd been in the hotel room. "I'm sorry. I'll come with you."

"You don't have to."

She reached out a hand and ran her fingers down his cheek. "I'm sorry. I just —" she gestured helplessly at the photos, then slid them back into their envelope. "But I am coming in with you."

He was ridiculously touched. "Thank you."

She grinned, something of her old mischief in it, relieving him greatly. And when he climbed out and went to open her door, she'd already done it and stood there waiting for him. He offered her his arm, she took it, James steeled himself, and they headed for the big white double doors.

The place looked as clean and unnatural on the inside as it did on the outside. More like a medical office than a place to live. The door opened directly onto what amounted to a waiting room with a pass-through about halfway down one wall. Behind the opening sat a woman in a nurse's uniform, who looked up and smiled at James as he approached her.

"I'm here to visit Mrs. Anna Schmidt."

"Your name, please?"

"James McManis."

"Just a moment." The nurse checked a list, and her face fell. "I'm sorry, sir, but she's listed for family only."

"I'm her great-nephew."

The nurse still looked sympathetic, but not like that information had changed her mind. Behind him, James could hear Jo rustling through that

240

ridiculous handbag. She thrust a piece of paper at him. "Have her call your cousin. She'll get you in."

Gratefully, James took the paper with its phone number on it. "Can you do that?" he asked the nurse, who nodded and took the paper.

But the phone rang and rang this time, without an answer. At last the nurse hung up. "I am sorry, sir."

All right, so he hadn't wanted to be here in the first place, but no one was going to tell him he couldn't see his aunt now that he was. All of a sudden it seemed incredibly urgent he do so, and rules, well, rules hadn't gotten him very far lately, had they? "I've driven here all the way from Denver," he told the nurse. "My cousin said this may be the last time I'll have a chance to see my aunt, and your protocol isn't going to keep me from doing so." James turned on his heel and headed toward the two large hospital doors at the end of the foyer.

Behind him, he heard the nurse call, "Sir, if you go in there, I will have to call the police."

Well, and what did he have to lose? It wasn't as if they were going to throw him in jail. He threw the words over his shoulder, "Do it," and pushed the swinging door out of his way.

Of course, now he had no idea which of the many closed doors along the far-too-long pale green hallway would lead to Aunt Anna's room. He glanced helplessly at Jo, right behind him. "Look," she said, pointing to the clipboards hanging on hooks next to each door. "Names."

"All right. You go that way and I'll go –"

"Sir." The nurse grabbed his sleeve. "I'm sorry, sir, but you must leave-" James jerked his arm free and strode down the hall peering at clipboards. He didn't even bother to look behind him, but he knew she hadn't followed him.

Not this one, not this one – A few minutes later he heard a commotion back at the double doors, but he paid no attention – "Ha." He'd found the door marked Schmidt. No young desk nurse was going to boss *him* around. He put his hand on the knob.

"James!" The voice behind him was newly familiar. He turned to see, was that Cousin Beth? Yes, it was. An older, worried-looking Cousin Beth, but she hadn't changed that much.

"Please don't just go barging in there like that. You might do her harm."

"Where were you?" he demanded." Why didn't you tell me there'd be a problem letting me in?"

"Why couldn't you have just waited a few minutes? You're as bad as he was –"

James froze. "As bad as who was, Beth?"

"Your grandfather," she told him flatly.

"Yes, he is," said a faint voice from through the open door. "Let him come in, Bethy. He won't kill me, I promise. Not today."

James put his head through the doorway, and smiled, although the sight of her made his heart hurt. "Hello, Aunt Anna."

"Hello, Jem."

* * *

He should have been prepared for how she looked, he thought. She *was* old, after all. She'd turned ninety-five this past spring. Her hair was not only pure white, but thin to where her age-spotted scalp showed through. Her face was less wrinkled than he'd expected it to be, but it was not a healthy color, more gray than pink. Her eyes still watched him intently, though, that deep, rich brown, shades darker than her sister's had been. But she was tiny. Not just petite as she'd always been, but thin to the point of gaunt. Her nightgown and bed jacket hung from her, and her hands, as she reached out to him, were nothing but age-spotted skin stretched over the bones of her once-delicate fingers.

He stepped inside. The first question that sprang to his mind was, "Don't they feed you here?" He barely kept it from jumping out of his mouth. "It's good to see you."

Her voice sounded old, too, when she answered him. "I'm not much to look at these days."

He couldn't very well deny what she obviously knew was the truth, so he said, "I've always thought you were something to see."

She smiled, and there were the wrinkles. Laugh lines, not wrinkles, James thought decisively. He could hear the commotion dying down behind him in the hallway, and he knew they wouldn't have much time alone, so he got right to the point. "You knew, didn't you?"

Her smile went wry, and she pointed at the chair by the bed. "Sit, child."

He sat. James supposed he would always be a child to her, but he felt like he was four years old again, meeting her for the first time, afraid she'd be like all the other strangers, staring and asking more questions like the ones Charley and Eliza had refused to countenance from everyone else. She hadn't, though, not then, and she didn't now. Instead, she reached out a hand and rested it on his arm, thin skin and sharp bones. And cold. Too cold. "Yes, I knew. I'm sorry I couldn't say anything before."

"I'm not." And James realized at last he wasn't. Oh, he still missed Chuck with an ache he supposed would never really go away, but he knew, from watching Jo just this morning, exactly how lucky he was to know what had happened to his son, that the boy had ended up happy – happier, perhaps, than he would have been if he'd stayed in his own time. *No perhaps about it.* The thought came down like a hammer, and something must have shown in James's face, because Anna's fingers pressed down on him. They felt like the feet of a bird.

"He was a mess," Anna said in her reedy voice, "when he stumbled into our camp. None of us suspected what he'd been through. How could we? Mr. Byrne thought he was a lunkhead for getting lost out in the wilderness alone, and even though Byrne was an idiot himself I'm afraid the rest of us didn't think much better of Charley then. We thought he'd gotten himself in trouble, and almost gotten himself killed.

"When Eliza told me what really happened –"

"Eliza *told* you?" And who else had she told? And what had they thought? And what had Anna been told about *him*?

"Years later," Anna said matter-of-factly. "After you showed up, actually. They bamboozled most people about where you'd come from, but they had to explain you to family."

He could barely ask. "And, and what did you think then?"

She smiled again." After I saw Charley's proof, and yours? What could I think? I was jealous, of course."

"Jealous?" He couldn't quite keep the incredulity out of his voice.

Anna sighed. It sounded, well, she sounded wistful. "I loved my life, Jem, don't get me wrong. It's been a good long full one, and I was lucky to find a husband who didn't try to lasso me down. I've had adventures, and I've had a family, and I've had just about anything a woman could want. I've loved and I've been loved." She gave him a sharp look. "Do you know how important that is?"

James nodded and thought of Catherine, and how she'd given him everything she could before she'd left him. Far more than he'd deserved. And of Jo, and how he wanted her. Needed her. Loved her and wanted to spend the rest of his life with her. "Yes, I do."

"Good, because I've wondered if you really did. The things Charley said about you when he first came to us – Well, that's water over the dam now. Don't waste any more of it, do you hear me?"

James thought he knew what Charley had said about him, and winced, but he said only, "Yes, ma'am."

"And don't look like you're sucking on a lemon while you're about it."

That startled him into a laugh. "Yes, ma'am."

"That's better." She sank back into her pillows and closed her eyes. Without opening them she said, "Getting old is for the birds." Her voice had gone faint, her skin even paler than it had been before.

It worried him. He started to get up, to go call for a nurse, a doctor, someone, but her hand tightened on his arm with a strength that amazed him.

"Don't fetch them yet," she whispered. "I've got one more thing to tell you, Jem."

It went against his better judgment, but he stayed. "Yes, Aunt Anna?"

"Chuck loved you very much. In spite of everything, or, he told me, maybe because of it. He told me to tell you, and I promised him I would. But we all do, Jem. We did from the moment we met you."

Her hand on his arm went limp. So did the rest of her.

James stood up, looking down at her for a moment, then went to fetch the doctor.

CHAPTER 23

"Are you all right?" Jo asked as they stepped out of the nursing home's big front doors into the bright sunlight.

James thought about it for a moment. "Surprisingly enough, yes, I am. I'm going to miss Aunt Anna, but, as she told me, she's had a good long life, and a lucky one. She told me she'd loved and been loved, and that was the most important thing." He stopped beside the Lincoln. "She told me Chuck loved me."

"Of course he did."

"No, you don't understand. We argued before he left. He was angry with me, really angry. And I was just as angry at him. It's at least partly why he ran off the way he did. And while he told me he wasn't still angry with me in the letter, it's not the same."

She opened the car door as usual without waiting for him to do it for her, and slid in. He supposed he'd get used to that eventually. Along with everything else about her. It would be his pleasure to get used to her, actually. "He was a teenage boy, James."

"Yes, but we never had the chance –" James closed the car door and went around to the driver's side, but she'd already scooted over behind the wheel.

Jo held her hand out for the keys. "Do you mind?"

"No." He strode back around to the passenger side and climbed in. "Anyway, it bothered me I'd never had a chance to make things right with Chuck, letter or no letter. It mattered." James sighed. "Aunt Anna is one of the few people I know who's honest about things like that.

And she's the only person I know who knew him in 1877, who's still alive. If Chuck hadn't told her to tell me, she wouldn't have told me he did."

"I think I understand." She paused, pulling the car out into the sparse traffic, and said, "Would you mind if we went on back to the park today? Any library research we did now couldn't possibly add anything more to what you already know."

He had to admit that was true.

She took a deep breath. "And would you mind if I skipped the trip to Denver?"

James blinked. Yes, he did mind. But did he have the right to ask – yes, he *did*. "Why?"

She was silent for a moment. "I need to be home."

"She's not there, Jo." No need to say who she was.

"I know. But I need to be home."

* * *

He'd put more miles on the Lincoln in the past three weeks than he normally put on his car in a year. Well, James thought as they drove under the Roosevelt Arch and back into Yellowstone once more, at least it was for a good purpose.

He still couldn't describe the way he felt. Relaxed, he supposed, in a way he hadn't been since before Will – before his real father had died last August. That was part of it. Part of it was relief, he was quite sure, knowing Chuck had forgiven him. Bless Aunt Anna for that. Part of it was being content in a way he hadn't been since – he couldn't remember when. Since he was four years old, he suspected. At last all of the puzzle pieces of his life fit, in a way he couldn't have begun to imagine three months ago. They fit in a way that actually worked for him, as nothing ever had before.

He wished the pieces were fitting together as well for Jo as they were for him. He glanced over at her as they headed up the hill after the obligatory stop at the entrance station. He'd insisted it was his turn to drive when they'd stopped for gas in Bozeman, and she'd given in, as she had to any suggestion he'd made since they'd left Helena, with increasing ill grace. But when the ranger started warning James that the only road open now was the one from Mammoth to Cooke City, just outside the northeast corner of the park, Jo stuck her head over his shoulder and told the fellow she was aware of that, thank you very much, Frank. The ranger had grinned at her and waved them on.

The sun had just disappeared behind the mountains when they arrived at her trailer. James fetched his suitcase and her duffel and followed her inside. "Would you mind if I stayed for a day or two before I head to Denver?" He smiled at her apologetically. "I'm really tired of driving right now."

"Then you should have let me drive." Her tone was sharp, and James stepped back, still holding their luggage. He'd known she was distracted. She had been ever since she'd seen the photographs. He was beginning to wish he'd never shown them to her, maybe even never had them developed. But he hadn't realized she was angry with him. For what?

He dropped her duffel. "I'm sorry. I'll sleep on the couch and leave first thing in the morning. You won't kick me out tonight, I hope?"

She squeezed her eyelids shut, then opened them to look at him. "No, I'm sorry. I didn't mean that the way it sounded. I'm just really, really tired."

"And hungry, I bet." The lunch she'd barely picked at in Butte was hours ago now. *He* was hungry, and he'd eaten his meal.

"Not really." But she wandered back into the kitchen. "I suppose we should eat, though."

"May I help?"

* * *

He hadn't been much help, James thought as he lay next to Jo's almost rigid body later that night. They'd eaten what she called her electricity's out meal, canned stew and canned fruit. She had pulled out more wine to wash it down with, but it hadn't seemed to relax her at all. He'd helped with the few dishes the bare bones supper had generated, but when he'd gone to the closet for the pillow and blanket for the couch, she only shook her head at him and gestured for him to put them back.

He'd never felt less welcome in her bed, though. They hadn't made love. They hadn't even snuggled. The lack of lovemaking was not the end of the world – they were both exhausted from the day –

but the lack of cuddling was, so far as he was concerned. He hadn't realized how used to it he'd gotten. And how comfortable it made him feel.

She wasn't asleep. He knew it. There was no reason why he couldn't reach over and hug *her*. Just because he'd gotten in the habit of letting her take all the initiative in their relationship – well, he supposed he had. That was going to stop, right now. He rolled over and snuggled up to her, rigid body or no rigid body.

When she rolled away from him, he almost despaired. But then she pushed herself back up against him, letting him spoon her body, the stiffness finally relaxing out of her a bit at a time, and James let out a breath, fluttering her hair. He wrapped himself around her and let himself sleep at last.

* * *

He was alone when he woke. He could hear the washing machine running, and glanced across to his suitcase, open and empty except for his shaving kit. Well, that was considerate of her, and he couldn't leave until his clothes were dry, at the very least, so she wasn't kicking him out first thing.

But when he went into the kitchen, still in his bathrobe, it was to find a note on the table. "Got called to an emergency. Don't know when I'll be back. I understand if you want to go on."

And how did anyone know she was back to call her to whatever emergency she might have to deal with?

He examined the note further. Not even an "I'll see you when you get back." All of his hard-won contentment vanished, to be replaced with determination. He'd finally got to a point where his life was where he wanted it. He wanted her life to be there, too.

He couldn't leave the house until he had something to wear, however. James wondered if it had been intentional on her part, to keep him from coming after her, then decided he was being paranoid, as Chuck would have said. To fill the time while the washing machine finished – its cycle was almost done, so she'd not been gone more than half an hour – and his clothes dried over the shower rod in the bathroom, he made a rudimentary breakfast for himself and cleaned up the small mess he'd made, then prowled the trailer, wondering how he would fit in here, or if they would move out of the park into a larger place. In Gardiner, perhaps, since her work seemed to be based in the Mammoth area. Somehow he suspected she hadn't thought that part quite through, but then neither had he. Could he be content here?

The trailer wasn't tiny, not for one person, not even for two people who didn't mind a certain amount of living in each other's pockets. Two bedrooms, the one they'd slept in and a smaller one she obviously used as a study, the living/dining room opening onto the kitchen. One rather tiny but adequate bathroom. James snorted. Maybe in a year or two he could talk her into building a new house in Gardiner, one where he wouldn't feel like he was fitting into the cracks of her life.

He went to check on his clothes again.

* * *

Once he was shaved and dressed and in the car, it dawned on him he hadn't the foggiest idea where to find her. Or what to do when he got there. He had no idea where her office was, although for some reason he was sure it was in one of the old Fort Yellowstone buildings. Sighing, he got out of the car and went back in the house for a reconnoiter of another kind. The telephone hung on the wall in the kitchen. No address book sat conveniently nearby or in any of the drawers or cupboards. A second phone sat on the nightstand in her bedroom. Nothing there, either. Or anywhere else in the house, James concluded after a methodical search that was probably more thorough than he had a right to make. Well, and so. He'd go see if any of the buildings in Mammoth were open, and ask there.

The sky hung heavy with clouds, and a cold wind picked up the dust in swirls when he went back outside. James wrapped his coat more tightly around himself and fished his keys out of his pocket. He wished Jo had left him a key to her trailer, but he had to leave it unlocked or risk not being able to get back in if he had to.

* * *

Mammoth Hot Springs was more like a ghost town this time of year than anything else. James headed for the one building with cars parked outside of it, and strode up to the door. It was open. He ducked in out of the wind, smoothing his hair down. He found himself in a long hallway with doors opening on either side. The first one he poked his head into was empty. So was the second, and the third. He finally found someone in the sixth office, a woman who looked to be in her thirties wearing a park service uniform, who looked annoyed at being disturbed, but said politely enough, in response to James's query, "I thought she was still out of town."

"We got back last night."

The woman shook her head. "She hasn't checked in."

"And you'd be who she'd check in with?"

"Yes."

"Her note said something about an emergency."

She shook her head again. "No emergencies. Not likely this time of year, anyway, but if there had been, I'd know about it, even if it was a concessionaire problem. This time of year," she said again, "there's so few of us in the park everyone knows what everyone else is doing. It's a matter of safety."

"Oh."

"Sorry I can't help you." She went back to her work. James left her to it.

Back in the car, he thought, well, that's the first time she's lied to me. Out and out lied. It didn't hurt the way he thought it ought to, for some reason. He knew she hadn't been thinking about him when she did it. She was used to doing things on her own.

But she'd bulldozed her way into his life, helping him whether he wanted her to or not. Even when he'd been extremely ungracious to her, well beyond a simple white lie. She'd stuck with him through thick and thin. For better or for worse, he thought, and almost chuckled. Then he climbed back out of the Lincoln. There was one question he hadn't thought to ask the park service secretary.

Annoyance squared was on the woman's face when he showed up in her office the second time, but she answered him readily enough, probably because she realized it was the easiest way to get him out of her office.

"No, she wouldn't have to report anywhere to take one of the concessioner vehicles. And if she did, she'd be reporting to herself, since she's the ranking manager here in the wintertime."

"Thank you." James turned to leave.

But the secretary had more to tell him, whether he wanted to hear it or not. "If you're thinking about going down into the park to look for her, you might want to reconsider. The roads are closed for good reason."

He nodded. "I know."

"Did you know there's almost two feet of snow on the ground at the higher elevations?"

He wasn't sure whether to believe her. "There's none on the ground here."

She shrugged. "That's not unusual."

"Well, thank you." James took one step, then two, but the secretary stopped him one last time.

"Do you know where she might have gone?"

"I think so. How much snow is there at Old Faithful?"

"Wait a minute." She gestured him to a chair and picked up the phone. James watched her for no more than a second, and was out the door, her call, of "Wait a minute, please!" trailing behind him.

* * *

The gate at the base of the hill south of Mammoth Hot Springs was closed but the lock was dangling. Someone's oversight, James thought as he closed it behind the Lincoln and got back in the car. He wondered if it had been Jo's oversight, and if it meant part of her wanted him to follow. If so, he wasn't going to let her down.

He saw the first snow on the edge of the road as it opened out onto Swan Lake Flat, but it was a mere dusting, a dry skim dancing across the surface of the road. The road itself was as clear as he'd ever seen it, all the way past Obsidian Cliff and the twin lakes and Roaring Mountain. He realized he was driving faster than was probably safe when he saw Norris far sooner than he thought he should have, looming up ahead of him in the cold air, steam blowing across the road, forcing him to slow down.

Still, the conditions could have been much worse, and he was grateful they weren't. Then the road started to climb alongside the Gibbon River, and the edges of the snow became deeper, encroaching onto the pavement until he was down to one lane, hoping he wouldn't run into anyone coming the other direction. Then down to two tracks, but at least he could see where someone, it had to be Jo, had been here before him since the snow had fallen.

He was very, very glad of the chains in the Lincoln's trunk, although he hoped he wouldn't have to use them. He slowed even further, as the sun glinted between the thick gray clouds, sparking off what was now a pristine blanket at least six inches thick. That's not even close to two feet, he thought, his hands gripping the wheel. He'd driven in worse than this back in Denver.

Madison Junction. He negotiated the curves at the junction, carefully watching the tracks in front of him. Yes, they were still headed south, and not west toward the park boundary. He kept the Lincoln's tracks aligned with Jo's. They had to be Jo's, and he was more and more certain of her destination, and why she was headed there. After all, he'd done much the same thing himself less than a week ago, and he'd gotten answers.

And if she didn't get her answer, too? Would she hate and envy him for the rest of their lives? He knew his story, even if he didn't know where it went from there. He'd been able to speak through that slip in time, and be spoken to. Would Jo? Or would she slip through altogether the way he had when he was young? He'd never see her again. *No.* But how could he know?

The Lincoln slipped and slid, and he steered out of the skid, his heart pounding. He needed to pay attention. He wasn't going to help her if he landed in a ditch. He was an old hand at driving in snow. He'd been doing it for decades, had done it in vehicles he wouldn't drive on a bet these days. Had done it without snow tires and power steering. And if worse came to worst, he had chains in the trunk.

More steam in the distance, across a wide meadow. The Paint Pots? As he crept his way closer he could see the geyser Marler'd told them hadn't stopped since the earthquake. Clepsydra? Strange name. The steam blinded him for a few crucial seconds as he slid past the two big springs, Grand Prismatic and Excelsior, the tracks in the snow deeper the farther he went.

There had to be a good foot on the ground here. Still not two, though, he told himself. And he could still see tracks. Then all of a sudden they veered off into nowhere, down the slope toward the river, the road in front of him blank and white. He didn't dare try to follow them. He couldn't see anything.

Carefully, slowly, James pulled the car to a point he hoped would be out of the way of any other fool stupid enough to be trying to drive out here. As he climbed out of the Lincoln, more flakes began to fall.

CHAPTER 24

"Jo?" he called experimentally, slipping and sliding as he followed the tracks. "Jo?"

"Here! I'm down here, dammit."

He almost collapsed with relief, but stiffened his spine and kept going.

The vehicle, an army surplus Jeep with "Hamilton Stores" painted on the side and the canvas top sagging with collecting snow, was leaning lopsidedly, one wheel at the edge of the Firehole River, the other three perched on the slope.

Jo peered around the side of the Jeep. "What are you doing here?"

She didn't sound pleased to see him. Well, wasn't that just too bad. She wasn't normally that obtuse, either. "I came looking for you."

"You're supposed to be on your way to Denver."

James just shook his head. "Come on."

She picked her way around the Jeep. James put out a hand, and when she didn't take it, he put it under her arm, got a good grip, and pulled her up the riverbank by main force. At least she didn't fight him about it, her expression only resigned, not indignant.

"Do you need me to fetch anything out of there for you?" He nodded toward the Jeep.

She scowled. "No."

"You sure? Because I suspect it's going to be a while before anyone can haul that thing back onto the road."

"You're telling me." Her shoulders slumped. "Yes. My duffel's in the back. I should have gotten it out, but I, well, it wasn't my main concern."

James looked her up and down, but didn't see any injuries. She made as if she were going to start back down the embankment. James tightened his hand. "You go on back up. I'll get it."

She didn't argue with him, but she didn't head back to the Lincoln, either. He could feel her watching him as he pried open the door to the Jeep and pulled her battered duffel out, then scrambled back up to her.

"You sure you're all right?" he puffed.

"Yes, I'm fine." But she shook him off when he took hold of her arm again and set off back up the Jeep's tracks to the road. James followed. But when they reached the Lincoln and she held her hand out for the keys, he just shook his head. And let her open her own door while he slung her duffel into the trunk where it belonged.

But when he started the car and began what he suspected would take quite a few more points than a three-point turn, she said, "No. I need to go on."

She couldn't be serious. "I don't want to risk it. We shouldn't be here in the first place."

She'd been avoiding meeting his eyes up till now, but she turned in her seat and gazed straight at him then. The only thing she said was, "Please, James," but it was enough, even against his better judgment.

"All right." He turned off the engine and opened the door again.

"Where are you going?"

"To put on the chains."

* * *

She insisted on getting out and helping him, even though he knew she hadn't anywhere near warmed up from her spell out there with the Jeep. But he also knew better than to try to stop her, and she obviously knew what she was doing as well as he did. It wasn't more than fifteen minutes before they were back in the car with the engine started. James took a moment to crank the heat up to full blast with the fan roaring.

Jo pulled her gloves off and put her hands down to where it was blowing near their feet. "Oh, that feels good."

"I hope so." James eased the car back out onto the blank white expanse, and was devoutly grateful for the Lincoln's weight helping the chains do their work of holding the road. No more tracks to follow. "You want to tell me what you're doing out here now?"

She swallowed audibly.

"I talked with the secretary at Fort Yellowstone," he told her easily, his eyes and hands on the road. "I know there wasn't an emergency."

"I'm sorry."

"For lying to me?" He shrugged. "I can live with it, this time." He paused. "If you tell me why you did it."

She hesitated so long he almost wondered if — no, he thought, relieved beyond measure when she finally spoke. "I'm jealous."

That was almost enough to take his attention off the admittedly dicey driving conditions, although the chains had made all the difference. "Of what, for heaven's sake?"

"Not what. Who. You, getting to talk with your mother."

"My mother died five years ago. You mean Shannon?"

"Yes." She sounded so forlorn he wanted to stop the car and hug her, in spite of everything. But now was not the time or the place. "You know what happened. I never will."

"So you decided to come out here and freeze to death trying to find out?"

"Well, when you put it that way. . ." Was that amusement or disgust in her voice?

He went with amusement. "It's kind of hard to put it any other way, from my point of view."

She put a hand on his shoulder. When he glanced to his side, she was turned toward him. "But do you understand?"

Her fingers were still icy, but he was quite sure it wasn't from the cold. For one thing, the interior of the car was warm enough he felt overheated in his jacket now. "Me, of all people?"

She sniffed. He risked another glance in her direction. She glared at him, even as the tears fell. "Keep your eyes on the road."

"Yes, ma'am."

"And turn right."

The sign to Black Sand Basin was half-obscured by heavy, wet snow. "We'll get stuck."

"I'll dig us out with my bare hands if I have to. Turn. Please."

James sighed. "I've got a shovel in the trunk." Standard gear for winter driving. He turned, eased his way onto the flat expanse of the parking area. It was a far cry from when he'd sat here in a lawn chair three days before. And he didn't think anyone would be out here in shirtsleeves again until next June. Praying he'd be able to get the car moving again even with the shovel, he eased the Lincoln to a stop.

Jo opened the door. James put a hand on her arm. "You can't do what I did now."

She closed it again. "I know."

"You do realize what the date was the other day, don't you?"

"Yes." She sounded utterly defeated. "October 23rd. Your birthday. That can't have had anything to do with it, could it?"

"I think it did," James said slowly. The air inside the car was already beginning to cool. He had no idea what the temperature outside was, except for ridiculously cold. Falling snow was already beginning to obscure the windshield. He turned the key and hit the windshield wipers. They provided only a momentary view. "We can't sit here and wait, you know, or we'll never be able to get out again."

"I know."

But instead of starting the engine again, he reached out an arm and, after a moment, Jo scooted under it. James snuggled her up closely to him, and laid his cheek on top of her head.

He wasn't sure how long they sat there, in their slowly-cooling white-windowed cocoon. He'd have sat there forever for her, he thought. As long as he had Jo, everything was all right.

But she shook herself and straightened. "You're right. We'd better get out of here."

He hated that defeat in her voice. "One more minute one way or the other isn't going to make a difference." He turned to face her. "I can't give you what you want. It breaks my heart that I can't. I would give anything for you to know Stacey is all right, and Marie. I just want you to know that. But you have more than you had," he told her.

She swallowed." Yes, I do. Thank you."

"I, I had an idea." It had been niggling at the back of his mind ever since he'd left Denver, wondering what he was going to do with a will whose beneficiary was beyond reach now. And now he knew, with a certainty assuring him it was exactly the right thing to do.

"I can give you something more. Not knowledge, but better than nothing."

"What?" She was just being polite now, he thought, although he could tell she appreciated his sincerity.

It was all he was going to get. He took a deep breath. "It isn't much, but we have her name."

"Yes."

"I need to change my will, anyway."

She stared up at him, astonished out of her, yes, it was grief. He of all people recognized that kind of grief. "Are you saying what I think you're saying?"

"I," he said carefully, wanting to be absolutely clear on this most important point, "would do anything for you. Do you understand that?"

She nodded, still astonished. He was going to have to spend a lot of time getting her past being astonished at that kind of thing. He was looking forward to it, actually.

"Good. Then it's settled." He grinned. "Besides, at least part of that money came from Charley's knowledge of things he shouldn't have known. I always wondered why he pulled his money out of the stock market in the summer of 1929. Everyone thought he was crazy at the time. I think, if he was here, he'd be laughing right now. I really do think he'd approve.

"It would change the future, but I was going to do that, anyway, for Shannon and Mike. And it's only money. It won't change her, but it might give her some options."

Jo almost squeaked. "You'd do that, for her?"

"I will do it for you. Pritchard can set it up. He won't bat an eye, given what he's already been a party to. I can't give you what you really want, and I'm sorrier than you know about that." She was still staring at him, and he didn't know what else to say, what else he could do. He wanted years with her, not the few hours they'd have staying here while she waited. And waited. In vain.

"But you would do that much, on the strength of my word. You're right, it's not what I really want. But I've never been able to have what I really wanted for Stacey, or Marie. I'll never know them. But at least I got to see Marie. That's more than I ever thought I'd have." Then her smile spread and warmed him inside and out. "I wish I could see her when Pritchard finds her and tells her, but I can imagine it, and it's a wonderful thing. You, James Whitehorse McManis, are an absolutely amazing and beautiful man."

He shook his head, but he could feel his own grin escaping. "Let's go dig ourselves out."

* * *

In the end, it turned out to be a good thing James had stopped and spoken to the secretary, because when neither he nor Jo arrived at Old Faithful they sent a snowplow out after them. James wasn't sure they'd have gotten out of the park without it, shovel or no shovel, chains or no chains. The fine was certainly steep enough, but at least they didn't arrest him, and while he figured Jo was responsible for him not being hauled away, especially when they passed where her Jeep sat already half-buried, he wasn't going to complain about the money.

They were safe. They were on their way to Denver. And he couldn't think of a better cause to celebrate.

They took the chains off at West Yellowstone, and drove completely out of the snow by Idaho Falls. They spent the night in the best accommodations, which wasn't saying much, in Rock Springs, Wyoming, but the steak house the desk clerk recommended more than made up for the room. And at least the heat worked, even if the shower grout was dirty. The bed was big enough for two, and that was what mattered. Jo wrapped herself around him as tightly as he wrapped himself around her, and they both slept as if they were working at it as hard as they possibly could.

The steak house, it turned out, converted itself to a pancake emporium in the morning, and, full of hotcakes and sausage, they headed east. A tail wind made it all James could do to keep from going too fast. It didn't help he was fighting his own inclinations on that front as well. He wanted to get back to Denver, get things settled and sold, and get back home.

Home. James didn't precisely know when he'd started thinking of Yellowstone as home again, but, "You know what?" he told Jo as they swung south at Laramie.

"What?"

He beamed at her and saw her blink. "You've made my home *home* again."

"You do realize that makes no sense whatsoever." But she squeezed his hand where she held it on the seat between them.

"Yes, it does. And you were the one who did it. You helped me find home again." He'd never felt more exhilarated. "And I can't wait to go."

AFTERWORD

Thank you for reading *Finding Home*. I hope you enjoyed it. Reviews help other readers find books. I appreciate all reviews, whether positive or negative.

Earthquakes and geysers are not, of course, able to send anyone back or forward or any other direction in time, but the earthquake that sent Chuck eighty-two years into the past at 11:37 pm on August 17, 1959, was real nonetheless. The Hebgen Lake Earthquake not only rattled Yellowstone and its thermal features good and hard, but it also caused a landslide west of the park that killed twenty-eight people, many of whose bodies were never found, and created an entirely new lake in the process.

Another real quake significant to this story, the Borah Peak earthquake, was centered in eastern Idaho on October 28, 1983, on an unseasonably warm day just before the park closed for the season, and also shook Yellowstone.

Would you like to know when my next book is available? You can sign up for my new release email list at mmjustus.com, or follow me on on Facebook at https://www.facebook.com/M.M.Justusauthor or on Twitter @mmjustus.

If you're interested in reading more about the actual history behind this story, please go to the Pathfinders page on my website at mmjustus.com, where I have put together links to resources about these earthquakes, as well as a collection of photos of locations in the story.

If you're interested in finding out more about the people who adopted the little boy who grew up to be James, please take a look at *True Gold*, the second Time in Yellowstone novel, and the short story "Homesick." If you're interested in reading the manuscript filling all those legal pads that Charley wrote for James, please turn the page for the first chapter of *Repeating History*, the first Time in Yellowstone novel.

It was just a geyser

The moon gleamed on the pool under the boardwalk, the ripples growing into small waves as the vibrations magnified. A splash, another splash, this one bigger than the first, a chugging racket that sounded like the propellers on an airplane about to take off.

The earthquake, it had to be an earthquake, hit like a giant pounding a sledgehammer. The boardwalk – bounced. With me on it. It was like riding a bucking bronco. I grabbed the edge of the boards and hung on. Grand Geyser's pool was churning like a crazy thing now. Water hit me on the back, the heat soaking through my jacket and shirt.

Then it all stopped. "That was a helluva ride," I said into the suddenly still darkness, the moon glimmering off the still sloshing pool.

Everything seemed to be holding its breath. Not a bit of movement, except the water draining under my feet. Not a sound, not even a breeze in the trees. I took a deep breath and started to get up.

That's when the big one hit.

CHAPTER 1

August 15, 1959

My summer school grades arrived the day after Granddad's funeral. I didn't bother opening them. I knew what was inside. Granddad would have appreciated the irony. I knew Dad wouldn't, and I was glad I'd got to the mail first. Dad was broken up enough over Granddad's death as it was. Although with him it wasn't easy to tell.

"It's time to go." He looked, as usual, like the accountant he is. Bland and smooth in his gray suit, white buttondown shirt, and navy blue tie.

"Sure." I wasn't wearing a suit, just jeans and a plaid shirt and my motorcycle boots. I didn't pat the pocket I'd stuffed the envelope in. Didn't want to draw attention to it. I pushed my glasses up and ran a hand over my dishwater blond buzz cut instead. Then tugged the sleeves of my leather jacket back down over my wrists. The curse of being a beanpole.

He looked me up and down and frowned but didn't say anything else as he locked the door behind us and led the way to his car. At least not until I went to my bike instead.

"You're not riding that *thing* to the lawyer's office."

I swung my leg over the Harley. "Sure I am."

"No, you're -" The rest of the rant, which I knew by heart, was lost in the rumble of the bike's engine. Music to my ears.

* * *

"And that's the last of it," Mr. Pritchard said, handing me Granddad's pocketwatch. So there had been something in the will for me, after all, as familiar as if I'd known it all my life. Which I had. I closed my hand around the smooth metal case, then stuffed it deep into the bottom of my jeans pocket. That was one thing I never wanted to lose. The lawyer straightened the sheaf of paper he was holding, and looked at Dad. I leaned back in my chair and stared out the window overlooking the street, wishing for a hamburger. Lunch had been a long time ago.

"I don't understand why he was so adamant about getting in here to see you two weeks ago," Dad said. "Nothing appears to have changed from the version he gave me last year."

Mr. Pritchard looked apologetic. "I should have said almost the last of it. The codicil he had me add at our last meeting doesn't have anything to do with the disposition of his property, but of his and your mother's remains."

That was creepy. Cremation was even worse than getting buried.

"I've bought a niche for both of them out at Cherry Hills," Dad said in that tone he has. *This is the way it is, period.*

Cherry Hills was the last place my grandparents would have wanted to end up, not that they were going to be able to tell the difference now. It's the ritziest cemetery in Denver, all carefully mowed lawns and fancy statuary. Besides, neither one of them liked Denver to begin with. Granddad had only given up and moved here to be closer to the Dad and me after Grandmother died and his health went downhill.

And when Dad had insisted. Granddad hadn't put up nearly as much of a fight about it as I'd thought he would, though.

"He was very specific about what he wanted done," Mr. Pritchard said, with almost exactly the same tone..

"Well, what *does-*" Dad broke off. I could almost see the blood draining from his face. *Why?* It couldn't be that bad. There's only so much you can do with a pile of ashes, after all. "No. Absolutely not."

Mr. Pritchard looked kind of surprised. "But I haven't even told you what he wanted done yet." Then he turned to me.

I could have sworn they'd completely forgotten I was there. God knows I was wishing I wasn't. What I wanted was to get on my bike and ride far away from this office, from Denver, from my grades burning a hole in my pocket, from the fact that Granddad was dead...

"Your grandfather wished for you to take their ashes back to Yellowstone and scatter them there. He wanted them left where he and your grandmother spent so much of their lives and were so happy together. I've arranged permission from the park service, and made reservations for you at the Old Faithful Inn for three nights starting tomorrow."

All I could think was *oh, my God. Really? Yes! Thank you thank you thank you, Granddad.* He couldn't have given me anything better if he'd tried. I sobered. Except to stay alive.

Mr. Pritchard paused, watching, smiling slightly at me. I could see Dad out of the corner of my eye, all the blood back in his face turning it red with – why was he so mad? Yeah, he didn't get it, wouldn't get it, but it wasn't that big a deal. Just four lousy days. In Yellowstone. Where I'd spent the best times with Grandmother and Granddad, growing up. A chance to get the hell out of here. "You should have plenty of time. If I understand correctly, you won't be going back to college this fall."

My jaw dropped, but before I could say anything, Dad took a deep breath. "And why not?" His fists were clenched on the arm of the chair, and he was past just red. He looked like he was going to explode. "What did you do this time, and why the *hell* didn't you tell me before it went this far?"

"I, uh." My tongue stuck in my throat. *Well, at least he knows now.* "I, uh, flunked Business Law. And Economic Analysis."

"*Again?*" He looked like he wanted to strangle me. I guess the only reason he didn't was where we were.

Mr. Pritchard was looking apologetic again. "I'm sorry. I thought you knew. I spoke out of turn."

I turned on him. Anything so I didn't have to look at Dad. "How the-How did you know about my grades? I just got them today."

His smile this time was almost a smirk. "Perhaps the two of you need to go home and talk this over."

Over my dead body. Which is what it was likely to be by the time Dad got done with me.

Dad apparently had the same idea, because he stood and grabbed me by the arm. I'm taller than he is, but he's got a helluva grip for a 65-year-old man. "Come on, son."

I glanced back at Mr. Pritchard as Dad dragged me out of the room. *Thanks a lot, Mister.*

* * *

I'm twenty years old. It's not like my father can stick me in my room and expect me to stay there. I packed up my duffel bag and snuck out that night while Dad was on the phone, talking to God knows who about God knows what. Well, not God knows what, although what Dad thought he could do to get Colorado State University to take me back again was sort of beyond me.

I spent what was left of the night at a diner, dozing with my coffee going cold on the table in front of me, and arrived at Pritchard's office at the crack of dawn the next morning. He got there pretty darned early himself, and he didn't seem to be surprised to see me. He handed me an envelope full of cash, gave me the paperwork for permission to pick up the ashes and the directions to the crematorium, which was one seriously strange place, and wished me good luck.

I was on the road to Yellowstone, duffel bag on the back of my bike, before rush hour even got started.

* * *

It was full dark and my legs were aching like a son of a gun by the time I came over the last rise to Old Faithful. I was so tired I was about to fall off the bike. But I'd made it.

Lights illuminated the valley below. The Inn, a huge pile of logs with windows, was surrounded by smaller buildings that made it look like the thing had had puppies, the river flowing between plumes of steam.

The road curved around past the low slung lodge and its cabins, past the visitor center, to the porte cochere, which had once protected fancy guests a long time ago, and now stood guard over people in jeans and pedal pushers towing their own suitcases.

I found a place to park the bike, and unhooked my duffle with one hand while swiping the road dust off my face with the other.

"Ooh," voices rose around me. "It's erupting."

I turned to watch with everyone else. I've seen Old Faithful go off dozens of times, but it had been a long time since Grandmother died, Granddad retired and I went off to college. I let my duffle drop to the ground and grinned. I could hear the roar over the people around me, through the memories in my head.

Dammit, I'd missed this place.

The geyser spent itself in a few minutes, and I watched, tickled, as people applauded. They always did, like the geyser was alive. Then, the show over, I picked up my bag and headed inside to claim my room.

* * *

I didn't bother with the Inn's dining room. Too pricey and too fancy. The store a few hundred yards away had a soda fountain. One of Granddad's and my favorite treats when Grandmother had gone to Jackson or West to go shopping for the day had been greasy hamburgers and fries at that fountain.

It was at the back of the store, a row of little round red stools and a metal counter, with a bunch of shiny chrome restaurant equipment and a pass-through behind it. As I approached it looked deserted. I hoped it wasn't closed. The rest of the store was busy with tourists buying souvenirs, but it was after the normal time most people ate supper.

Then, as I sat down on one of the stools, I saw this cute little rear end, round and sweet in a red and white striped skirt, bent over behind the counter.

"Hi," I said, and she shot up, straws spraying out of the box in her hand as she squeezed it.

"Oh! You startled me." She seemed to realize what she was doing to the box, and dropped it on the counter. Straws slithered everywhere, and she and I both made grabs for them.

Her front view was as good as the back. Nicely stacked, pretty face, brown curly hair escaping from a net.

She caught my eye, then fumbled for an order pad. "What can I get for you?"

I smiled at her. She smiled back. *Good.* "A hamburger, please. Fries. A Coke."

She scribbled it down. "It'll be just a minute." She turned to stick the order on the spindle in the pass-through window, and called out, "Joe! Order!"

Joe turned out to be Jo, a middle-aged woman wearing an apron shiny with grease who filled out her red-and-white dress a lot more solidly than my waitress did. She scowled at the order slip. "Grill's supposed to be closing."

"I know, Jo, but–"

"Yeah, you're a soft touch for a cute guy."

I smiled at her. The scowl melted from her eyes, although she tried to keep it on her mouth, and she slapped a burger on the griddle. I could hear it sizzle.

"Thanks, ma'am," I told her. "I've been on the road since six a.m."

"Yeah, yeah." Her gaze shot to the other end of the counter. "Loverboy at two o'clock."

The girl and I both turned to look. Her gaze fell, and she went back to picking up straws.

"Hey, Alice, what's a guy got to do to get some service around here?"

So much for my idea to ask her if she'd like to go for a beer later.

The guy was almost as tall as I am, and I'm six foot two, but he was a lot broader, and it looked like mostly muscle. He scowled at me. I shrugged and shoved my glasses up my nose. She'd been fair game till he showed up, but I wasn't going to muscle in on him now.

Reluctantly, as if pulled by strings, Alice made her way to the other end of the counter. As soon as she got within arm's length, he reached out and snagged her by the elbow, tugging her around the end of the counter so she practically bounced off of him. She sent an apologetic glance back towards Jo, who waved her off.

I sighed, and Jo turned towards me.

"Know anyplace a guy can get a beer around here?" I asked her. She smirked at me.

"Only place in the village licensed to sell liquor is the bar in the Inn, and they don't sell to underaged."

I ignored the dig since I was used to that kind of thing, swallowed my last french fry, and paid her.

Beer at the Inn would probably cost an arm and a leg, but what the hell. It had been one long day. There was enough money in Pritchard's envelope, and I'd earned it.

* * *

When I woke up it was pitch black and freezing. I was in my room, sprawled on top of the covers, with my head at the foot of the bed. I still had all my clothes on, which was a good thing or I probably would have frozen to death. I still had my boots on, as I discovered when one of them clunked against the log headboard. The vibration made my head rattle. I couldn't remember how I'd gotten there, but I must have managed it under my own steam. Nobody here I knew to do it for me. I sat up, and immediately decided the last couple of beers had been a mistake. My head rang, the room spun, and oh, man, I had to piss. Bigtime. Good thing the sink was handy, since the toilet was down the hall.

When I was done, I plunked myself back down on the bed and realized I wasn't going to get back to sleep anytime soon. The radiator was hissing, which didn't explain why I was freezing my ass off. Something was ruffling the curtains. I went over to look and discovered the window was open. That explained the temperature, at any rate. I closed it, and stayed to stare out into the night. The moon was full, shining off the river in the distance, illuminating the boardwalks and the trees, the occasional plume of steam. Not a soul to be seen. I pulled out Granddad's pocketwatch. Past eleven. Why not?

I hoisted my duffel onto the bed. The box was at the very bottom, tucked into one end where it had settled. I pried at the plastic lid with a fingernail. It refused to open. I sat for a minute, staring at it. Knife. I stood and began rooting through my pockets. That turned up nothing besides the watch but my room key and an unwrapped breath mint, growing a nice case of pocket crud. I brushed it off and stuck it in my mouth to get rid of it. Bad move. If I thought my mouth had tasted scuzzy before, it was twice as nasty now.

After I spit the mint into the garbage can, I found my pocketknife in the toe of my spare shoes, strangely enough. Gingerly I slid the blade along the seam of the box. With no warning, the lid snapped open and a poof of dust rose, straight into my face.

I snapped the lid back down, cussing. It wouldn't stay. "Okay. Okay." I set the box down on the little table next to the bed and backed away from it, swiping at my face, hoping I wasn't inhaling Grandmother and Granddad. Once the dust settled, I approached it again, and carefully closed the lid, feeling for the catch and pressing hard. This time it stayed. I let my breath out in a long whoosh.

I picked my pocketknife up off the floor, grabbed my leather jacket and the box, and headed out the door.

* * *

It was even colder outside, too cold for August even up here. And eerie, with no one around. I could hear sounds coming from the lodge across the road, music, thumps, and somebody's muffled laughter. They seemed very far away.

My momentum got me as far as the beginning of the boardwalk, where my boots sounded like somebody banging on a door out there in the middle of the night. I tried to straighten out my steps, but I guess I was still more toasted than I'd thought I was. No railings to lean on, either. I could have used one just then.

The bridge over the river echoed, too, but the water rushing underneath drowned some of that out. And it had railings. I stopped and watched the current for a while, leaning on the railing, but not too hard. I didn't want to topple over into the river, which seemed way too possible right then. Too much beer. *Sorry, Granddad.*

I took a better hold on the box. Time to move on. Granddad's will hadn't been all that specific about where to scatter the ashes, as long as it was in the park. I stopped and tried to think about it. Around Old Faithful seemed like kind of a cliché, and, anyway, I couldn't get close enough to the geyser anymore to scatter them properly. Not like when I was a kid and the only thing keeping a person from striding up and peering down the hole was his own good sense. Or his Granddad the park ranger. Besides, I was already on the other side of the river.

Observation Point seemed like a good idea until I started up the hill, grasping at tree branches and tripping over rocks in the dark. But I was halfway up before that dawned on me, and by then it was a matter of principle. So I kept going, and eventually I stood at the top, overlooking the whole valley in the moonlight.

The quiet was almost too much. No breeze, no sounds of animals – *they're all asleep, you idiot, everything with any sense is sound asleep* – no, wait a minute. I could hear splashing, muted by distance, and sank down on a rock to watch Old Faithful go off, as if it had waited for me to take my seat. I stared at it, spellbound, as if it was the first time I'd ever seen it. It certainly was the first time I'd ever had it all to myself, water spraying in the moonlight, steam clouds lifting into the sky.

Too soon, it was finished, and the night sounds took over again. A breeze picked up in the trees, and something chittered, then fell silent again. The scene below me looked like a painting. I felt like one of the early explorers, watching something no one would believe existed. The half-dozen remaining lighted windows of the inn might have been stars, the distant fires in the campground on the other side of the lodge might have belonged to an early expedition, or to old Colter himself. Or to the Indians. I shivered.

Here you are. Get it over with and get back to bed. I fished my pocketknife out and pried at the lid.

The box opened easily this time, and the dust wafted away into nothing in the slight breeze, more quickly than I expected. I shook out the last few bits. "Hope this does it for you, Granddad," I said into the night. "Miss you. Grandmother, too." I did. They were my real parents, the ones who'd taken me in and raised me after my mother died when I was born and Dad couldn't handle the whole situation. They were the ones who'd taught me who I was and who I wanted to be, who'd given me everything. Who'd understood me.

I didn't cry then. I don't cry much, at least not on the outside. But my chest was tight and my eyes burned, even though I knew I was doing the right thing. This trip felt like one last present they'd given me. Suddenly I was very glad things had worked out this way. In spite of having to sneak out on Dad. "You're home," I told them. "So am I. Thanks. I'll come back some day. I promise."

I tucked the box back under my arm and headed down the hill.

It was a fine night. Yeah, it was freezing, but my leather jacket kept me warm. The stars were shining like high beams against the sky and the beer was finally wearing off and I felt good about what I'd done. Sad, but good. I couldn't quite bring myself to go back inside. Not yet. To go back inside was to say the whole thing was over. I had three nights, so I didn't have to go back and face my real life yet – *this is real life, dammit.* Flunking out of college was what felt like a dream right now. Or a nightmare. So I didn't go in. I got myself down the trail to the valley, and decided to take a little stroll instead. It wasn't likely I'd ever have the place to myself like this again, unless I got drunk for the next two nights, which didn't feel like a bad idea now that the hangover was wearing off.

I'd wandered a ways down the path when the ground began to vibrate under my feet.

I looked up from my thoughts to find myself in front of Grand Geyser. I grinned. The tremors meant I might get to watch another eruption before I went back in. I sat down crosslegged on the planks to wait and watch.

The moon gleamed on the pool under the boardwalk, the ripples growing into small waves as the vibrations magnified. A splash, another splash, this one bigger than the first, a chugging racket that sounded like the propellers on an airplane about to take off...

The earthquake, it had to be an earthquake, hit like a giant pounding a sledgehammer. The boardwalk – bounced. With me on it. It was like riding a bucking bronco. I grabbed the edge of the boards, and hung on. Grand's pool was churning like a crazy thing now. Water hit me on the back, the heat soaking through my jacket and shirt.

Then it all stopped. "That was a helluva ride," I said into the suddenly still darkness, the moon glimmering off the still sloshing pool. My thumb hurt. I held it up a few inches from my nose. A splinter was lodged under the nail. I grasped it between my teeth and yanked it out. Tugged the tail of my shirt out to stanch the blood. And stared around.

Everything seemed to be holding its breath. Not a bit of movement, except the water draining under my feet. Not a sound, except for the now-fading hiss of the runoff. I took a deep breath and started to get up.

That's when the big one hit.

Available on Amazon and from other retailers.

About the Author

M.M. Justus's first visit to Yellowstone National Park was at age four, where it snowed on the Fourth of July. She spent most of her childhood summers in the back seat of a car, traveling with her parents to almost every national park west of the Mississippi and a great many places in between.

She holds degrees in British and American literature and history and library science, and a certificate in museum studies. In her other life, she's held jobs as far flung as hog farm bookkeeper, music school secretary, professional dilettante (aka reference librarian), and museum curator, all of which are fair fodder for her fiction.

Her other interests include quilting, gardening, meteorology, and the travel bug she inherited from her father, including multiple trips back to her favorite Grand Geyser and the rest of Yellowstone. She lives on the rainy side of the Cascade mountains in Washington state within easy reach of her other favorite national park, Mt. Rainier.

Please visit her website and blog at http://mmjustus.com, on Facebook at https://www.facebook.com/M.M.Justusauthor or on Twitter @mmjustus.

BOOKS BY M.M. JUSTUS

Much Ado in Montana

*Cross-Country: Adventures Alone Across
America and Back*

UNEARTHLY NORTHWEST

Sojourn

TIME IN YELLOWSTONE

Repeating History
True Gold
"Homesick"
Finding Home

Carbon
River
Press

Made in the USA
Columbia, SC
15 November 2017